I0645431

HEAL ME

LINDA SEED

This is a work of fiction. Any characters, organizations, places, or events portrayed in this novel are either products of the author's imagination or are used fictitiously.

HEAL ME
Copyright © 2022 by Linda Seed

ISBN: 979-8407556565

All rights reserved. No part of this book may be reproduced in any form or by any means without the prior written consent of the author, excepting brief quotes used in reviews.

The author is available for book signings, book club discussions, conferences, and other appearances.
Linda Seed may be contacted via e-mail at linda@lindaseed.com or on Facebook at www.facebook.com/LindaSeedAuthor. Learn more about Linda Seed's novels at www.lindaseed.com.

Cover design by Kari March

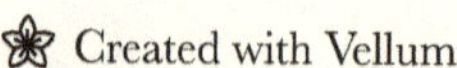 Created with Vellum

By Linda Seed

The Main Street Merchants
Moonstone Beach
Cambria Sky
Nearly Wild
Fire and Glass

The Delaneys of Cambria
A Long, Cool Rain
The Promise of Lightning
Loving the Storm
Searching for Sunshine

The Russo Sisters
Saving Sofia
First Crush
Fixer-Upper
Loving Benny

Otter Bluff
The Icing on the Cake
Christmas in Cambria
Love and Joy
Then, Now, and Always

The Bridge Street MDs
Heal Me

Sign up to Linda's newsletter and get a free gift

Sign up for Linda's twice-monthly newsletter and get her free ebook starter library: three full-length romances and a bonus short story available only to newsletter subscribers. Your information will never be shared or sold, and you can unsubscribe at any time.

To subscribe and get your free ebooks, go to the following address:
https://claims.prolificworks.com/free/hDF1LvnI

Chapter One

Shane Brody was acting like an ass, and he knew it, but he couldn't seem to do anything about it. The harder he tried to dam up his bad mood, the more it seemed to squeeze out around the edges, leaking onto everyone around him. He was a professional, so he managed to maintain a positive tone around his patients.

His brothers were another matter.

"Brittany's here looking for you," Rowan, Shane's younger brother and a pediatrician in the Brody family's medical practice, called to him from behind the reception desk. "I told her she needs to dump you and try a real man for a change."

"Sure, but where would she find one?" Shane shot back. "Surely you wouldn't know."

Shane had just emerged from an exam room, where he'd been counseling an elderly man about his diet. The guy had diabetes, yet he refused to adopt any lifestyle changes. He was going to kill himself with neglect, and there wasn't a damned thing Shane could do about it. The devastation to the man's family, the grief—and all of it preventable. It was just one of the things pissing Shane off right now.

Usually, after a remark like that, Rowan would come right back at him with some cutting comment about Shane's sexual prowess or his penis size. Instead, he looked at Shane with concern, his brows furrowed.

"Dude, are you okay?"

How could he be okay? It was nearly February eighth. He was never okay on or around February eighth. The fact that his family expected him to be fine mystified him. The fact that all of them seemed like it was just another day confused and hurt him.

Shane scoffed. "What do you think?"

"I think Brittany's been waiting half an hour, and she doesn't look happy."

———

SHANE AND BRITTANY had been dating for a while now. It had gone fine until it hadn't. He liked her, and she liked him. But when the New Year had come and gone and February had drawn closer and closer, his mood had darkened, and Brittany didn't understand why. Of course she didn't—Shane didn't want to talk about it, with her or with anyone.

He'd known she was about done, so when he went to the waiting room to greet her and saw her grim expression, he knew what was coming.

"Shane, we need to talk."

"Fine. You want to come back to my office?"

She spun to face him the moment the office door was closed behind them. "Shane, this isn't working. You know it and I know it. Maybe it's time we just walked away."

Brittany paced in front of him on the hardwood floors as Shane leaned his butt against his desk, his arms crossed over his chest.

"If that's the way you want it," he said.

"Of course it's not the way I want it! None of this is the way I want it!"

"Could you lower your voice, please?" he asked. "This is my place of business."

Brittany stopped and closed her eyes. She took a deep breath, let it out, then started again in a voice that was quieter but no less intense. "I don't want any of this, Shane. But it's where we are. Unless you want to tell me what's wrong. If you'd just let me in—"

"I do let you in. You're in."

"That's bullshit, and you know it."

He did know it. He hadn't let her in about anything real—anything that mattered to him—in the entirety of their relationship. At first, he'd deflected because he didn't know her well enough to tell her his deepest secrets. Then he'd deflected because it seemed kinder to shield her from all of it. And then, it was just habit.

Now it seemed to him that she was about to abandon him when he needed someone most. That wasn't fair, but feelings weren't fair, were they?

He checked his watch. "I have a patient in five minutes."

"Fine. I've said what I needed to say. I'm finished. With this conversation *and* with our relationship. I hope you and your … your weird, free-floating misery will be very happy together."

When she turned and left the room, all Shane felt was relief.

———

LILY HART HAD THOUGHT her new life in Cambria would be more relaxed and slow-paced than the lifestyle she'd had before, but that hadn't turned out to be the case.

Before, she'd had only one job. Now she was juggling three: freelance editing, the online newsletter she'd launched to provide local news to a community that had next to none, and, of course, the novel she was writing.

Just because she was technically unemployed, that didn't mean she wasn't busy as hell.

She sat at the desk in the corner of her bedroom, her laptop open and a cup of coffee next to her, copyediting a book on essential oils for one of the publishers who regularly sent her freelance projects. The book was a mess, both in terms of organization and the quality of the writing, but Lily told herself to stay in her own lane. Her job was to correct grammar, punctuation, and factual errors, ensure consistency, and impose a coherent style for things like capitalization and hyphen use. Her job wasn't to ponder the sense in the publisher paying actual money to produce a piece of crap like this in the first place.

In any event, she didn't have time for the bigger questions. Her deadline was looming, and she'd still barely gotten through the first four chapters.

"Lily?" Her sister, Brittany, knocked softly on her bedroom door.

"Working!" Lily called out.

"Um … oh-oh-okay." Brittany's shuddering voice sounded like she was near tears.

Lily got up from her desk and opened the door to find her sister red-eyed and wet-cheeked. She burst into tears, and Lily pulled her sister into her arms. "Oh, Brit. I guess you must have told him, then? I'm so sorry."

Lily had only lived with Brittany for a few months, and she didn't know Shane well. What she did know was that he had been friendly, pleasant, and generally lovely—at first. But over the past month or so, he'd grown more and more surly until, finally, Lily had started avoiding him whenever he came to the house.

Brittany had been telling Lily for a while that she was tired of Shane's sullen moods, but apparently, that hadn't made it any easier for her to break things off.

"Come on. I'll make us some tea and you can tell me about it." Lily, her arm around her sister, ushered Brittany out to the kitchen, sat her on a barstool, and went to put water in the kettle. Lily boiled the water, poured it over tea bags in two mugs, and brought Brittany her drink. Then she sat down on a stool next to Brittany and faced her sister.

"So, what happened? What did he say when you told him you're done?"

"He said, 'If that's what you want.' Then he said he had a patient in five minutes. Like it was nothing. Like he didn't even care."

Lily rubbed her sister's upper arm in a circular motion she

hoped was comforting. "Oh, Brit. I know it hurts. But this relationship was never right for you."

"I know it wasn't. But this still sucks."

In truth, Brittany had been considering breaking things off even before Shane had gone all dark and broody. She'd discussed it with Lily more than once. But just because the end was inevitable, that didn't mean it wasn't painful.

"You didn't love him," Lily said. "Not really."

"And he didn't love me," Brittany said. "I wanted to think he did, but …"

"Well, this is a good thing, then." Lily smiled and tried to look encouraging. "It means you can move on and find someone who really is right for you."

"I know." Brittany nodded and took in a shuddering breath. "God, I wanted it to work. He's so …"

She didn't have to finish her sentence. Lily already knew what the *so* meant. Shane was what? So smart. So accomplished. So wealthy. So damned hot. All of those things were why Lily had a hard time making coherent conversation with him whenever he was around.

They were also the reason Brittany was a mess, even though she really did want out—really did want it to be over.

"Oh … crap." Lily's eyes widened. "I'm supposed to interview him and his brothers next week about their practice. Is it okay if I still do that?" A new medical practice in Cambria—which had always had a shortage of doctors—was a big deal. Lily planned to write an article for her newsletter.

Brittany waved her hand in the air. "Of course it is."

"Are you sure? I'm not being disloyal?"

"The Brodys are doing a good thing with Bridge Street Wellness. That doesn't change just because Shane is my ex."

The term *ex* sent Brittany into a fresh bout of crying, and Lily hugged her and rubbed her back. "It's going to be okay," Lily murmured.

"I know. I know." Brittany pulled away, grabbed a napkin from a holder on the counter, and wiped her eyes. "I know it is. But I'll tell you what: even if we're not together anymore, I'm still worried about Shane. I don't know what's wrong, but it's something. And if he won't tell me, I hope he'll tell *someone*."

———

ONCE BRITTANY HAD TAKEN her tea into her room to brood over Shane, Lily considered what she knew about him and about Bridge Street Wellness.

The Brodys had come to town several months before, bought a big Victorian house on Bridge Street, and spent considerable time and money renovating the house to turn it into a medical office.

Five brothers, five specialties. But the interesting thing was their payment model: cash only, no insurance accepted. And they claimed never to turn anyone away for lack of ability to pay.

There had been a lot of buzz in town about the Brodys, some of it simply curious and most of it good. Lily's instincts as a reporter made her want to peel back the layers of the onion to find out what was underneath. Was Shane harboring some kind of secret?

Just because Lily had been laid off from her job at the *San Diego Union-Tribune*, forcing her to move in with her sister until she found something else, that didn't mean she was any less of a reporter. It wasn't the kind of thing that went away just because she didn't have anyone paying her.

Shane Brody's personal issues are none of my business.

If he were still dating Brittany, Lily would feel compelled to get to the bottom of things for her sister's sake. But he wasn't, so digging around to find out what was going on would just be prying.

I will not pry.

And, okay, it was true that for Lily, that was much like saying *I will not breathe* or *I will not exist.* Still, she could at least try to behave herself.

Chapter Two

On the morning of her interview with the Brodys, Lily dressed in a professional-looking pants suit, took time with her hair and makeup, gathered her notebook, pens, camera, and digital recorder, and looked over the list of questions she'd prepared.

It felt good to be going through the routine again as though she were back in San Diego, heading out to research a school board story or an examination of a new city ordinance.

She'd loved reporting. It wasn't a surprise when she got her layoff notice—how could it be, when journalists all over the country were experiencing the same thing? But it was a shock nonetheless. At first, she hadn't known who she would become if she couldn't be a journalist.

Only after a great many tears and phone calls with her sister had she decided to see this change as an opportunity to decide where she wanted to live and how. To try new challenges. To be her own boss. To reinvent her life.

And to finally find someone to build that life with.

The long and unpredictable hours of her newspaper job had made it hard to date anyone, so she hadn't really tried. And when she did try, she was unbearably awkward with any man she found truly attractive. So she'd just let it slide. And now here she was, well into her thirties and still single.

Time to change that, but first, she had a job to do.

She packed her things into her bag and set off for Bridge Street Wellness.

———

SHANE WAS IN A TERRIBLE MOOD, and he didn't want to be doing this interview, especially on what was supposed to be his day off. And especially when Brittany's sister was the one conducting the interview.

But his brothers had insisted, arguing that the practice needed more publicity in the community. So here he was, on a Saturday, when he should have been sleeping in or watching Netflix or walking on the beach, for God's sake.

"It's not even a real newspaper," he grumbled as he and his brothers assembled at the big Victorian on Bridge Street.

"It's got real subscribers," Nolan said. "About a thousand of them. Are you too busy to tell a thousand locals about what we do here? Because I'm not."

"He's just pissy because Brittany dumped him," Rowan said.

"That's not why he's pissy." Finn said it in a gentle way that made Shane want to punch him. And Shane was a pacifist.

"No. It isn't," Aidan agreed. "Shane, if you'd just talk to someone …"

"I don't even want to be talking to *you*," Shane said. "When's she getting here? I just want to get this over with."

The five of them were assembled on the second floor of the building, in the office suite where Finn saw his psychiatric patients. It was homier up here and it looked less like a doctor's office—the decor was designed to be soothing—so they'd decided to talk to Lily here instead of downstairs.

Finn checked the clock. "She's still got five minutes."

"Well, shit." Shane fidgeted on a leather sofa Finn had chosen from Pottery Barn. Shane knew he wasn't acting like himself. Hell, he didn't feel like himself. But he never did this time of year.

"You got somewhere to be?" Rowan got a bottled water out of the refrigerator in the unit's kitchenette and came to sit down on the opposite side of the sofa from Shane. "I'd ask if you've got a date, but what woman in her right mind would want anything to do with you when you're like this?"

"Rowan." Finn gave his brother a warning look.

"I'm just saying."

"Seriously, Ro. It's not cool to kick a man when he's just been dumped," Aidan put in.

"Yeah, yeah. Whatever." Rowan was not the least bit chastened. "All I'm saying is, he wouldn't have been dumped if he'd just deal with his shit once and for all."

"Fair point," Nolan said.

"I'm right here." Shane waved a hand to demonstrate. "I can hear you."

"And I can hear you," Finn said. "So if you ever want to talk about it …"

"You want me to lie on your sofa and release my inner pain while you make notes on your little pad?" Shane said. "I don't think so."

"People very rarely lie down," Finn said. "Although, there are studies—"

As much as Shane had been dreading the interview, he was relieved when the doorbell rang, bringing an end to what was becoming a very uncomfortable conversation.

"That must be her," Shane said.

"You think?" Rowan put in. "You guys just keep lazing around. I'll get it."

———

THE MAN who opened the door was stupidly attractive, with dark, wavy hair, broad shoulders, and a seductive smile. Lily worried about her tendency toward awkwardness with attractive men, but when she put out her hand to shake his, she felt surprisingly fine.

"Lily Hart," she said. "Thank you for agreeing to see me today."

"Rowan Brody." He shook her hand and held it a beat too long, that smile still fixed on her. "What do you say we ditch my brothers and go get to know each other, just the two of us?"

It should have been unsettling, but Lily got the idea he wasn't serious—it was just his shtick. In any large family, Lily knew, the siblings assigned themselves roles to play. Rowan's, apparently, was the incorrigible ladies' man.

"If it's all the same to you, I'd like to meet your brothers."

Rowan shrugged. "Once you meet them, you might wish you'd chosen differently. Come on up." He ushered her inside and led her upstairs to where his family was waiting.

———

WHEN THEY WERE all settled upstairs and the introductions had been made—Lily and Shane greeting each other without any mention of Brittany—the Brodys sat in various states of relaxation on the sofa and in an array of upholstered chairs. Lily sat with her notebook open on her lap, a pen in her hand.

The Brodys, to a man, looked like they could have appeared in a *Doctors of Cambria* spread in *GQ.* Which wasn't a bad idea, now that she thought of it. She made a mental note to pitch the idea to the magazine.

Rowan, in particular, looked good enough to be an actor or a model with his dark, unruly hair and his mischievous grin. Nolan, with his thick-framed glasses and his studious expression, would probably be considered the awkward one, but even so, he had a charming sweetness about him that would have grabbed her attention had she not been surrounded by an overwhelming amount of male magnetism.

Still, Shane was the one who drew her gaze. He was the one whose presence she could feel even when she wasn't looking at him. He was the one who had her so rattled she had to actively avoid thinking about him so she could focus on her job. She told herself it was just because he'd hurt her sister, but that was a lie. Shane Brody had rattled her since the day they'd met, when Brittany brought him to the house one night on their way out to dinner.

That thick, rich brown hair. Those broad shoulders. One eyebrow that quirked upward when he was curious or amused.

I should not be thinking this way about my sister's ex.

"Uh … maybe I should start by telling you a little about my newsletter," she said. "I noticed when I moved to Cambria a few months ago that there wasn't much local news. As a trained journalist—I covered city government in San Diego for ten years before I was laid off due to budget cuts—I decided to fill the void. I write local news articles and make them available to readers for a monthly subscription fee. I have about a thousand subscribers at this point, but that number is growing. I've had requests that I write something about all of you and your practice, so … here I am."

There. Shane's presence hadn't caused any major missteps in what she'd said. Of course, she'd simply offered the scripted introduction she used before pretty much any interview with a subject who didn't know her well.

Aidan—at least, she thought it was Aidan—leaned forward, propping his forearms on his knees. "As someone who's only been in Cambria a few months, do you think you're familiar enough with the character of the town to step forward as its local news source?"

"As someone who's been in Cambria"—she checked her notes —"less than a year himself, do you think you're familiar enough with the character of the town to step forward as its local source of medical care?" she asked, keeping her tone pleasant.

"Fair point," Nolan said, pushing his glasses up on his nose.

Finn spoke up. "We might be relatively new in town, but our parents have lived here for five years, since they both retired. He was a cardio-thoracic surgeon, and she was in plastics. This was their idea. A cash-only practice with a range of specialties, offering high-end concierge care to those who can afford it and low-cost or free service to those who can't. The five of us might still be learning what this community needs, but our mother and father already know. And we're doing our best to provide it."

"Since they've had such a large hand in things, it would be great if they could be here for this interview," Lily said. "Is it possible that—"

"They're on a cruise," Nolan said. "To Alaska. Mom wanted to see the glaciers."

"But mostly, she likes the free buffets," Shane said. "Now, if we could just get on with the questions?"

———

SHANE KNEW he'd sounded annoyed and irritable with that thing about just getting on with it. That made sense, because he *was* annoyed and irritable. And Lily was probably predisposed not to like him, given what had happened with Brittany.

The last thing their practice needed was bad publicity in Lily's newsletter just because Shane couldn't keep his inner angst in check. He made a mental note to keep quiet and let his brothers do most of the talking.

It was a wise move. The interview seemed to go well, with Shane's brothers talking about their specialties, their decision to go cash-only, their medical training and philosophy of care, and their impressions of Cambria. Photos were taken and information was exchanged.

Then Aidan offered to take Lily on a tour of the facility. They went downstairs together, leaving four Brodys upstairs.

"That seemed to go okay," Nolan said.

"Yeah, if you don't count Gloomy Gus over there telling her to just get the hell on with it already," Rowan put in.

"That's not what I said. I—"

"It wasn't what you said so much as the way you said it," Finn added.

"Your words said *let's do this* but your voice screamed *fuck off*," Rowan remarked.

"It kind of did," Nolan agreed.

Shane closed his eyes, let out a sigh, and rubbed at his face with both hands. "Look, you all know what time of year it is. If you could just cut me a little slack?"

Finn leaned forward, close to Shane, and spoke softly. "It's hard for all of us, Shane. Not just you. The way you blame yourself for what happened isn't healthy. If you'd just try to deal with your feelings …"

"You know what? Now all of me is saying *fuck off*."

He shot to his feet and stormed out of the room.

———

SHANE WAS HOPING to get downstairs and out the front door without interference. But he timed it poorly, because somehow, he and Lily ended up on the front porch, heading down toward the street at the same time. Lily must have felt as awkward as he did, because she visibly flinched when she saw him.

"Oh. Shane. Ah … I wasn't …" She fumbled a little with her bag, putting her pad and pen inside. "I'll just …" She indicated the street, where her car was parked.

"Yeah," he said, as though she'd actually made sense.

He was going to just walk away, but then he remembered what his brothers had said about his attitude and how that might affect the article.

"Look," he said, stopping her. "The thing with Brittany … I didn't mean to hurt her. I really care about her. I hope she knows that."

Lily stopped messing around with her bag and looked at him. "I'm … I don't … I'm not sure she does know it."

He stuffed his hands into his pockets and looked at the pavement instead of at her. "I'm going through some things. Personal things."

"Yes. Right. Only …"

He waited, eyebrows raised.

"We all go through personal things," she said at last. "That doesn't mean we all get to act like total dicks."

———

LILY GOT into her car and banged her head lightly against the steering wheel. Why had she said that?

Something about Shane Brody flipped her AWKWARD WITH MEN switch. When she'd talked to his brothers, she'd been fine. But when she talked to him? She was either stammering incoherently or calling him names.

What was wrong with her?

When she got home, Brittany was sitting at the kitchen table with her laptop and a cup of coffee. It was Saturday, and it was still relatively early, so she was still in her pajamas and a pair of fuzzy slippers.

"Well, there's good news and bad news." Lily plunked her bag down onto the table and sank into a chair. "The good news is, it's going to be a nice article, and I was impressed with the Brodys' practice."

"So, what's the bad news?"

"The bad news is, I did that weird-with-men thing and made a fool of myself. Then I called Shane a dick."

Brittany's eyes widened. "I can't wait to hear how that came up in the course of the interview."

"It didn't. The interview was over, and we were standing outside, and he said he didn't mean to hurt you, but he's going through something personal. And I said it didn't give him the right to act like a total dick. God. I don't know what's wrong with me. Why do I say these things? Why does my brain turn off when I'm talking to a man?"

Brittany regarded her sister. "I'll take those things one at a time. One, you said it because he is, in fact, acting like a total dick. And two …"

"Do we have to do two?"

"And two," Brittany went on as though Lily hadn't spoken, "you don't act that way when you're talking to men in general. Only when you're talking to men you're strongly attracted to."

Lily didn't say anything, but she could feel her cheeks reddening.

"Which means," Brittany continued, "you're strongly attracted to my ex."

"No, I'm not."

"Bullshit." Brittany pointed one finger at Lily.

Okay, it was true. Lily had avoided being caught out before this because she'd avoided Shane as much as possible while he and Brittany were dating. If she'd been in her right mind, she'd have kept her mouth shut about how she'd acted with him at Bridge Street Wellness. But she'd blurted it out, and now here they were.

Lily tried a new approach. "Well, Shane is objectively attractive. And we know I'm bad with attractive men. It only stands to reason—"

"The other Brodys are objectively attractive, but you didn't say anything about blurting out stupid things to them."

Damn it.

"Does it matter?" Lily said. "Whatever I think of him, it's not like I'd ever in a million years make a play for my sister's ex."

"No. I know you wouldn't." Brittany's voice softened, and she put a hand on Lily's arm. "And even if you did? He's not exactly a joy ride. You'd get exactly what you had coming to you."

Chapter Three

T he next day, Lily settled in at the desk in her room and wrote her article about the Brodys. She included information about how their parents had gotten the idea for a cash-only practice in Cambria; how the Brody brothers had come together to plan the practice and redesign the historic building on Bridge Street; how the cash-only structure worked, with the doctors' high-end services helping to pay for treatment of low-income patients; and some background on each of the Brodys.

The brothers all had a healthy amount of family money—their mother, Fiona, had ancestors who had immigrated from Ireland and had made a fortune in banking—but Rowan, Lily learned, was some sort of tech whiz who'd sold an app for a jaw-dropping price and was covering most of the startup costs for the business.

Lily had interviewed a few patients who'd discussed their experiences with the practice in a Cambria Facebook group. The reviews ranged from pleased to gushing. One woman told Lily she hadn't seen a doctor in years because of the high cost of health insurance, until the Brodys had taken her on pro bono. She talked about Shane as though he were some kind of health-giving saint.

The best she could do for an opposing view was a quote from

one man who pointed out that the Brodys only provided whatever care they could offer at their practice—if you needed hospitalization or some other kind of specialist, you'd be out of luck if you didn't have insurance.

That wasn't the Brodys' fault, of course, but at least it kept her piece from being one long love fest.

She proofread the article, then posted it to the website for her newsletter with a selection of photos she'd taken the morning before. Maybe she'd do an article on the trend toward cash-only healthcare, which more and more doctors were providing nation-wide as a response to the increasingly dysfunctional health insurance industry.

She typed the idea into a file she kept for story ideas, then closed her laptop, ready for a break.

She couldn't stop thinking about what that one woman had said about Shane. To hear her tell it, he was a deeply caring, selfless hero. That didn't jibe with what Brittany had said about him or what she'd observed herself.

He was going through something personal, he'd said, but he'd been unwilling to tell Brittany what it was. What was going on with him? What kind of secret was he keeping?

Part of Lily knew it was none of her business, but another part was one hundred percent reporter. That part saw any kind of secret as an irresistible challenge. And maybe if she poked around a little and found out the truth, it might help Brittany get closure. So it would be altruistic, a way to help her sister.

That's what she told herself, anyway.

———

LILY'S NEWSLETTER came out at ten a.m. that Monday, and within a few minutes of its release, the Brodys were already talking about it.

Shane was just getting ready to go on a house call—something they could do at Bridge Street Wellness because they weren't beholden to the health insurance companies—when Nolan poked his head into Shane's office.

"Did you see it?"

"See what?"

"The article. Lily Hart. It's up." He held up his cell phone to demonstrate.

"Ah." Shane was half convinced that she'd put a negative spin on the practice just because he'd been dumped by her sister.

"You can unclench," Nolan said. "It's very positive. A veritable love letter, in fact."

Shane's eyebrows rose. "Really?"

"Here." Nolan offered Shane the phone, which was already displaying the article in question.

Shane took the phone and scanned what Lily had written.

"This isn't so bad," he said.

"Not so bad? It couldn't be better if we'd written it ourselves."

A moment later, Finn came into the office. "Did you see it?"

"Yes, I saw it."

"'The darkly handsome Rowan Brody,'" Rowan called to them from the hallway. "Did you get that part? I'm darkly handsome."

Shane had seen that part, and it rankled him. Why it should have that effect on him, he couldn't have said. He was just rankled in general these days.

Fortunately, Aidan was out of the office, or Shane would have had to hear him chime in, too.

Iris, one of the receptionists, called out to them from the front desk, "We've had three calls already from people who read the article and want to give us a try. And it's only been out fifteen minutes!"

Well, shit. Now Shane guessed he couldn't stay irritated with Lily Hart, as much as he wanted to.

———

AS IT TURNED OUT, Shane actually liked making house calls.

When his family had suggested it, he'd been skeptical. Now,

though, he had to admit he'd been wrong. Visiting a patient at their own residence had a lot going for it—for one thing, it got him out of the office, which was always nice. For another, it allowed him to assess the patient's home environment, and that had proved valuable on more than one occasion.

Now, as he straightened up after listening to Orin Delaney's heart and lungs, he took off his stethoscope and put it back in his bag.

"How's his heart? It still in there?" Orin's wife, Sandra, asked with a cackle that, Shane supposed, was actually a laugh. The woman, dressed in a 49ers football jersey, jeans, and bunny slippers, stood by with her hands planed on her hips as Shane worked.

"It's there, all right," Shane affirmed. "But, Orin, you might want to give it—and the rest of you—a break by taking it easy. At your age—"

"*Mmf.* My age," Orin grumbled.

"Protest all you want," Sandra said. "The man's a doctor, and I'd say he's got a point. You're supposed to be retired. You're supposed to let the boys do all the work on the ranch, and yet there you are every day, out there on a damned horse, working like you think you're twenty years old. My God."

Orin shifted in his seat, fidgeting. "Well, I figure I can still work. I'm not dead yet."

"You will be if you don't use some damned common sense," his wife said. "Because I'll kill you myself."

Regarding the thing about house calls being informative, the Delaneys were a case in point. Shane now knew two things he hadn't known before as a result of visiting the Delaney home on their expansive cattle ranch: one, Orin had a loving but cantankerous wife who would look after and advocate for him—an important consideration when it came to a senior citizen's health. And two, Orin seriously needed to change his diet. Shane had shown up just before lunchtime, and Sandra had invited him to stay for a meal of pot roast, mashed potatoes, gravy, and rolls with butter.

"That's very kind of you, but I have another patient in twenty minutes," Shane told Sandra. "And I'd be remiss if I didn't mention the fact that Orin's cholesterol and blood pressure are a little high. The gravy alone …"

"Aw, don't tell me I'm going to have to eat dry salads and bran and that stuff that starts with a q. I don't know what that word is."

"Quinoa?" Shane suggested.

"That's the one." Having found the correct word didn't make Orin look any happier at the prospect of having to eat it.

"You'll do what the doctor is telling you, I guess," Sandra said.

"Not dry salads and quinoa, necessarily," Shane said. "Though a few leafy greens wouldn't hurt you. I'll have my office staff send you some information on a heart-healthy diet."

"The paper it's written on is probably going to taste better," Orin grumbled.

———

NOW THAT THIS week's newsletter was out, Lily turned her focus to other things, such as her freelance editing assignments, her novel —which was still in the outline stage—and basic housekeeping tasks like doing laundry and shopping for groceries.

"I'm going to the market. Do you need anything?" she called to Brittany on her way out the door to go to the Cookie Crock.

Brittany stuck her head out the door of the bedroom. "Could you get me some of that iced tea that I like? Oh, and tampons. And I need some milk, and … I better make a list."

Lily rolled her eyes, but she wasn't really annoyed. Brittany seemed perky and happy this morning, less than a week after her breakup from Shane. It confirmed what Lily had suspected—Brittany hadn't been fully committed to the relationship anyway.

Brittany and Shane had turned out to be one of those couples who spent a pleasant stretch of time together while each of them waited for their real match to come along. Lily was certain Brittany's would come sooner rather than later.

Brittany came out of her room with the list and handed it to Lily.

"You seem good," Lily told her sister.

"I am good."

"I'm glad. After the thing with Shane—"

"Ugh." Brittany put up a hand to stop her. "Let's not talk about Shane. Except to say I read your article. It was good. People need to know about what the Brodys are doing."

"So you really don't mind that I interviewed them? After everything?"

"Of course not. Shane's brothers deserve the publicity."

"I liked them," Lily said. "His brothers, I mean."

"Oh, I do, too. I'm probably going to miss them more than I'll miss Shane. Well, off you go. I really need those tampons."

———

LILY WAS at the Cookie Crock, pushing her cart through the canned beans section, when she heard a familiar voice behind her. The voice made her go tense and stupid—until she realized it wasn't Shane, but someone who sounded very much like him.

"Hey, Lily."

She turned to find Finn Brody with his own cart half full of corn tortillas, beans, ground beef, salsa, and a six-pack of beer.

"Oh. Dr. Brody. Hi."

"Call me Finn. If we went with 'Dr. Brody,' you'd call one of us and five people would answer. Or, with my parents, seven."

"Okay. Finn, then."

Finn Brody was the practice's psychiatrist. He had the same Brody good looks as his brothers—tall, broad shoulders, hair so thick and wavy you wanted to plunge your hands into it—but he seemed … softer. Not less masculine, but somehow more relaxed, as though the stick that was up some of his brothers' butts was inexplicably missing from his.

"Listen, since I've got you, I wanted to thank you for the article."

A middle-aged woman was trying to get her cart past them, and Finn moved his to the side so she could pass.

"You read it, then."

"I did. We all did. It was very positive."

Lily cocked her head to the side, regarding him. "You sound surprised."

"Well, maybe a little. I know you're from a big metro paper, and a completely positive article—"

"Would make me look like I'm on your payroll," she finished for him.

"Something like that."

Lily shrugged. "A big metro paper is different from a small-town newsletter. There are different expectations. I'm filling a different need. People need to know about the services you offer. And I didn't have anything particularly negative to say."

"Shane was relieved."

Lily's skin prickled at the very mention of his name. "Why is that? Did he think I was going to slam your practice just because he and my sister broke up?"

"And because he was in a bad mood during the interview."

"I'm not that petty," Lily said.

"I never thought you were."

"But Shane thought I would be."

Lily didn't particularly want to continue this line of conversation, because she didn't like the direction it was going. She didn't want to talk about Shane and her sister. One interesting thing, though—Lily was talking to a supremely attractive man and was neither awkward nor nervous.

Intriguing.

Any time she tried to talk to Shane, she was a bumbling mess. But Finn didn't provoke any such reaction.

"Anyway," Lily said, "I'll let you get back to your ..." She peered into his basket. "Taco preparations?"

"All right. It was good to see you."

She started down the aisle when he stopped her. "Lily?"

She stopped pushing her cart and turned to face him.

"I make a hell of a taco," he said. "Do you want to join me?"

Okay, that did make her awkward and nervous. Shane's brother was asking her to have dinner with him? And why was she thinking of him as *Shane's brother* and not as Finn?

"That's very nice of you, but I can't. I have plans."

"Ah, well. Another time, then."

She got out of there before she could change her mind.

Chapter Four

"And then he asked me to join him. For tacos!"

Lily spilled the whole thing to Brittany the moment she got home. Because it was ridiculous, one Brody brother asking her out after another Brody brother had broken her sister's heart.

Except Brittany didn't seem particularly broken at the moment, nor did she react the way Lily had expected.

"He did? Oh, my God, why aren't you there, eating tacos right now? Finn is great!"

"I'm not over there eating tacos because it's not even noon."

"You know what I mean." Brittany was standing in the kitchen holding a dish towel, and she threw it at Lily. The towel smacked her in the shoulder before falling to the floor.

Lily bent over to pick up the offending towel. "I can't believe you think I should have said yes."

"Why not?"

"Because he's Shane's brother, and we don't even like Shane! Which would make it weird."

Brittany shrugged. "We don't *not* like Shane."

Lily's eyes widened in surprise. "We don't?"

Brittany came over to where Lily was standing and sank down onto a stool at the counter, her shoulders slumped. "No. We don't. I mean, yeah, he acted like an ass to me there at the end. But he's going through something, and I don't know what it is. And he doesn't feel close enough to me to tell me. Which pretty much doomed the relationship. But that doesn't mean he's not a good person."

It was one of the reasons Lily loved her sister—Brittany's unfailing kindness and sympathy toward the people in her life.

"Well, okay," Lily said. "But it would still be weird. Me dating the brother of my sister's ex."

"If I'm fine with it, and Finn's fine with it, why shouldn't you be fine with it?"

It was a fair point.

"What if Shane's not fine with it?" Lily asked.

"Who cares?" Brittany threw her hands into the air. "I said we don't hate him. I didn't say we're letting him run our lives."

———

THE MORE LILY thought about going out with Finn, the more it made a certain kind of sense. Objectively, he was everything she wanted in a man: successful, intelligent, handsome as hell. But because there was no immediate, intense chemistry with him, she wasn't gripped by that awful sense of awkwardness and discomfort that overtook her whenever she was instantly hot for someone.

The way I'm awkward and uncomfortable around Shane.

Okay, but that was a special circumstance. She wasn't awkward around Shane because she wanted him. Obviously. She was awkward around him because of what had happened with Brittany, and that was all.

That was the only reason.

In any event, she *wasn't* awkward with Finn, which might mean she'd have a chance to get to know him before the discomfort kicked in and ruined everything.

She shared her theory with Brittany one night after Lily had finished with the various tasks related to her cobbled-together career and Brittany had gotten home from the salon where she cut hair. Brittany's friend Candace was over, and the three of them were preparing for an evening of pizza, wine, and romcoms.

"So, it makes sense, right?" Lily asked after she'd laid out her reasoning. "I should date someone who doesn't throw me off balance. Like Finn."

Candace—who had gone out with Shane a few times herself and who, in fact, had briefly worked for the Brodys—screwed up her face in an expression of uncertainty as she poured herself a glass of Chardonnay from the bottle on the coffee table. "I don't know. The fact that he doesn't throw you off balance means you're not really into him, right?"

"Yet." Lily put up one finger. "It means I'm not really into him *yet*. But that could change. Especially if I'm in command of my faculties during the early dating period."

Brittany rolled her eyes. "You always do this, though."

"Do what?"

"Date guys you're not really into because it's more comfortable. And then you realize—surprise, surprise—that you're not really into him, and it ends."

"Okay, but—"

"I mean, she's kind of right," Candace said. "I've seen you do that."

"Your relationships always end, too," Lily told Brittany. "Every one of them has ended. That doesn't mean you're doing something wrong, it just means you haven't found the one yet."

"Mine haven't all ended," Candace said with the smugness of the happily coupled. She and her boyfriend, Evan, were stupidly in love, and she couldn't help gloating about her happiness.

"You're proving my point." Lily whirled around to face her. "You weren't into Evan at the beginning. It had to develop over time. Much as things between me and Finn might if I just give it a chance."

"Well …" Candace looked skeptical.

"Well, what?" Lily asked.

"I was into Evan at the beginning. I was always into Evan. I just tried to hide it."

"There you go," Brittany said.

The three of them sat on the sofa in front of the dark TV with their wine, a pizza box open in front of them. They hadn't even started the arduous process of choosing a movie yet.

"But you said I should date him," Lily reminded Brittany.

"That's before you said you felt comfortable. Your lack of discomfort changes everything."

Lily slumped on the sofa, feeling disheartened. Brittany did have a point. She did tend to choose men who made her feel at ease, and that did tend to work out badly when she got bored or restless.

She could sum up the problem in two words: Trevor Drake.

Trevor had been the first man Lily had truly and deeply fallen for. Her love for him had been all-consuming. So all-consuming, in fact, that she'd chosen to ignore the numerous signs that he'd been cheating: the constant text messages he wouldn't let her see; the nights when he had "late meetings" at work; the money from their household budget that had gone unaccounted for; the spare cell phone she'd found in his jacket pocket. The endless, unconscionable gaslighting.

He'd hurt her so thoroughly that now, the very idea of feeling that strongly for someone again terrified her. She only felt safe in a relationship if her heart wasn't in it.

"It's Trevor goddamned Drake's fault," Brittany said, as though she'd read Lily's mind.

"Just because I'm not goofy and stupid around Finn doesn't mean there's no potential there," Lily insisted. "Now, somebody give me the damned clicker. And another slice of pizza."

———

"WHAT DO you think about Lily Hart?" Finn was in the break room at Bridge Street Wellness, pouring himself a mug of coffee, when Shane walked in.

"I try not to. Why?"

Finn opened a packet of sugar and poured it into his coffee. "No reason. I just ran into her at the Cookie Crock yesterday, and I wondered. Since you know her a little."

Only three sentences from his brother, and Shane was already intensely uncomfortable about where this might be going.

"First, I don't know her. I know her sister. And second, you just ran into her in the produce section and now you want to know all about her?"

"It was the canned beans section, actually." Finn added cream to his coffee, stirred, then tasted it. "And I don't want to know *all* about her. Just your general impressions."

"My general impression is that you should stay away from my ex's sister."

Finn gave Shane that look that meant he was about to analyze his inner pain. "That's a stronger reaction than I might have expected. Interesting."

Shane had come into the room to get a bottle of juice out of the refrigerator, but he was standing there, juiceless, having forgotten his mission.

"Coffee?" Finn inquired.

"Ah … no." Shane remembered the juice, went to the refrigerator, and took it out. Then he uncapped the bottle and took a long swig, giving him a moment to gather his thoughts. Finn wasn't wrong—he'd reacted more strongly than he should have, though he wasn't sure why.

Finn was heading for the door, which meant this conversation could be over if Shane wanted it to be. But he couldn't help poking the wound.

"Why did you want to know? And don't give me that *no reason* shit."

Finn turned toward Shane and sighed, making a show of how supremely patient he was being with his irrational brother. "If you must know, I asked her out. Or in, really. I invited her to join me at my place for dinner." He shrugged. "It didn't work out, but I was thinking of giving it another go. And I wondered what you thought of her. Though, in retrospect, I imagine your opinion isn't exactly objective, given your relationship with her sister and your overly emotional reaction when I asked, so …"

Shane stopped cold. Finn had asked Lily out? On a date? The wheels in his head spun and spun, refusing to make sense of what Finn was telling him.

"Shane? Anybody in there?" Finn said.

"You are *not* going to date Lily Hart." It just popped out before he'd even known he was going to say it.

Aidan came in, his white coat in place, his hair so neatly groomed that Shane could see the comb tracks. "Who isn't going to date Lily Hart?"

"I'm not," Finn said. "Except I am, if she says yes."

"Goddamn it, Finn." Shane banged his half-full juice bottle onto the table, causing juice to slosh out.

"I see." Aidan brushed past both of them to get his own mug of coffee. "I just don't care." He filled his cup, then left as abruptly as he'd come in.

"Why is this an issue for you?" Finn asked. "Just because Brittany is her sister? I hardly think that should make Lily off-limits."

The thing was, Shane wouldn't have thought so either, but here he was, making a huge deal of it.

"Look, it just is, all right? You're not going to see her."

"Except I am. If she wants to." Finn kept his voice infuriatingly calm. All of that psychiatric training, probably. He was well-practiced at keeping his tone neutral in the face of irrational people.

Shane had two choices: he could either throw down with his brother right in the middle of the workday at his place of business, or he could go see his next patient, keep his day on schedule, and think about all of this later.

He chose to think about it later.

———

THE WHOLE THINK-ABOUT-IT-LATER thing came back to bite Shane in the ass that evening when he was home alone with nothing to do but brood.

His place on Happy Hill was quiet and serene, which was nice most of the time—except when he needed distractions from his own thoughts and worries and his neighborhood offered him nothing but peace and silence.

What he needed was to get out of his head and stop thinking about February eighth.

He decided to take a jog at Fiscalini Ranch since it was still light out, so he put on his workout clothes and running shoes and made the short drive to the trail head.

About a mile into the run, with a light sheen of sweat forming on his skin and his breath coming steady and hard, Shane had stopped thinking about the upcoming anniversary. But without that to consider, his mind turned to Lily Hart, which wasn't much better.

It irked the shit out of him that Finn wanted to date Lily. But why? Why did Shane care so much?

If Lily was in Finn's life, that meant Brittany would be, too, and the whole thing would be a constant reminder of how Shane had tanked the relationship. Surely that was enough of a reason for him to oppose Finn seeing her.

Also, it seemed … disloyal. If Shane was cutting ties with the Harts, then the rest of his family should, too. Intellectually, that was irrational, but emotionally, if felt right.

He continued on the trail leading up toward the pines and away from the bluffs and the crashing waves. His muscles felt loose and good, and the rhythmic pattern of his shoes on the dirt lulled him into something resembling calm.

Was it possible he was upset about Finn and Lily because he, himself, felt just a hint of attraction to her?

Well, yes, if he were being honest. He'd always been attracted to Lily, from the moment he'd met her. But that moment had come months into his relationship with Brittany, so he'd shoved the attraction down into some place inside him that he could lock up and forget about.

He wasn't a cheater, and he certainly wasn't the sort of man who would make a play for his girlfriend's sister. Or even his ex-girlfriend's sister, come to that.

But that didn't mean he wanted to see her with his brother.

And there was more to it than that. Even if Lily weren't Brittany's sister, and even if she didn't seem to unravel every time she talked to him, he still wouldn't put her through the trauma of a relationship with him.

Things with Brittany had shown that Shane wasn't good for any woman.

Oh, he was fine most of the time. Right up until the middle of winter. Then …

Goddamn it. That brought his thoughts right back to February eighth and everything he was trying so hard to forget.

Yes, it had occurred to him more than once to get therapy, the way Finn kept suggesting. Not with his own brother, of course, but Finn kept pointing out that he could refer Shane to someone good, someone who had no stake in any of this.

But that meant he'd have to get closer to the issue than he felt comfortable doing, so every year when the dark cloud settled over him, he became broody, snapped at all of the people in his life, drank too much, then waited for it to pass.

Brittany simply hadn't been willing to wait that long without knowing what was happening or why. Not that he blamed her.

Why would he want to do the same thing to Lily? He didn't. He wouldn't. He'd just keep the attraction locked in its little box.

If she did end up dating Finn, he'd have to find a few more locks for the box, because it was bound to fly open if he didn't, spilling those uncomfortable emotions all over everything.

And that would be a mess he didn't know if he could clean up.

Chapter Five

Lily was at her desk on Monday morning, wrestling the essential oils book into some sort of coherent order, when Finn called on her cell phone.

"Oh. Dr. Brody." She blinked a few times, surprised to hear from him.

"Finn," he reminded her.

"Right. Finn. What can I do for you?"

"After you refused my tacos," he said, "I thought maybe it's because you don't trust my culinary skills. Nor should you, without anything to go on. I wondered if maybe you'd be more amenable to restaurant tacos? Tonight? I know a good place."

That was cute. She found herself smiling.

Okay, yes, she experienced a distinct lack of chemistry when she spoke to Finn. And yes, since Trevor, she had displayed a certain tendency toward playing it safe with men—choosing to date people who couldn't hurt her because she didn't care enough about them to give them that kind of power.

But that didn't mean dating Finn was a bad idea. Objectively, he was an excellent choice for any woman. And chemistry could develop over time, couldn't it?

"I might be amenable to restaurant tacos," she said.

———

LILY MET Brittany for lunch that afternoon when Brittany was between clients. They had sandwiches and salad at Linn's Easy as Pie Cafe, enjoying the afternoon sunshine on the patio.

When Lily told her sister that she had a date with Finn Brody, Brittany scowled. "I'm not sure about this, Lily."

"If this is about the whole Brody family being off-limits just because you dated Shane——"

"It's not, and you know it's not. I was all in favor of it until I realized you don't really like Finn. I don't want him to waste his time. He's a good guy and doesn't deserve that."

"I do like him." Lily picked at the crust of her sandwich.

"Sure. You like him in the way people like each other when everyone's perfectly agreeable and there's nothing objectionable going on. But the very sight of him doesn't melt your panties, and it should. He's a definite panty-melter, objectively speaking."

Lily kept her eyes on her sandwich instead of her sister. She plucked more crust from the bread. "It takes time for panty-melting," she said.

"Bullshit. Trevor melted your panties the moment you laid eyes on him."

"And look how well that worked out."

"Okay, point taken." Brittany sipped some olallieberry lemonade through a straw. "All I'm saying is, playing it safe isn't doing you any favors."

As much as Lily wanted to protest that her sister was wrong, she wasn't. Ever since Trevor, Lily had gone through a string of perfectly nice guys who didn't do anything for her. Each time, she reassured herself that she'd develop feelings eventually.

She didn't.

But when had dating a panty-melter ever resulted in anything but pain and heartache? She'd learned to avoid that kind of man for her own safety.

And that was why she wanted to stay as far away as possible from Shane Brody.

Dating Shane's brother would serve two purposes: it would give her the possibility of developing something meaningful with Finn, and it would make Shane even more off-limits than he already was.

Which was just how she wanted him.

———

SHANE LEARNED about Finn's date with Lily as he was getting ready to leave the office. He'd just seen a patient who probably had cancer—he'd ordered a biopsy, but he wasn't optimistic—so his mood was even worse than it had already been.

"Hey." Finn poked his head into Shane's office just as Shane was hanging up his white coat and putting on his jacket. "I wanted to mention, I'm seeing Lily tonight. I hope that won't be a problem."

That was how he said it—so casually it was like he was asking Shane what kind of coffee he wanted for the next restock of the break room.

"Like hell you are." Shane had been calm a second ago, but now his fists were clenched at his sides and his pulse sped.

"I am, but I'm more than happy to talk about it with you if—"

"Fuck off."

"Very mature." Finn looked at him the way a tired parent looked at his child. "If this is just because of Brittany, I don't think—"

"I am not okay with this, Finn. For your information? I am not okay."

"I know you're not." Finn's voice was soft and understanding, letting Shane know he meant more than just the topic at hand. "And I'm here if you want to talk. I really am."

He left before Shane could say anything more.

When he was gone, Shane stood there with a hot pressure building in his chest. He waited for it to dissipate, and when it didn't, he reached out and slapped the pen holder off his desk, sending it to the floor with a crash.

Even he didn't know why he was having such a strong reaction to this. It wasn't like he wanted Lily for himself. Even if he did, she was out of bounds because of Brittany. He knew he'd hurt Brittany, and he didn't want to rub salt in the wound by parading around with her sister.

But there was something about Lily that put him on edge, made him feel unsettled and a little bit crazy. Of all the women on the Central Coast, Finn couldn't have chosen someone else to pursue?

And why did it have to be Finn? If it had been Rowan, Shane would have been able to be fully pissed off without remorse or reserve. Rowan changed women more often than he changed his socks. And he treated them about as well. Shane would have had firm ground to stand on if Rowan had been going after his ex's sister.

But Finn? Finn was … nice. Kind. Thoughtful and deeply principled. If Shane had a daughter and had to choose a husband for her, he'd pick someone very much like Finn.

Which kind of made Shane an asshole for raising an objection.

He took a deep breath, let it out, and began picking up his pens.

What he needed to do was just ride this out. Wait until the anniversary had passed and he began to feel better. Wait until this thing between Lily and Finn faded. Wait until he was himself again.

By then he'd have forgotten about both Brittany and her sister, and he'd have gotten himself back on some kind of even keel.

Hell, maybe Finn was right that he needed to talk to someone, though he couldn't see what difference it would make. No amount of talking would change what had happened or what he'd done.

He straightened the pen holder on his desk and went home to begin the process of obsessing about his brother and Lily.

———

THE TACO PLACE Finn had mentioned turned out to be a truck at the corner of Main Street and Burton Drive. Not the kind of thing she'd come to expect from a first date, when the man was generally still trying to impress her.

She was disappointed at first, until Finn drove her and their tacos to Moonstone Beach, where he laid out a blanket on the sand and produced a bottle of cold wine and two glasses.

Maybe not such a disappointment, then.

They ate their food and drank their wine as the sun set, the crashing surf in front of them and a riotous display of orange and yellow on the horizon.

After they ate, Finn put the blanket and the remains of their meal into his car, and they walked barefoot on the beach. Usually, she might have expected a bit of hand-holding at a time like this, but neither of them went there. Instead, they simply walked and talked, one or the other of them occasionally bending to pick up a shell or a particularly interesting rock.

"Hey, Finn?" Lily asked. "Is Shane okay?"

She wasn't sure why she was talking about Shane while on a date with Finn, but she couldn't seem to help it. She'd been thinking about Shane a lot lately—about his personality change and the way he'd acted with Brittany.

"He will be."

"So you know what's going on?"

Finn smiled apologetically. "I do, but I don't know you well enough to tell you about it."

"That's fair. It's none of my business, really."

Finn turned to her, his hair blown by the ocean breeze. "It's not, but it's nice that you care."

Lily knew she shouldn't be talking about Shane while she was on a date with his brother. But she couldn't seem to help herself.

"It's just, when he was with Brittany …"

"Lily?" Finn stopped walking and turned to face her.

"Yeah?"

"I can't talk about this with you. If Shane wanted people to know what's bothering him, he'd tell them."

Lily nodded. "Okay. Yes. You're right." She had to appreciate the fact that Finn was keeping his brother's confidence, and she promised herself not to talk about him anymore. She promised herself she would focus on Finn, the sunset, and the lovely evening they were sharing.

———

WHEN LILY GOT HOME that night, Brittany was still up. She was lying on the sofa in pajamas and fuzzy socks, reading a book.

She put the book aside and sat up. "So? How did it go?"

"It was fine." Lily put down her purse and kicked off her shoes.

"Wow. The enthusiasm is overwhelming."

Lily plunked herself down on the sofa next to her sister. "Very funny. It was better than fine. It was very nice."

"You've elevated it to *very nice*." Brittany assessed her sister. "At least that's better than total disaster. Where did he take you?"

Lily told her about the taco truck, the beach, their picnic with wine and tacos, and their walk on the sand. She didn't mention the part where she'd kept trying to talk about Shane.

When she finished describing the date, Brittany looked impressed. "I've got to tell you, that sounds romantic as hell."

It did. It should have been. And yet …

"So. Did you hold hands? Did he kiss you?"

"No, no. It was just a first date." Lily waved it off.

"So you don't hold hands on a first date now? I don't want to say that's prudish, but …"

The fact was, they hadn't held hands because Lily hadn't wanted to. And they hadn't kissed because, whenever they'd been in a situation where it seemed like that might happen, she'd made an excuse to step away. But her sister didn't need to know any of that.

"We're taking things slowly."

Brittany looked like she was going to make some kind of sarcastic remark, but then she nodded. "Fair enough."

"Really?"

"Yes. If you're just dating Finn because he's comfortable, because you don't have feelings that might cause you to freak out, then it's better this way. It's best if everybody can walk away before they've taken their pants off, you know?"

Lily did know. She'd had similar thoughts herself all evening. But it seemed as though she should protest, so she did.

"Brittany, come on," she said. "We're just getting to know each other, that's all."

She went to her room, closed the door, flopped down onto the bed, and tried not to think about Shane and whatever it might be that Finn wasn't saying.

Chapter Six

Over the next few weeks, Lily continued to see Finn, and things did progress to hand-holding—and then to kissing. Kissing Finn was nice. Better than nice. It made Lily feel comfortable, which was just what she'd thought she wanted.

When Finn invited her to join him for a family dinner at his parents' place, the trajectory of their relationship took a precipitous turn away from comfort.

"You"—she swallowed audibly—"you want me to meet your parents?"

Finn laughed. "Yes, but not in the way you're thinking. It's not a big thing. It's just casual." His parents had a big family dinner every Sunday, he explained, and it wasn't unusual for any or all of them to bring people along—dates, friends, coworkers. Whomever.

He wanted to go to the dinner and he wanted to see Lily, so why not combine the two?

"That's all it is?" she asked, uncertain.

"That's all it is."

She mentioned it to Brittany, who had attended more than a few Brody Sunday dinners.

"You're fine," she said, waving a hand dismissively. "It really is casual, like he said. You're not being evaluated for possible daughter-in-law potential. This isn't that."

"Okay. If you're sure."

Still, all of those Brodys in one place? Including Shane?

She'd just have to forget he was there and keep her focus on Finn.

As though anyone, ever, could forget Shane Brody.

———

DECLAN AND FIONA BRODY were not what Lily had expected. And their Sunday family dinner would have been unexpected, too, if Lily hadn't gotten a heads-up from Brittany.

Given that the Brodys were a family of doctors—and certainly wealthy, considering their spacious house in the upscale Leimert neighborhood—Lily might have imagined a long dining table, gleaming silver, and some kind of elegant and well-thought-out meal.

She also might have expected Finn's parents to be somehow dignified. Sedate.

Instead, she arrived at the Brody house to find Finn's father in shorts, a T-shirt, and flip-flops, wearing a BITCHIN IN THE KITCHEN apron and manning a gas grill in the back yard. Finn's mother, who was somewhere in her sixties, was wearing artfully ripped jeans cuffed halfway up her shins, a close-fitting red T-shirt tucked in, and high-heeled sandals. Her toenails were painted a vivid, sparkly green, and her silver hair, bobbed at the jawline, bore streaks of dark blue.

Lily would have thought such a look on a woman in her senior years would be somehow embarrassing, as though Fiona Brody were trying to deny her age, but instead, it worked. Lily's first thought was, *I want to look like her when I grow up.*

Lily came into the back yard tentatively, having followed a sign on the front door that directed her around to the back. Fortunately, she saw Finn right away and waved him over.

She'd brought a bottle of wine, and she wondered if she should have brought beer and chips instead.

"Lily, hi." Finn gave her a quick kiss on the cheek, accepted the wine bottle, and led her over to where his father was flipping burger patties on a grill that looked so complicated it might double as a 747 should the need arise.

"Hey, Dad? This is Lily."

Declan Brody looked up from what he was doing and offered his hand. "Welcome," he said. "How do you take your burgers? Is medium okay? Please don't say well done, or I'll have to send you home."

Lily laughed. "Medium is fine, Dr. Brody."

He waved a hand as though batting away the whole idea of *Dr. Brody*. "Call me Declan. If you call someone Dr. Brody, seven of us are going to answer."

Finn had used the same line, and Lily wondered if all of the Brodys did. The thought made her smile.

On the grill, in addition to the burger patties, were a line of hot dogs and another line of vegetables on wooden skewers. Declan used a pair of tongs to turn each one carefully.

Finn's mother, who'd just come out of the house bearing a plate of buns in one hand and a bowl of potato salad in the other, set everything down on a long folding table and offered Lily her hand.

"I'm Fiona. Honey, you're too dressed up. Didn't my boy tell you it was a barbecue?"

"Well …" She looked down at her cotton dress doubtfully.

"Never mind. Next time you'll know."

Lily was struck by how certain Fiona was that there would be a next time, that Lily would just seamlessly meld into the fabric of the Brody family.

The back yard was overgrown with oaks and pines interspersed with paved seating areas that looked like they'd been plunked down in the middle of an enchanted forest. Amid all of it, the Brody brothers were scattered around in various states of relaxation.

Aidan was chatting with an older man whom Lily took to be a friend of Declan and Fiona. Rowan had his arm around a blonde woman in cutoff shorts and a crop top. Nolan was sitting in an Adirondack chair with a bottle of beer in his hand, talking to … oh, God. He was talking to Shane.

Of course Lily had known Shane would be here. But knowing it and seeing him in the flesh were two different things. How was she supposed to act around him? How did one treat the man who'd had a messy breakup with her sister?

And how was Lily supposed to interact with someone who made her stammer and act stupid every time she encountered him?

Stammering and acting stupid were not Lily's default mode, and she didn't want the Brodys to think they were.

The only thing she could do was avoid Shane as much as possible. Which is what a good sister would do, under the circumstances.

"You want something to drink?" Finn asked.

It took her a while to answer, because she was staring at Shane with trepidation.

"Lily?" Finn tried again.

"What? Oh. Right. Yes. I'd love a beer."

"Coming right up." Finn went to a big Igloo cooler and brought out a longneck bottle that was cold and sweating with condensation.

Lily screwed off the cap and took a long drink, hoping it would help her to relax.

Then she turned her back to put Shane out of her line of vision and directed her attention to other, less intimidating Brodys.

"It's so interesting that your entire family are doctors," Lily said to Fiona. "How exactly did that happen?"

———

SHANE WAS SITTING WITH NOLAN, sipping a beer and talking, when Lily showed up. When he saw her, he stopped in mid-sentence.

"Shane?" Nolan said. "Everything okay?"

"What the hell is she doing here?"

"Who?"

"Her. Lily Hart." He gestured with his beer bottle.

"Oh. Finn said she was coming."

"Well, he didn't say it to me."

Shane had gone from zero to outraged in less than five seconds. It seemed to him to be an affront that his brother would bring his ex's sister to their family gathering. What was he thinking? Didn't he care how Shane felt?

When Lily saw him and then pointedly turned her back, he felt that his indignation had been validated.

"You see that?" he said. "The way she took one look at me and turned away? There's hostility there, man. God only knows what Brittany told her about me."

Nolan shrugged. "She probably said you were great until you weren't, and then you wouldn't tell her why you'd changed. You know, the usual."

"Goddamn it. You know why I—"

"Yeah, I know. But Brittany didn't. If you'd maybe let her in …"

"I didn't want to let her in."

"Well. It's probably good that it ended, then."

"Yeah, yeah." Shane had heard it all before. He'd heard how he needed to let out his feelings about February eighth—to someone, if not to the woman in his life—if he was ever going to move forward emotionally. He'd heard how his many breakups were all his fault. He'd heard how the women who'd left him were right to do it.

He knew all of that. But that didn't help him right here, today, with his ex's sister twenty yards away drinking his beer.

"But what happened with Brittany isn't your real problem," Nolan said. Which meant he was about to tell Shane what his real problem actually was. "Your real problem," Nolan went on, "is that this person here right now?" He waved a hand to indicate the entirety of Shane. "This isn't you. You were showing her a person who's different than the one she fell for, and until you can reconcile those two Shanes, you're never going to make things work with a woman."

"Ah, fuck off," Shane said, but without heat.

The thing was, Nolan was wrong. This *was* the real Shane. The friendly, easygoing version of him and the angry, hurt one who emerged every winter were both real. Pretending they weren't wasn't helping anyone.

"You sound like Finn," he told his brother.

"Well, if he and I agree on something, that's food for thought."

———

LILY TRIED to avoid Shane while making it look like she wasn't.

She chatted with the Brody brothers—all of those who weren't Shane, anyway—exchanged basic biographical information with Fiona and Declan's friends, ate a burger, drank a beer, and generally tried to pretend she was having a good time.

In fact, she would have been having a good time, genuinely, if Shane's presence hadn't made her so uncomfortable.

But why was he making her so uncomfortable? Maybe because every time she sneaked a look at him, she found him sneaking a look at her.

Finn let Lily know this hadn't escaped his notice.

"Are you expecting him to go on a murderous rampage? Or maybe grow an additional arm?"

Finn's voice jolted Lily out of her daze. "What?"

"You keep looking at Shane with a worried expression. Yes, he's going through something, but I don't think he's going to turn violent." His voice was wry, and a hint of a smile played on his features.

"Oh. I wasn't looking at him."

"Yeah, you were."

She sighed, and her shoulders fell. "Okay, I was. It's just … weird. Being here with my sister's ex. Knowing what I know about him."

"What do you know about him?"

Lily set her plate and her bottle on a patio table and threw her hands into the air. "Not enough. I know that for the first few months he and Brittany were dating, she thought he was perfect. Kind, considerate, smart, thoughtful. And then it all changed, and he wouldn't say why! It's … Well, it's a mystery, and I've never been able to leave a mystery alone."

"Really? Why can't you?"

She tilted her head and narrowed her eyes. "You can take a reporter out of the newsroom, but she's still a reporter. Always."

"Well, you need to let this go. It's not your business." He said it so calmly, so gently, that she couldn't even be offended at the rebuke.

"I know it's not."

"Does that mean you'll accept that this just isn't yours to know?"

She should. She knew that. It was the right thing to do.

"Yes," she said.

She even meant it at the time. She really did. But sometimes, good intentions weren't worth nearly as much as they should have been.

———

SHANE TOLD himself not to confront Finn about bringing Lily here. He urged himself not to do it. And yet here he was, getting a beer he didn't want just because Finn was at the cooler and it gave him an excuse to talk to him.

"You brought Lily," he said.

Finn looked at him, eyebrows raised. "Why, yes. I did. Very observant of you."

"Don't be an asshole. You know how I feel about her."

Finn turned to face him more fully. "And how is that?"

"Uncomfortable! Things ended badly with her sister. Which means Brittany's probably been talking smack to her about me. How would you feel?"

"I don't know how I'd feel," Finn said. "But I can tell you how I do actually feel right now. I feel puzzled and more than a little bit concerned that my date can only think about you. And apparently, it's mutual. Which means you're not the only one who's uncomfortable right now."

Shane started to say something, stopped, then started and stopped again.

"She's talking about me?"

"Yes, shithead. She is. And now you're talking about her. Which makes me wonder if she should be your date instead of mine."

Shane knew he should deny it, but he didn't. Yes, it was true that he didn't like having his ex's sister here. But it was also true that he found Lily Hart to be distractingly attractive. She was short and curvy, with thick, dark hair and a sprinkling of freckles across her nose that he found mesmerizing. But what difference did any of that make? You didn't make a move on your ex's sister, and you didn't make a move on your brother's date. Especially when they were the same person.

Not that he would make a move on any woman in the state he was in. His dark mood wasn't going to ease for another few weeks, and he was in no condition to inflict himself on anyone.

"Don't be stupid," Shane said, finally finding the words to deny what Finn was suggesting. "There's nothing there. You're imagining things."

"Am I?" Finn asked. "Fine. Then maybe you and she should have a few words and clear the air. This is likely not the only time I'll be bringing her around."

The idea that Finn might keep seeing Lily bothered him, but he had no right to be bothered.

"Fine," he said.

"Really?"

"Yes. I'll talk to her."

Chapter Seven

Shane had been ignoring Lily just as much as she'd been ignoring him. So she was surprised when she looked up from the food table, a plate loaded with a burger and potato salad in her hand, and saw Shane standing next to her.

Well, *surprised* wasn't quite the word for it. She was so startled she nearly dropped her plate.

"Lily," he said.

"Oh. Shane. I was … I just …" She held up her plate to demonstrate. "Burger."

"Yeah, I saw that."

God, why couldn't she talk like a normal human being around him? What was wrong with her?

"I wondered if I could have a word with you for a moment?" he said.

He could have a word with her. If she tried to have a word back, that's where she was going to run into problems.

"I … yes." She nodded. "Okay."

He took her lightly by the arm and led her to a corner of the yard where they would not be overheard. The whole way there, she felt as though every nerve in her body were concentrated on the spot where his hand touched her arm.

They came to a stop under a big oak tree, Lily still holding her plate.

"I just wanted to clear the air a little." He stuffed his hands into his pockets and rocked back and forth on his feet as though he were nervous. Of course, he couldn't be. Why would he be? She was the one with the nerves.

She waited, but he wasn't saying anything.

"So clear it." She waved her free hand at the air in a mime of blowing away some invisible fog.

"Right. Look. I know I was awful to Brittany, and I'm truly sorry. I never meant to hurt her. It's just that …" He ran a hand through his hair. "I'm going through a difficult time, and she took the brunt of it. But I don't want things to be awkward between us. Between you and me, I mean. With you dating Finn and all."

With Shane standing so close, looking down at her, she'd forgotten Finn so completely that the sound of his name gave her a jolt.

"Oh."

Lily had so many things she would say if she could only form a coherent sentence. *Why didn't you tell her what was bothering you? Why couldn't you let her in? How bad can it be? And would you ever consider letting me in? Would you ever tell me your secrets?*

Instead, she said, "She—Brittany, I mean—cares. Brittany cares. If you had just." She cleared her throat. "She would have …"

He nodded as though he knew exactly what she was trying to say. "I know. None of it was her fault. She did her best."

The admission was more than Lily had expected to hear. She'd been so predisposed to blame him that now, looking at the stubble on his chin, the dark circles under his eyes, she had to reconsider. Whatever was bothering him, it was giving him hell. If he hadn't opened up to Brittany, maybe it wasn't his fault. Maybe he'd done his best, too.

"It doesn't have to be," she blurted out. "Awkward, I mean. With us. Just because …" She gestured vaguely toward Finn.

"Okay." He nodded. "Good. That's good." She was still holding her plate, and Shane gestured toward it. "Well. I should let you eat."

He wandered off, and her eyes followed him for far too long.

————

SHANE FELT REASONABLY good about his conversation with Lily. That didn't mean he liked the fact that she was dating his brother, but at least they'd come to some sort of understanding. At least, he thought they had. It was hard to tell, the way Lily seemed to come unglued whenever he talked to her.

Why was that, anyway?

He was still wondering when Finn came over to stand next to him.

"So, you talked to her," Finn said.

"I did."

"How did that go?"

"Okay, I think."

"Then stop glaring at her. It's unsettling."

Was he doing that? He hadn't thought he was, but now, he realized his eyes were on Lily and his expression was stormy. He made a conscious effort to look elsewhere and to put on a neutral face.

"I'm not glaring," he said.

What he was doing was *gazing*, not glaring. Lily was, undeniably, pleasant to look at. She couldn't have been more than five feet tall, so adorably pint-sized, and those curves …

"You're doing it again," Finn said. "Are we going to have a problem?"

"No. No, we're not." Shane went off to get a plate of food he didn't really want just to make it look like there were other things—or people—he didn't want.

————

WHEN LILY SAID goodbye to Finn at the end of the evening, she could tell something was bothering him. She just wasn't sure what it was.

"I had a good time," she told him.

"Did you?"

She cocked her head, regarding him. "What does that mean?"

"It means you and Shane seemed distinctly uneasy with each other all evening. I'm wondering if that's about more than just Brittany."

"Why would it be?"

That wasn't an answer, and Finn wasn't naïve enough to think it was.

Finn shrugged. "I don't know. It just seems like there's more going on there."

"You're off duty right now, Finn. You don't need to be my psychiatrist." She smiled to soften it. She softened it further by stepping closer to him and putting her arms around him.

"*Hmm*. Maybe there are other things I can do for you." His voice was a low growl, and he leaned in to nuzzle her ear with his nose.

Lily and Finn hadn't gone there yet. Kissing, yes. Some warm embraces. He'd been hinting about more for a while now, but Lily kept putting him off.

"I'd better get home," she said.

"I could drive you."

"I have my car."

"I could bring you back for it. You know, in the morning." He caught her earlobe gently between his teeth.

She hesitated. "Another time?"

He released her ear and straightened, looking down at her. His hands rested on her upper arms, and that felt nice. But it didn't feel like the electricity she'd experienced when Shane had put his hand on her.

"Sure," he said. "Of course."

She kissed him goodbye, got into her car, and drove home thinking about the Brody boys—two of them in particular. The one she should have wanted, and the one she shouldn't want but did.

———

WHEN SHE GOT HOME, Brittany was on the sofa watching *When Harry Met Sally.*

"That movie again?" Lily said as she put down her purse and took off her jacket.

"Always." She picked up the remote and paused the movie. "How was the Brody family get-together?"

"It was nice. I like Finn's parents."

"I do, too. How were things with Shane? Not too weird, I hope."

"It was a little weird, yeah." She sat down next to Brittany and put her feet up on the coffee table. "We talked about you."

"You did?"

"Yes. Shane said he never meant to hurt you. He said the breakup wasn't your fault."

"I know it wasn't." Brittany pulled a throw pillow onto her lap and hugged it. "But that doesn't mean I didn't feel like crap, breaking up with him when he was obviously upset about something."

Lily seized on the one point she kept bringing up to herself whenever she thought about Shane. "But you two weren't even a match, right? I mean, it would have ended eventually, even if he hadn't gone all silent and gloomy on you."

"Honestly, yes. I think that's true." Brittany sighed. "I think I wanted it to work because it looked so good in theory, you know? But the idea of marrying him, having his kids someday?" She shook her head. "I just couldn't see it, even before things went wrong."

Lily had known that, but hearing it from her sister lifted her spirits. Not because it would ease Lily's guilt if she ever made a move on Shane herself. She would never do that. Obviously. It made her feel better because it meant Brittany and Shane both were better off.

Strictly altruism.

Chapter Eight

Over the next week, Lily finished the essential oils manuscript and sent it to the production editor who'd assigned it to her; interviewed someone from the Rotary Club about a fundraiser they were doing to create scholarships for local high school students; wrote an article about a fire on Burton Drive that destroyed a longtime business; and wrote the first two chapters of her novel.

She went out with Finn twice—once for dinner, and once for a casual lunch and a walk at Fiscalini Ranch. She was getting ready to see him again on Friday night, primping in front of the bathroom mirror with mascara and eyeliner, when Brittany peeked in and looked into the mirror over Lily's shoulder.

"Seeing Finn again?" she asked.

"We're going to a movie in San Luis Obispo."

"So it's going well, then?"

"Sure it is. Why wouldn't it be?"

Then Brittany gave her a mischievous look. "How is he in bed? I'm imagining he's super sensitive, what with the psychiatry and all. Concerned about your feelings, that kind of thing. Then again, he could have a dark alpha side."

Lily didn't answer. She focused on getting her eyeliner straight instead.

"Oh, come on," Brittany said. "If you can't tell this kind of thing to your sister, who can you tell?"

"It's not that." Lily, satisfied with her eyes, put the cap back on the tube.

"Then what?"

Lily shrugged. "We haven't done that yet."

Brittany's eyes widened. "You haven't? But you've been dating for weeks!"

"So? Does that mean I just have to jump into bed with him? We're taking it slow."

"How does he feel about that? The whole taking it slow thing? Are you both on board, or is it just you?"

"Does it matter? If one person in a couple wants to take it slow, then you take it slow."

"Fair enough. But you haven't always been this cautious. What's going on? Is there something wrong between you? If you're not sure about him—"

Lily spun to face her sister. "You're right. I haven't always been this careful. But look at the mistakes I've made in the past. I'm trying to do better. I'm trying to do things differently to get a different result."

She'd jumped into things with Trevor, and look how that had turned out. Following her heart hadn't done much for her, so now she was following her head.

Neither her head nor her heart wanted to sleep with Finn, but that would change once she got to know him better. Once they felt more comfortable as a couple.

Brittany pointed one finger at her sister. "This plan of yours? The one where you're not into him but you're trying to be because it seems, logically, like the two of you should make sense? It's not working. That's why you haven't taken your panties off yet."

The fact that Brittany had pegged the situation so exactly irritated Lily, so she denied it.

"I haven't taken my panties off because it just hasn't been the right time."

"*Mmm hmm*," Brittany said, clearly not believing a word of it. "If you wanted it, you'd make it the right time."

———

LILY DECIDED that she just hadn't been trying hard enough to have a good attitude about Finn. She was lucky to be dating him. He was successful, handsome, kind, smart, and considerate. What more was she looking for?

So she kissed him with enthusiasm when he picked her up. She held his hand while they watched the movie, resting her head on his shoulder during the most romantic parts. Then, when it was over, she suggested they keep the evening going. She wasn't ready to bring him back to her place—or to go to his—so she suggested Ted's, a bar off Main Street.

"Are you sure you want to go there?" he asked. "It's kind of a dive."

"Oh, I know. But it's got a certain charm. Come on, it'll be fun."

And it might have been, she supposed, if not for the fact that Ted's was a favorite spot for many of the Cambria locals. Which meant that people she knew were already at the bar when they arrived. Including Brittany and Candace.

And Shane Brody.

If Lily had spotted Shane right away, she'd have made an excuse for them to go elsewhere. But she didn't. She saw Brittany and Candace and made her way over to them to say hello, and it was only afterward that she noticed Shane standing over at the pool tables.

"Hey, you guys." Brittany greeted them with enthusiasm. "How was the movie?"

"Oh, it was fine," Lily said. "Funny in places and all warm and squishy at the end. Just the way I like them."

"It wasn't as bad as I thought it would be," Finn said, giving

Brittany a wry smile. "I didn't have to fake an emergency text or anything."

"You'd do that?" Lily asked.

"Only if it was urgent. An Adam Sandler movie, for instance."

That was the moment when Lily saw Shane and heard his voice. She couldn't make out what he'd said over the din in the room, but it was definitely him.

Her head swiveled toward him, the three people in her company forgotten.

There he was, all tall and thick-haired and brooding. Her heart sped up and her palms started to sweat. She told herself it was only because he made her uncomfortable—only because she was afraid she'd have to talk to him and would say something stupid.

Eventually she realized Brittany was talking to her.

" … Lily?"

Lily blinked a few times. "I … what?"

Brittany looked at Lily, then at Shane, and then at Finn.

"I need to use the ladies' room," she announced. "Lily, you're coming with me."

She grabbed Lily by the arm and pulled.

————

WHEN THEY WERE IN THE LADIES' room together, Brittany spun on her, arms crossed over her chest.

"What the hell do you think you're doing?"

"What are you talking about? You're the one who wanted me to come in here with you."

"That's not what I mean, and you know it. What are you doing ogling Shane? And don't give me some line of bullshit, either. I want to know the truth. Do you have a thing for my ex-boyfriend?"

"No! Of course not!" Lily pressed one open hand to her breastbone.

"*Mm hmm.*" Brittany narrowed her eyes at Lily.

"I don't like what you're accusing me of," Lily said. "Do you really think I'd make a move on your ex? Do you think I don't understand the rules of sisterhood? Or that I do understand the rules and would just … would just break them willy nilly?"

"Maybe not." Brittany glared at her. "But that doesn't mean you're not experiencing a certain amount of lust and longing."

Okay, Brittany had her there. Not that she was about to admit it.

"You know what the worst part of it is?" Brittany went on.

"I'm sure you'll tell me."

"The worst part is that Finn is a really great guy who likes you a lot and who would make a great partner. And you barely look at him when Shane is in the room."

"What you're seeing is not lust and longing." Lily threw her hands into the air. "It's outrage for you and for the way he treated you. That's all it is!"

"That's all," Brittany repeated.

"Yes!"

"If you say so." Brittany pointed a finger at her. "But for the record? Finn deserves better than what you're giving him. And you know it."

———

SHANE DIDN'T IMMEDIATELY LOOK up when Lily came into the room, but he knew she was there, all the same. He felt her. Almost as though a certain electric charge filled the air as soon as she entered a space.

He was playing pool with Rowan in an effort to distract himself from all of his messy feelings. Rowan was good for that kind of thing—usually, when you were with him, you couldn't focus on anything but how annoying he was.

Case in point, it was Rowan's turn, but he was too busy staring at a blonde in a short skirt to notice.

"Hey, dickhead. It's your turn. You think you can tear your eyes off that woman long enough to bungle your shot?" Shane asked. It was the kind of brotherly banter Rowan particularly enjoyed.

"We'll see who bungles what when I sink the nine into the corner pocket." Rowan took a slug from his mug of beer, then lined up for the shot. That was when he saw Lily with Finn.

"Oh ho." Rowan straightened up again before he could even play.

"Oh ho what?" But Shane knew. He'd already seen Lily and had already made the decision to try to ignore her.

"Brittany's sister is here with Finn. Don't tell me you didn't notice."

Shane didn't even try to deny it. "What am I supposed to do about it? Am I supposed to leave just because those two decided to have a drink? Like hell."

That was exactly what he wanted to do, though. He wanted to put down his cue, leave his beer unconsumed, and walk out of here so he wouldn't have to think about Lily with his brother.

Because, increasingly, he knew he wanted her for himself. He'd started out claiming to be uncomfortable because of bad blood between himself and Lily. He'd even believed it. But more and more, he knew that was bullshit. He wanted her, and he *couldn't* want her, because she was both his ex's sister and his brother's girlfriend. Two reasons she was strictly on his one-woman list of eligible women he could never date.

He accepted that he couldn't date her. That didn't mean he had to like it.

You're in no shape to date anyone anyway.

That was another thing. What would happen if he did start something up with her? It would go okay at first, and then he'd turn dark and silent and brooding, and she'd run like hell.

Just the way Brittany had.

So there was no point, anyway. But that didn't mean he liked seeing her with Finn.

He hated the way Finn had his arm around her waist like he owned her. The way Finn was whispering something into her ear. The way Lily laughed in response. And the idea of what they might get up to later, after they left here …

"Hey. Are you going to take your turn, or what?"

Shane awoke from his thoughts to realize Rowan was talking to him. Rowan had finished his turn God knew how long ago, and now he was standing with his cue in one hand and his beer mug in the other, smirking at Shane.

Shane took his shot—six in the side pocket—and missed by a mile. No wonder. He was so distracted it was a surprise he remembered which end of the stick to use.

He was watching Lily while trying not to look like he was watching her. At the same time, she was watching him while trying to look like she wasn't.

What a pair they made.

And that was exactly the kind of thing he shouldn't be thinking.

He lost the game by far more than he should have, then paid Rowan the twenty they'd bet.

"Look. I've gotta go," he told Rowan.

"It's not even ten o'clock," Rowan protested.

"I've got an early morning."

"Bullshit. Tomorrow's Saturday."

Shane racked his cue and put on his jacket, the muscles in his jaw bunching up as he thought about Finn's hands on Lily.

"Don't you even want to say hello to Finn?" Rowan asked.

Shane's lips pressed into a tight line. "That's about the last fucking thing I want to do."

AS SHANE WALKED out of Ted's, weaving his way past patrons in various states of intoxication, Lily couldn't take her eyes off him.

She only realized she'd been staring when the front door closed behind him and she emerged into consciousness to find that Finn, Brittany, Candace, and even Rowan, who was across the room, were looking at her.

All of them had been watching her watch Shane.

She couldn't quite read Finn's expression, but it was clear he'd taken notice of her interest in Shane, and he had thoughts about it. She was willing to bet they weren't happy, encouraging ones.

"Should we go over and say hello to Rowan?" she asked, just to get the attention onto someone other than herself. Then she noticed that Rowan was talking to the blonde, penning her in with one hand propped against the wall on either side of her. "Or, maybe not," she said.

Chapter Nine

S hane drove to his house on Happy Hill thinking of Lily, but she wasn't the only woman on his mind.

February eighth was just a week away, and he felt it approaching like a gathering storm.

The anniversary of his sister's death. His *twin* sister.

That would have been bad enough on its own, but the accident that had taken her life had been Shane's fault.

His parents, his brothers, his friends—hell, everyone in his life urged him to get therapy, work through it, feel better. But he didn't *want* to feel better. He wanted to suffer like this every year for the rest of his life. He deserved to suffer, and no matter how much he did, no matter how bad he felt for how long, he would never begin to make up for the suffering he'd caused to everyone he loved.

It was a debt he would never be able to repay.

So, yes, he wanted Lily. But what right did he have to inflict this on her? She needed someone emotionally stable, and he wasn't it. Oh, he put on a good show of it most of the time. But the weeks preceding and following February eighth? Well, he just couldn't fake it anymore.

He got home, unlocked the door, and walked into the dark

house. He didn't bother to turn on a light—the moonlight was bright enough, and anyway, the darkness fit his mood.

He went into his bedroom, took off his jacket, and fell onto the bed, lying on his back and looking at the ceiling.

He didn't deserve to get married, have kids, build a family of his own. If Molly couldn't do those things, then neither should he.

For that reason if no other, he needed to put Lily Hart out of his mind.

———

FINN WAS quiet as he drove Lily to the house she shared with Brittany on Lodge Hill.

Lily wanted to ask if everything was all right, but she knew it wasn't. He'd seen the way she'd looked at Shane, and he was processing it. If she asked, they'd have to talk about it, and what would she say? How could she explain herself?

Better to pretend nothing had happened. And it hadn't, really. She hadn't spoken to Shane, nor had she spoken about him. What had she done wrong? Nothing. And she needed to act that way.

When he pulled up at the curb, she turned to him. "Do you want to come in for a while?"

Usually when you asked a man to come in at the end of the date, you were inviting him to have sex. But that wasn't Lily's intention. She just thought they could have a glass of wine and be together as friends. Because that's how she was beginning to think of him—as a friend.

"I don't think that's a good idea," he said.

Despite everything, Lily felt stung. "Why not?"

"Because I'm tired. It's been a long day."

"Finn ..."

"Really, Lily. I've got to go. I'll talk to you tomorrow."

She got out of the car, and he drove away while she was still standing there.

———

LILY WAS LYING on her bed, fully clothed, staring at the ceiling when Brittany came home from Ted's. She poked her head into Lily's room.

"Hey. Are you okay?"

"Why wouldn't I be?"

Brittany rolled her eyes to indicate she could not be fooled. She swayed a little on her feet, and her gaze seemed unfocused. Lily sat up on the bed.

"You're drunk," she said.

"Just a little."

"You didn't drive home, did you? Because—"

"Of course not. What do you take me for? Candace didn't drink. She drove me home."

"Candace didn't drink?" Lily processed that. Candace usually wasn't a heavy drinker, but she did enjoy a glass of wine or two on an evening out.

"No. She didn't. Because she's pregnant!" Brittany looked like she'd been overflowing with the news, and now, having told it, her face was glowing with happiness for her friend.

"She is? Oh my God! When did she tell you? How far along is she? What did Evan say?"

Brittany sat down on the bed next to Lily. "She told me tonight. She's five weeks, which means she just found out. And she hasn't told Evan yet. She's planning a big thing—dinner, candlelight, a WORLD'S BEST FATHER T-shirt."

"Wow. That's so great."

Candace and Evan were going to make great parents, and Lily was happy for them. And yet she seemed to have tears running down her face.

"Wait. You're crying. What's wrong?" Brittany grabbed Lily's forearm.

"Nothing. It's nothing."

"Bullshit," Brittany said.

Lily shrugged. "I think Finn is going to break up with me."

Brittany let go of Lily's arm. "Oh." She didn't sound surprised.

"Oh? Just oh?"

"Well, I'm not sure what else to say. I mean, you've had to know it was coming."

Brittany's reaction surprised Lily. How could Brittany have known it was coming when Lily herself hadn't?

"What do you mean? Why would I know? Things have been going … fine. They're fine!"

"Lily. You've been dating him for weeks and you haven't slept with him yet. You can't take your eyes off his brother. And the best adjective you can come up with for your relationship is *fine*. But you're telling me it's a complete surprise that he's going to end it?"

Well, when she put it that way.

"It's just … I wanted it to work, that's all."

"I know you did," Brittany said. "You always do, and then it never does. And it never will until you figure out that you deserve to get what you want." She paused, then pointed a finger at Lily. "As long as what you want isn't Shane."

———

SHANE WAS STANDING in front of the TV in sweatpants and a T-shirt, trying to decide whether to watch something to slow his mind down or to try just going to sleep. He wasn't expecting a knock on his door at this time of night, but there it was.

He opened the door to find Finn standing there, his face stormy.

"Well, who ate your Snickers?" Shane asked.

"Shut up and let me in."

Shane stood back so Finn could come into the house, and he braced himself for whatever it was he'd come here to say.

He didn't have to wait long. Finn spun around and glared at him. "What the hell is going on between you and Lily?"

Shane sighed. "Literally nothing is going on between me and Lily."

"That's crap."

"No, it's the truth. We're not seeing each other behind your back, and we don't have simmering feelings for each other. We don't even talk."

"Well. I figure that's two-thirds true."

"What the hell do you mean?" Shane knew exactly what he meant, but he wanted Finn to say it.

"I believe you're not talking or seeing each other. But the part about you not having simmering feelings? That's the biggest load of steaming horse shit I've ever heard. And I'm a psychiatrist. The amount of steaming horse shit I've heard could fill a barn."

At this point, Shane could either admit it or deny it. He went with obfuscation.

"What makes you say that?"

"I say it because it's true. Are you going to stand there and lie to me?"

Shane ran both hands through his hair and sank down onto the sofa. "If we've got feelings, they're feelings of discomfort because of Brittany. That's what you're seeing."

"That's not what I'm seeing. And you're insulting me by pretending it is."

"Fine. So, why don't you tell me what you think is going on, Dr. Freud?"

Finn sat down on an ottoman facing his brother. "I think you're attracted to her, but you're pretending you're not because of some idea about brothers and exes and rules about what you are and are not supposed to do. And I think it's wrecking any chance Lily and I have together."

"Oh, come on. That's—"

"And." Finn stopped him, pointing one finger at Shane's face. "I think you're also so deep in your self-pity about Molly that you're using Lily to torture yourself on purpose. And I think I could stop wasting my time with her if you'd just admit it."

The way Shane felt, the last thing he needed was Finn in his face being right.

And decades of sibling rivalry meant that admitting Finn's rightness was not an option.

"If you can't get things going with Lily, don't blame me," Shane said. "Maybe she just doesn't respond to your touchy-feely approach to things. Maybe it reminds her of talking to her sister."

One of the most annoying things about Finn was that he was mostly unflappable, and he didn't react to Shane's jab. Instead, he softened his voice and gave Shane a meaningful look. "You've got some kind of feelings about Lily, and I'm not sure what they are, but I'm certain they're going to make it impossible for me to keep seeing her."

"I told you. Don't blame me if—"

"I'm not blaming you for anything," Finn said. "What I am doing is urging you to get your shit together. Not for my sake, or for Lily's, but for yours."

When Finn left, Shane closed and locked the front door behind him. Then he rested his forehead against the smooth wood and breathed. He'd messed things up for himself and Brittany, and now he'd messed things up for Finn and Lily.

Just more evidence that he wasn't in the right head space to be with any woman right now. Maybe ever again.

Chapter Ten

Lily had known things with Finn were nearing their end. But when he asked her out for lunch a few days later, she tried to tell herself that maybe he'd forgiven her for how she'd acted.

Maybe he was willing to give her another chance.

The fact that she wasn't sure she wanted another chance was something she pushed to the back of her mind.

They met at the Moonstone Beach Bar and Grill and sat on the patio with a view of the ocean. The sky was lightly overcast, and a breeze ruffled the umbrella over their heads.

Finn ordered a sandwich and Lily ordered a salad, and they sipped ice water while they waited for their food.

Lily knew from the look on Finn's face and from the way he was fidgeting with his napkin that she was going to be single again before her food arrived.

"Just tell me," she said. "You've got something on your mind, and I think you should get it out."

"Okay. Lily, this isn't easy."

"You talk about difficult things all the time with your patients," she said. "Just pretend I'm one of them."

Finn pressed his lips together and gave her a crisp nod. "I don't think we should see each other anymore."

Exactly what she'd expected from the way he'd been acting since she'd arrived. And her salad hadn't even come yet, as she'd predicted. Were they expected to eat lunch together now that they'd broken up? Were they really supposed to deal with that kind of awkwardness while they tried to digest their food?

"I can't say I'm surprised," she said.

"I didn't think you would be, given that you want my brother instead of me."

Lily stared at him. She hadn't expected this kind of directness. Somehow, she'd thought they would skirt over the issue with bland statements of *just bad timing* and *it's not you, it's me.*

"I should go," she said.

He reached out and took her hand. "Please don't. I think we should talk."

"What's there to talk about? If it's over, it's over."

"Not about us. I want to talk about you and Shane."

Her butt was two inches off the seat as she'd been standing to go. Now she slowly lowered herself back into her chair. "There's nothing between me and Shane."

"Well, I don't actually believe that's true. I do believe that nothing's happened between you. Yet. But I'm not blind, Lily. I see the way you look at each other. And I want to know what's going on. For his sake and yours."

Lily's expression hardened. "If there were anything going on between me and Shane—which there isn't—it wouldn't be any of your business. Not now that you've broken up with me."

"It is, because I care about him. He's fragile right now. And I don't want anyone playing games with him."

Lily had thought this talk was going to be about Finn's feelings for her and his jealousy because he thought she wanted Shane. But it was turning into something different. Finn knew where his loyalties lay, and they were firmly with his brother.

That was fair enough, but he seemed to think Lily was some kind of threat to Shane, which was just ridiculous.

"I'm not playing games with anyone," she said.

Finn crossed his forearms on the table and leaned toward her. "I certainly hope not. You've been stringing me along when you obviously have no real interest in me. If you do that with Shane …" He left it open as an expression of worry. Or maybe as an implied threat.

"I'm not doing anything with Shane," she insisted. "Though …"

"Though what?"

"I am interested in him, but not in the way you think."

"In exactly what way, then?"

Lily picked up her water glass, took a sip, then put it down precisely inside the ring of condensation it had created on the table. "The way he acted with Brittany … He was wonderful. Caring, warm, considerate. And then everything changed. Something happened, and I want to know what it was."

"That's none of your business."

Finn, usually so warm and caring and considerate himself, was now looking at Lily with an expression that said she shouldn't mess with him or his family. The look he was giving her was intimidating, but she was a reporter. She resolved not to be intimidated.

"It's my business because I care about my sister. Just like you care about your brother." He opened his mouth to say something, but Lily stopped him, holding up one finger. "And," she continued, "I have to wonder if you're doing him any favors by supporting all of this secrecy. People who have emotional,"—she struggled for a word—"*things* to work out benefit from talking about them. You of all people should know that."

"And not all emotional *things* are for public consumption." He made finger quotes around the word *things*. "As a reporter, I doubt you do know that, but it's true."

He got up from the table just as the waitress arrived with his sandwich. Finn, ever courteous, opened his wallet and put a couple of twenties on the table before walking away.

———

THAT NIGHT when Brittany came home, Lily tried to act like nothing had happened, but she was upset about her conversation with Finn, and Brittany could see that. She started grilling Lily immediately.

"What happened? Is it Mom?"

Their mother, who was diabetic, had been sick lately. It hadn't occurred to Lily that Brittany would jump to the conclusion that she'd gotten worse.

"What? No. Nothing happened."

"Then why does your face look like that?"

Lily didn't know what, exactly, her face looked like, but Brittany had an unerring ability to read her emotions. She always had, ever since they were kids.

"This is just my face."

"It's your face after something upset you." Brittany was still holding her purse, having just come in the door. She plunked it down on the dining table. "You might as well tell me, because I'm not going to stop hounding you until you do."

Lily sank down into a dining chair and threw her hands up. "Fine. Finn broke up with me. There. Now you know."

Brittany pulled out a chair and sat down next to her sister. "He did? Oh, no. What happened?"

"I don't want to talk about it."

"Oh, Lily. That sucks. But what did he say?"

"I don't want to talk about what he said!"

If they talked about what he said, then they'd have to talk about Shane, and Lily didn't want to go there, especially with Brittany. How could she admit to her sister that Finn was right—she did have feelings for Brittany's ex? She also didn't want to admit what he'd implied about her being nosy and insensitive, poking into things that were Shane's personal business.

And finally, she did not want to talk about the fact that her theory had been wrong—the one that said she could have a healthy, functional relationship with a man as long as it was someone who didn't set off her personal defense mechanisms. She'd been counting on that strategy, and now that it hadn't worked, she worried she was doomed to grow old and die alone.

The more she thought about it—about how unlikely it was that she would ever want a man who actually was good for her—the more hopeless it seemed. And the more hopeless it seemed, the more she found it difficult to hide her emotions. Before she knew it, tears were leaking down her face and she was making a kind of *huh-huh-huh* noise. Much to her horror.

Brittany immediately flew into protective sister mode.

"Oh, Lily. It's okay. It's going to be okay." She rubbed Lily's shoulder. "I didn't even know you cared that much about Finn. I thought he was just one of your placeholder boyfriends."

"My *puh-puh*-placeholder boyfriends?" Lily stared at her sister through blurry eyes.

"Well, yes. You know—someone you were dating because he's safe and unthreatening but who you could never really have serious feelings for."

That was exactly what Finn was, and Lily was ashamed of having used him that way. Which made her cry harder.

Brittany's eyes narrowed, and she stared at Lily. "Tell me what he did to you."

"I … I … He … He …" It sounded more like Lamaze breathing than any kind of response.

Brittany stood up, grabbed her purse, and slung the strap over her shoulder, an angry and determined expression on her face. "Don't worry, Lily. I've got this."

"You've got what? Brittany? What—"

Brittany was out the door before Lily could stop her.

———

IF SHANE HADN'T BEEN at Finn's place that night, he might never have known what happened. But he was there, so he saw the whole thing when Brittany pounded on the door, barged in, and started ripping his brother a new bodily orifice.

"I don't know what you said to Lily or what you did to her, but I swear to God, Finn, you'd better tell me right this second or I'll make you sorry."

"What the hell are you talking about, Brittany?" Shane stepped between her and Finn.

"I didn't come here to talk to you, Shane. I came here to talk to Finn. So please step aside and let me talk to Finn."

Shane was many things, but he was not a fool, so he stepped back while Brittany poked a finger into his brother's chest.

"Lily is at home crying right now." Poke. "Because of you." Poke. "So whatever you did," poke, "you're going to make it right."

Finn remained as calm as a still spring day. "I didn't do anything to her. If she said I did, she misled you."

"She didn't tell me anything! She was too upset!"

"Well, I'm sorry about that. Truly. But what was said between us is just that. Between us."

Shane tried to stay out of it, but he found he couldn't. "Finn, goddamn it. What did you say to her?"

Brittany looked at Shane and then back at Finn, apparently willing to put aside her feelings about him in order to have an ally.

Finn rubbed his forehead as though the whole thing was giving him a headache. "What I said to her, and what she said to me, is private. But … our relationship wasn't working out, so I ended it. I'm allowed to do that. And that's all either one of you needs to know."

Brittany demanded a few more times to know what was said, and Finn refused a few more times to tell her. She left angry, scowling, her face red with fury.

When she was gone, Shane turned to his brother.

"All right, she's gone. You can tell me what happened."

"Weren't you listening?" Finn said. "That's private. It's between me and Lily."

"Look. I realize I've got nothing to do with this, but——"

Finn scoffed and rolled his eyes, and Shane stopped in mid-sentence.

"What is that supposed to mean? That sound you made. And

the eye roll. What the hell is that supposed to mean, Finn?" Shane stared at his brother, his hands planted on his hips.

"All right. You want to go there? That sound and the eye roll mean you're not as irrelevant to this situation as you'd like to pretend."

"Meaning?"

"Meaning, we broke up because of you. Okay, asshole? Happy now?"

"Me? But Brittany said she was crying. She said—"

"I'm not talking about this anymore, Shane. If you're going to keep asking, maybe you should go."

"Goddamn it, Finn."

"You want me to hold the door open for you, or you think you can manage it yourself?" Finn asked.

Shane scowled at his brother and stormed out of the house.

Chapter Eleven

Over the next couple of days, the thing with Finn ate at Shane. He knew what happened between Finn and Lily was none of his business, and yet he wanted to know who'd said what and why. Lily had been crying, Brittany said. She'd been upset. Shane felt an overwhelming urge to fix it, but that was stupid. People dated, then they broke up. It happened all the time. It wasn't a crisis. There was no need for intervention.

He pulled weeds in his yard and went to work and did his laundry and attended to all of the things a responsible adult should attend to.

But the entire time, his mind was on Lily.

The fact that his mind was on Lily and not on February eighth, which was a mere week away, should have seemed significant to him, but somehow, he didn't realize it. All he could think about was whether Lily was okay, and if not, whether he needed to kick his brother's ass.

He had a follow-up appointment with Orin Delaney, provided the full concierge medicine service to a wealthy patient a few miles up Santa Rosa Creek Road who wanted a checkup, and gave care to three low-income patients at no charge: one for asthma, one for diabetes, and one for a nasty skin rash.

The entire time, Lily was on his mind, so when he ran into her at Soto's on Main Street one day after work, it almost felt as though he'd conjured her.

She was carrying a plastic container from the deli—dinner for one—and Shane was holding a basket bearing an organic frozen dinner and two apples. Apparently, neither of them had plans.

"Oh. Lily," Shane said, coming to a halt in the cereal aisle.

When she saw him, she looked stricken and immediately began to engineer her escape.

"Oh. Hello. I was just … Oh, God." Lily turned around as though she was just going to walk away from him, then she must have realized that would be rude. She stopped and turned to face him again. "I have to go," she said.

"Wait."

She hesitated, and he plunged right in. "Finn said you two broke up, and Brittany said you were upset. What did he say to you? What did he do? Lily …"

To his horror, her eyes reddened and grew damp, and her face went all blotchy with emotion. "I just … I can't talk about this. Please. I have to go." Then she turned and fled as though gunmen were chasing her.

Shane didn't know what Finn had done to get her this upset, but he was damned well going to find out.

———

LILY LEFT Soto's flustered and in tears. It seemed she couldn't have even the simplest conversation with Shane without bungling it, but more than that, seeing him and hearing him mention Finn were reminders that she couldn't talk to the men who really interested her, and she couldn't make it work with perfectly good men who didn't.

Where did that leave her? Was she doomed to be alone forever?

The way she'd acted, Shane probably thought she was a

completely unhinged fool. And, hell, maybe she was. All she wanted was a normal, functional relationship, and it seemed she was destined never to have one. But why? Others managed it. Why couldn't she?

She went home but no longer had an appetite. She put her food in the refrigerator and went to take a hot bath.

———

SHANE WENT HOME, put away his purchases, and called Finn.

"I want to know what the hell you said to Lily, and I want to know now." He launched into it before Finn could say anything other than *hello*.

"This again?" Finn said.

"Yes, this again. I just saw her at the market and she's still crying at the very mention of your name. What did you do to her?"

Finn didn't answer.

"Fine," Shane said. "If that's the way you want to play it, I'll find out myself."

"What are you going to do? Shane?"

"I'm going over there, and I'm not going to leave until I have answers. It's what I should have done from the beginning." He hung up while Finn was still protesting.

———

SHANE SHOWED up at Lily's house with a full head of steam and determination. He pounded the door with the side of his fist, ready to break the damned thing down if he had to.

"Lily? It's Shane. Let me in. I need to talk to you. Lily!"

She didn't answer, but her car was out front. He had images of her barricaded inside, weeping and mired in despair.

"Lily!" He banged on the door a few more times. Nothing.

He'd just pulled out his cell phone, thinking to call her and tell her to open the door, when he heard the lock unlatch and the door swung open.

And there stood Lily, hair wet, wearing nothing but a bathrobe.

The idea of what might be under there struck him momentarily stupid.

———

"WHAT ARE YOU DOING HERE?" Lily held the bathrobe tight at her throat with one hand, conscious of how she must look. Wet hair, no makeup, feet bare, only a thin robe covering her. She'd been taking the bath to help her forget about him, for God's sake. Instead, it was like she'd manifested him out of thin air.

"Let me come in."

"No."

"Lily, please?"

The way he said it—the worry in his voice—swayed her. "All right. But not … I mean … Just for a minute."

She stepped back from the door to let him enter, but not far enough, it seemed, because he passed so close to her she could smell his earthy scent. It nearly made her swoon.

"I want to know what Finn did to you." He said it before she'd even fully closed the door.

"He didn't do anything."

"That's crap. Brittany said you were upset, and today at the market, you barely heard his name before you started tearing up. I want to know what he did, and I want to know now. And then I'm going to go kick his ass from here to next week."

This was something Lily hadn't expected. Protectiveness? Why? Because she was Brittany's sister?

"Look, Shane, I—"

"You don't have to protect him. If he hurt you, he deserves whatever he gets."

"He … he didn't."

She was stammering, the way she always did when Shane was near. She willed herself to stop it, to hold herself together. She was a capable adult, and she needed to act like it.

"Lily?"

"He didn't do anything, Shane. Except tell the truth."

"The truth about what? Why did he break up with you?"

This was the pivotal moment when she could either lie or tell the truth. If she lied, it was likely Shane would hear it from Finn anyway. *I'm a capable adult.* She closed her eyes, took a deep breath, then opened them.

"He broke up with me because he thinks I have a thing for you."

Shane froze. She didn't know what she'd expected him to say, but she'd surely expected him to say *something* instead of standing there, speechless and wide-eyed.

"Shane?"

"He said …"

"That's what he said, yes."

"Well, do you? Have a thing for me?"

She opened her mouth, closed it, then tried again. "I don't know that I'd call it a *thing*. But … he's not entirely wrong. There might be something. Some kind of *thinglike* situation. Not that I would act on it. You're my sister's ex and Finn's brother, and …" So much for her composing herself.

Shane drew his hand across his mouth, looking at her. Devouring her with his eyes, more like. Suddenly, Lily felt hot all over. And when he reached out and gently touched her face, she thought she might burst into flames.

––––––––

SHANE KNEW he should not be here. He should not be touching Lily. And he sure as hell should not be thinking about kissing her. But he *was* thinking about it. And then, before he'd even thought it through, he was doing it.

He touched his lips to hers, his hand on her cheek, and she whimpered in a way that sent a bolt of electricity straight to his groin.

"Lily." He murmured her name, and she parted her lips to him, accepting the kiss and then deepening it.

All rational thought fled his brain. He pulled her into his arms, his mouth on hers, his tongue caressing hers. He wasn't thinking about Finn or Brittany or even Molly, only about how she felt in his arms, how she tasted, and how one tug of the belt around her waist would have her naked and pressed against him.

Before he knew what he was doing, he had her down on the sofa, his body over hers, his hand on her waist inside the robe. He smelled the scent of her soap, of lavender shampoo.

"Shane." She breathed his name.

He tried to gather his senses, tried to remind himself to be responsible, to do the right thing.

"Do you want me to leave?" he whispered, his voice ragged.

"No." Then she kissed him harder, deeper, pulling him to her. The robe fell open, and he cupped her breast in his hand.

He didn't notice when the door opened. Didn't notice that someone was in the room, saying something. And then he did notice. He let go of Lily and sat up abruptly, dizziness swimming in his brain as his ears started working again.

That was when he realized both Brittany and Finn were here and yelling at him.

———

THE FIRST THING Lily noticed when Shane leaped off her was that Brittany and Finn were in the room—though where they'd come from, she didn't know. It was almost as though they'd materialized out of thin air. The second thing she noticed was that her robe was open and she wasn't wearing anything underneath it.

She jumped off the sofa and pulled it closed, tying the belt and then holding the front together with both hands for good measure.

"What the hell is going on here? Shane? Lily?" Brittany gaped at them.

"I knew it. I goddamned knew it." Finn stood with his hands on his hips, his expression thunderous.

"Let's everybody just calm down," Shane said.

"Calm down? Calm down?" Brittany's face was a mask of

almost comical shock. "Our relationship is barely cold and you're here banging my sister? In my own home?"

"Nobody's banging anybody," Lily said.

"Could have fooled me," Finn put in.

Then everybody was yelling at once, and it was hard to make out any one person's protests or exclamations.

"Stop. Stop!" Lily put both hands up, traffic-cop style, then realized she'd released her robe and grabbed it again. "What are you two doing here in the first place?"

"I live here," Brittany said.

"And I came to defend myself." Finn's eyes narrowed. "After Shane said he was coming here to confront you about what I'd done to you, I thought I'd better make sure what was said was the truth. Though neither of you seemed to be doing much talking."

Lily wanted to claim righteous indignation, but of course both Brittany and Finn had a right to be upset. Brittany had just found her ex making out with her sister, and Finn had just witnessed his ex being felt up by his brother.

None of this would make for pleasant conversation around the various family dinner tables.

"Oh, God. I'm so sorry," Lily said.

"You've got nothing to be sorry for," Shane told her.

"Like hell she doesn't," Brittany said.

"Yeah, I've got to side with Brittany on that," Finn added.

"How long has all of this been going on?" Brittany gestured vaguely with her hands to indicate the *all of this*.

About ten minutes, Lily wanted to say. But that wasn't true, was it? She'd wanted Shane longer than that. And apparently, he'd wanted her. The fact that nothing had happened until now didn't absolve them.

"It hasn't been going on," Shane said. "This was just …"

Lily waited to hear what he thought it was.

"Spontaneous," he said, finally settling on a word. "It just sort of *happened*."

"Rain just happens," Finn said. "Earthquakes just happen. This right here?" He waved a finger back and forth between Lily and Shane. "This was a decision."

"Yeah, well, it wouldn't have happened in the first place if I hadn't had to come over here to find out what you did to Lily," Shane said.

"What I did to her? What I *did* to her? What the hell were *you* doing to her?"

Lily listened to the two of them and felt pure horror at what she'd set in motion. After the way she'd hurt Brittany and Finn, the last thing she wanted to do now was cry, and yet here came the tears, her eyes hot and blurred, her breath coming in gasps.

Brittany noticed Lily's distress and took action. "Guys. Guys! Shut up." She held up two hands to stop the Brodys. "Anybody who doesn't live here needs to go now."

"I'm not finished yet," Finn said. "I want—"

"I don't care what you want. Not right now. You need to go." Brittany went to the door, which was still standing ajar, and held it wide open, gesturing toward the front porch with a sweep of one arm. "I'm serious," she said when neither Shane nor Finn moved.

"Lily, are you okay?" Shane began.

Brittany cut him off. "She's fine. She's got me. Now, out. Both of you. Don't make me start throwing crockery."

Apparently, the threat of cookware flying at their heads got the job done, because they both left, casting regretful glances back at the women until Brittany closed the door on them.

"Well, that was a shit show," Brittany observed.

Lily felt a surge of gratitude toward Brittany for protecting her, for putting aside her own anger and hurt in order to see to Lily's well-being.

"Brittany, thank you for—"

"Stop." She put up a hand to silence her sister. "I'm so mad at you right now I could throw you out a window. But you're my sister, so I won't."

"Brittany ..."

"I mean it. Stop. Just because I didn't want to let those two yell at you while you stood there and cried, doesn't mean I can listen to you right now. You're okay? He wasn't taking advantage of you or anything?"

"God, no. No, he wasn't."

"Fine. Then I really need to not see you or hear you right now." She went into her bedroom and closed the door, leaving Lily to stand there in her bathrobe and wet hair, sniffling and wondering how she would ever make this right.

————

SHANE AND FINN continued their fight out at the curb, even though Shane suspected that, morally, he didn't have a leg to stand on.

He expected Finn to yell at him, but that didn't happen. Instead, Finn looked at the ground, his arms crossed over his chest, and said, "I've always admired you, Shane. I've always respected you. Sure, you're kind of a dick for several weeks out of every year, but I get that. We all do. But this? Moving in on my girlfriend? That's just …" He shook his head sadly.

Shane kind of wished he'd gone with the yelling.

"She's not your girlfriend anymore, Finn. You dumped her. Remember?"

"Yeah, well. I broke up with her because I thought she had feelings for you. Are you going to stand there, in light of everything, and tell me I was wrong?"

Shane rubbed his face with both hands. "Ah, hell. No. I guess not."

"And if you want to talk about who's hurting whom," Finn went on, "How do you think Brittany feels right now? You think she's feeling good about what just happened?"

"No."

Finn sighed. "Get your shit together, Shane. For your sake and for everyone's. Acting like an asshole won't bring Molly back." Finn got into his car and drove away before Shane could say anything else.

Chapter Twelve

B rittany didn't talk to Lily at all the next day. When Lily tried to talk about routine things—the fact that they needed milk, for instance—Brittany ignored her. When Lily tried to apologize, Brittany held up a hand and said, "Not yet."

Lily tried to feel encouraged that *not yet* implied that the time for her apology—and, presumably, Brittany's acceptance of it—would come at some point.

Lily tried to give Brittany space. She tried to focus on her work: an article about the new skate park on Main Street for her newsletter, a book editing project that had come in, and her novel—which happened to involve the bond between two sisters—but she couldn't give any of it her attention, knowing how she'd hurt Brittany.

She almost texted Shane more than once—she wrote and deleted one message after another—then decided there was no point. He had his own sibling issues to work out, and telling Lily what their make-out session had meant, if it had meant anything at all, was probably the last thing he wanted to deal with.

Lily marveled at the fact that she'd managed to bungle things so spectacularly with not one, not two, but three people in her life. Brittany had taken Lily in when she'd been out of a job, and what had Lily done to repay her?

Sad and remorseful, her head swimming with memories of Shane touching her body, Lily did what she often did in times of trouble: she looked to her mother for advice. Partly because Janice Hart was the one person Lily could count on to always believe the best of her, and partly because she worried her mother had already heard a one-sided version of events from Brittany.

"Mom?" she said tentatively, when her mother answered the phone a day and a half after the Shane incident.

"Oh, Lily." The withering way in which she said it told Lily she'd already heard everything.

"Brittany told you."

"That she found you half naked on the sofa with Shane? When you'd just broken up with his brother? Yes, she might have mentioned it."

Janice's arch tone made Lily feel awful, but at the same time, she knew her mother would hear her out and would try to see Lily's point of view.

With Brittany at work, Lily had the house to herself. She leaned back on the sofa, still in her pajamas at nearly ten a.m., her feet clad in fuzzy socks. She told her mother everything: how she'd felt an immediate attraction to Shane even though she'd tried not to; how she'd dated Finn as a way to cleanse herself of those feelings; how Finn had broken up with her over it; and how Shane had stormed into the house demanding to know what had happened.

And then, how she'd ended up half naked under him on the sofa.

"I'm not making excuses for myself. I know what I did was awful. I feel terrible. And now Brittany won't even talk to me. God, it's bad enough to have all of this … this *chaos* going on with Shane and Finn. But if I lose Brittany …" Her voice grew thick with emotion.

"You're not going to lose Brittany."

Lily sniffled and grabbed a tissue from the box on the side table, blowing her nose noisily into it. "How can you be sure?"

"Honey. Your sister adores you. That won't change just because you got into a mess with a man she doesn't love anyway."

Lily dabbed at her eyes with a fresh tissue. "She really doesn't love him?" Brittany had said as much to Lily herself, but now Lily needed reassurance.

"She really doesn't. But that doesn't mean you weren't unkind, Lily. What you did with Shane was unkind."

"I know. I didn't mean to be. I just … I wasn't thinking."

"Well. You'll make things right with Brittany, sweetheart. I know you will," Janice said. "What I'm wondering, though, is where this thing with Shane is going."

Lily was astonished that her mother would even ask. "Nowhere! It's going nowhere. Obviously. How can it, with Brittany and Finn?"

"Honey. We've already established that Brittany and Shane don't love each other."

"Okay …"

"And I assume you and Finn don't, either."

"Well … no."

"Then the damage to their egos will heal. Sooner rather than later, probably. Which means you shouldn't rule out things with Shane if you really have feelings for him."

Lily was silent.

"So?" Janice said. "Do you? Really have feelings for him?"

Lily sighed and squeezed her eyes shut. "Mom. Do you really think I'd have done something so epically stupid if I didn't?"

"And does he have real feelings for you?"

"I don't know." She rubbed at her eyes with her free hand. "I just don't know."

"You should probably find out, then."

"But … but …"

Janice waited for Lily to continue.

"I can't even talk to him," Lily went on. "I go all stupid, and I stammer, and … Ever since Trevor …"

"Trevor." Janice made a rude noise. "Please don't tell me you're letting *that person* decide your love life for you."

The way Janice said *that person*, it was clear she really meant *that fly-infested pile of shit.*

"Of course I'm not, but—"

"If you're making decisions out of fear because of the way he treated you, then you are. Look, honey. I'm not saying this thing with Shane is going anywhere, or that it even should. What I'm saying is that it should stand or fall on its own merits, not because of the way you were hurt by someone else—someone who's not Shane."

Lily didn't say anything.

"It's just something to think about," Janice said.

After that, they talked for a while about Janice's plan to sell her house and move to the Central Coast so she could be closer to her daughters.

"Are you sure?" Lily asked her. "I mean, I'd love to have you close by—we both would—but moving is so stressful."

"It is," Janice agreed. "But with both of you in Cambria now? It's the right thing."

Janice had raised Lily and Brittany in Cambria, but of the three of them, only Brittany had stayed. Now, it seemed, they were all returning to where they'd started.

———

SHANE WANTED TO CALL LILY. He wanted to call Finn. He wanted to set things right with both of them. He wanted to make up with his brother and make out with Lily, in the best-case scenario.

But he was mired in despair. Paralyzed.

From February sixth onward, he didn't leave his house, and he barely got out of bed. He didn't have the energy to make things right. He didn't have the capacity. He didn't go to work, and he didn't answer his phone when his brothers or his parents called. He barely ate, and he didn't sleep. He lay wallowing in his misery, which, to his mind, was just where he deserved to be.

His family, who knew his pattern, mostly let him be until the morning of February eighth. Then they started showing up at his door.

To Shane's surprise, Finn was first. Shane tried ignoring the pounding on his door, but then, as he heard it open, he realized he'd given Finn a key the last time he went out of town. And he'd never asked for it back.

"Shane?" Finn called as he let himself in. "Where are you?"

Shane didn't answer. He was lying in bed, unshaven, unwashed, smelling terrible. He hadn't eaten in a while, but he wasn't sure if what he was feeling in his belly was hunger or existential angst.

Finn poked his head into the bedroom. "There you are." He flipped on a light. "I'll make coffee."

"I don't want coffee."

"Well, you need some, so I'm making it anyway."

Rowan came next. He arrived just as the coffee was finished brewing. "Excellent," he told Finn. "Pour me a cup, would you?"

"Bite me. You can pour your own," Finn said.

Shane heard all of this from his bed—he still hadn't gotten up.

"Where is he?" Rowan asked Finn.

"Still in bed. Wallowing."

"I can hear you. I'm right here," Shane called.

"Still alive, then," Rowan observed. "That's a positive sign."

Rowan came into the bedroom with a mug of black coffee and put it on the table next to Shane's bed. "Drink up," he said.

Shane peered into the cup. "It's black. I take cream and sugar."

"Fine. Then get your ass out of bed and get some."

Nolan and Aidan arrived together, presumably in the same car. Aidan asked Finn if there was any food in the house, and Finn said it appeared there was not.

"I'm on it," Aidan said. Then Shane heard him leave.

A few minutes later, his parents showed up. His parents, to whom he owed the biggest debt of all for what he'd done. He groaned and pulled the blankets over his head.

From under the pile of blankets, he heard footsteps coming into his room, and then his mother's voice.

"Oh, Shane. I wish you'd stop punishing yourself." She pulled the blankets down off his face and ran a hand through his dirty hair.

His mother's touch—his mother's mercy—made tears spring to

his eyes.

"Sweetheart, drink your coffee and then take a shower, won't you? We're all here for you. And we all love you."

He nodded and got up, wearing just a pair of flannel pajama pants. He took his mug of coffee with him as he went to take a shower.

As soon as the water was running to muffle the noise, Shane broke down. He stood under the hot water and cried, for himself, for Molly. And for his family, whom he'd hurt so deeply, and who still showed up for him when he needed them, who never blamed him, who were willing to put aside whatever issues they had with him to come here and help him heal.

He didn't deserve a single damned one of them. Especially Finn, who'd arrived first despite what happened with Lily. Finn, in Shane's kitchen making coffee. Finn, who'd probably arranged all of this.

This family, who loved him no matter what.

He cried until he couldn't anymore, then he washed and shampooed and shaved. It didn't make him feel any better, but at least he was trying.

By the time he came out, Aidan had arrived with a couple of bags of groceries, and Fiona was making Shane a sandwich he didn't want but that, nonetheless, he appreciated.

"Sweetheart, eat this." Fiona put a plate bearing the sandwich and some cut fruit on the dining room table. "You'll feel better."

He wouldn't feel better—couldn't feel better—but he wanted his family to think he was making an effort, so he picked up the sandwich and took a small bite. His body didn't want to accept it, but he forced the bite down.

This was how it went, most every year. Shane's despair, his family's steadfast presence, Shane's guilt and shame, his family's rock-solid, reliable love.

They didn't talk about Molly on this day. Shane had always thought they should, but his family preferred to commemorate her birthday rather than the day of her death. They chose celebration over grief.

Shane only wished he could learn to do the same.

Chapter Thirteen

Lily had finally gotten up the nerve to text Shane, but he hadn't answered. Now, she felt like she had in high school when she'd let Troy Summers get to second base only for him to act like she didn't exist afterward.

This had something to do with Shane's dark mood—the one Brittany had ended the relationship over—but she didn't know what.

Lily was still a reporter. Of course she'd Googled Shane. She'd had to when she'd been preparing her article on Bridge Street Wellness. But she hadn't dug deep because she'd worried it would be an invasion of his privacy and possibly even a breach of her journalistic ethics.

Now, though, when she was being ghosted so soon after kissing him that she could still feel the touch of his lips, she decided, to hell with her ethics. To hell with his privacy. She wanted to know what was going on.

Lily settled in at her computer and started to go through all of the steps. His social media? Check. Mentions of him in professional publications? Check. Public records? Check.

By now, she had enough information that she could compile a

decent resume for him, but she was still no closer to unearthing the reason for whatever was going on.

Going further, she found an obituary with Shane mentioned as one of the next of kin. His sister, Molly Patricia Brody, date of death, February 8, 2003. Today was the anniversary.

More than that, she learned that Molly's date of birth—July fourteenth—was the same as Shane's.

He wasn't just mourning his sister. He was mourning his *twin* sister.

No wonder he was having a difficult time. No wonder he was out of touch right now. Her heart hurt for him.

Lily had to wonder, though—his sister had died eighteen years earlier. She figured it was normal for him to still be mourning. Did you ever stop mourning when someone that close to you died? But this completely black mood followed by a withdrawal from people this many years after the tragedy? Was there something more going on?

She made a note of Molly's date of death and the city in which it had happened. The Brodys had been living in a suburb of Boston at the time. She found the daily newspaper for their community and was relieved to find that it still existed—a small miracle given the current state of the newspaper industry.

She went into the paper's online archives and searched for news printed the day after her death—February 9, 2003. She looked, in particular, for reports of accidents. Given Molly's age, that seemed most probable, though if she'd died of an illness, it was much less likely to be reported anywhere other than in the obituary she'd found.

Just when she'd about given up, she found it. A two-paragraph brief on page B-3. A single-vehicle accident with one fatality—a seventeen-year-old girl whose name was withheld pending notification of next of kin. It had happened the previous night, around ten p.m. Given the workings of a daily newspaper, the article probably had been filed within an hour of the accident, the paper printed a mere two or three hours after that. There hadn't been time to gather more details.

One detail, though, glared at her: the girl's teenage brother, her twin, had been driving. He'd been transported to a nearby hospital with unspecified injuries.

"Oh, God," Lily whispered, her hand clamped over her mouth.

That's what Finn had known but had not told her, saying it wasn't her business. And he was right—it wasn't her business. Except it seemed to her that Shane's secrecy wasn't helping matters. Maybe if people knew, maybe if they reached out to him …

His family knew, and they hadn't managed to bring him out of his guilt and grief. Surely they'd tried. Surely they were trying right now. If they couldn't manage it, what made Lily think she could?

I can't, she reminded herself. *This isn't my business. Shane is not my boyfriend, and he never will be. None of this has anything to do with me.*

The kiss was addling her brain, marring her judgment, making her think she needed to wade into waters where sharks awaited her. Better to leave the sharks to someone else.

The kiss, though.

It had been more than a kiss. Shane's hands on her, his body covering her, his scent filling her senses.

He's Brittany's ex. He's Finn's brother.

On top of all that, he was clearly emotionally unavailable. Lily shouldn't want him. She could not want him.

And yet she couldn't seem to stop.

She closed the windows on her computer that displayed his past, his secrets, his pain. What was she supposed to do with all of this information? Nothing, she decided. She could do nothing, and she *should* do nothing.

If she longed to hold him and comfort him, stroking his hair and whispering gentle and loving things into his ear, well, it wasn't her job and it wasn't her place.

She needed to remember that.

SHANE GOT through the anniversary and the days after that. He still felt like shit, but he was surviving. He was getting by.

He was back at work, so that was something. He managed to get up in the morning, shower, shave, dress, and make his way to the practice on Bridge Street. He needed to do those things—it was important. He tried to imagine that the harm he'd caused Molly could somehow be mitigated by the good he was doing now, especially for his low-income patients.

He improved lives, and sometimes he even saved them. If he could never really balance the scales, well, at least he could keep trying.

Two days after the anniversary, he was at work, keeping his head down and his mind on the job, trying to avoid the pitying looks from his brothers, when he went into an examining room and his knees nearly buckled.

The woman sitting on the edge of the examining table waiting for him looked exactly like Molly would have if she'd lived to her midtwenties. The dark hair, the shape of her nose, the blue eyes. Even the dimple in her left cheek.

The effect was so eerie, so uncanny, that for a few moments he couldn't speak.

"Dr. Brody?" she said when his silence became distinctly uncomfortable.

"I … yes. Pleased to meet you." He put out his hand to shake hers, and his fingers trembled.

"Are you okay?" she asked.

He told himself to act like a professional. "Yes. Of course." He tried to smile, but it felt wrong on his face. "You look very much like someone I know, that's all." He looked at the computer tablet with the information the nurse had filled out about his patient. "So, you're here because of pain? Tell me about that."

———

SHANE'S PATIENT told him she was there because, over the past few weeks, she'd been experiencing pain in her joints—something that was unusual for her. Shane asked her some background questions: What was in her medical history? Had she

been sick lately? Had she been engaging in any strenuous physical activity?

She laughed at this last question. Not only hadn't she been
engaged in strenuous activity, she'd been on vacation from work the
past couple of weeks. She'd just come back from a trip to Mexico,
where she'd spent her time sunbathing on the beach. That
explained the redness on her cheeks—it seemed she'd gotten a bit of
a sunburn.

Probably the flu, he thought, given that February was peak flu
season. In a couple of days, she'd probably report the classic symptoms: fever, cough, headache, fatigue. Even now, her temperature
was slightly elevated. Maybe she'd picked something up while
traveling.

She'd been on a plane, and everyone knew airplanes were flying
petri dishes of viruses and bacteria.

He prescribed ibuprofen for the joint pain, sent her for blood
work, and told her to follow up with him in a week. Her flu would
likely be on its way out by then.

He told her to call if she had any questions, then stood up to go.
Just as he had his hand on the doorknob, she stopped him. "Dr.
Brody?"

Shane turned to face her.

"I read that article about you and your brothers in Lily Hart's
newsletter."

"You did?"

"Yes. It's what made me come here. I usually go to an urgent
care in Morro Bay. I think it's great what you're doing here. You
know, the cash only thing. The sliding scale. It's important. It helps
people."

Shane didn't know what to say. He knew he should gracefully
accept the compliment, but right now, he felt anything but virtuous,
and hearing this woman praise him—this woman who looked so
much like Molly—felt wrong.

He smiled tightly and nodded. "I'll see you in a week."

———

THE WHOLE TIME Shane was gradually coming out of his cave of self-loathing, he thought about Lily.

After he'd kissed her at her house—after he'd put his hands on her—he'd told himself he was doing her a favor by disappearing. It wasn't cruel or thoughtless not to call her or text her. She was better off this way.

But thinking about Molly made him think about how he would feel if some guy put his hand inside her robe on a sofa somewhere, then cut her off as though she didn't exist.

It would piss him off. Maybe enough that he'd want to find the guy and punch him in the face. Not that he would actually do it. But he would *want* to do it, and more than that, the guy would deserve it.

And yet here he was, being that guy.

Lily was entitled to some kind of explanation about his disappearance. She was entitled to be treated like she mattered, which she did. Even if they both knew nothing would come of the two of them.

"You talked to Lily yet?" Finn asked as they were passing in the halls at Bridge Street Wellness, as though he'd read Shane's mind.

"Ah … no."

"Asshole," Finn said.

Shane spun to face his brother. "I'm an asshole? Because I haven't called a woman who you think I should have nothing to do with in the first place?"

Finn held a computer tablet to his chest as though it could shield him from his brother's idiocy. "You're an asshole because you engaged in half-naked groping and then haven't called her since. I hate guys like that. *You* hate guys like that."

Finn was right—he did.

"Well, what am I supposed to say to her?"

"I don't know. Maybe that you have no intention of pursuing things with her because you'd only make her miserable—which you would—but that she deserves the courtesy of a conversation about it. Which she does."

Shane didn't contest the thought that he would only make Lily miserable. He'd made Brittany miserable. And Brittany hadn't been the first.

Shane opened his mouth to … what? If not to protest, then to state his side of the story, maybe. But instead, what came out was a plea for help.

"Is that it, then? Is this the best I can do? Am I always going to ruin things with every woman I get involved with?"

Finn sighed and looked at his brother with something like compassion.

"Yes."

Shane blinked. "Yes?"

"Yes, until you meet a woman you're willing to open up to. Until you're ready to talk about things and give her the chance to accept you as you are, scars and all. Until then? Yeah, I'd say you're doomed to a life of loneliness and regret."

Damned Finn and his precious talk therapy.

Still, maybe he was onto something.

"So, you think if I told Lily—"

"Not Lily." Finn pointed a finger at him. "Someone, yes. But not my ex. I mean, I want you to heal, Shane, but that doesn't mean you get to be a dick."

Chapter Fourteen

L ily thought about what to do with the information she'd learned about Shane.

Her first impulse was to tell Brittany, who'd suffered so much over the mystery of Shane's moods. Her second impulse was to talk to Shane about it, reasoning that if she could just get him to open up, it might help him feel better.

She rejected both of those ideas. The first, because it felt like an invasion of Shane's privacy. If he'd wanted Brittany to know, he would have told her. The second, she set aside for much the same reason. If Shane had wanted Lily to know, he'd have said so.

So here she was, having stuck her nose in where it didn't belong, having learned a key insight that she couldn't use.

At least now, she didn't have to wonder helplessly what was going on with him. And she didn't have to make up scenarios about why he'd never called her after all of that kissing and groping on the sofa.

It wasn't about her. Clearly. His failure to call had nothing to do with Lily, and neither had the make-out session, apparently. He'd been in pain, and he'd sought to ease that pain in the only way that was available to him—with Lily's attention. And her body.

Part of her felt a little bit used, and another part of her felt regret that he likely wouldn't be using her again.

Her dominant feeling, though, was compassion. She wanted to help him. She wanted to reach out to him. But she didn't know how to do that without revealing the fact that she'd been snooping.

She decided to give him a little more time, then contact him in a casual, low-key way to see how he was doing.

As it happened, she didn't have to. He beat her to it.

———

THE IDEA of Lily had been nagging Shane. Now that he was beginning to come out from under the dark cloud he'd been living in, he had to confront the fact that he'd groped her, kissed her, laid atop her half-naked body, and then vanished without a word.

He wasn't that kind of guy, usually. That was Rowan, not him. He didn't use a woman for temporary comfort and then forget she existed.

Except, Lily probably thought he had. How could she know she'd been on his mind? If he never called her or saw her again, she would just assume she'd meant nothing to him. That he didn't care.

He did care, but the whole thing was so complicated, he had no idea how to proceed. He couldn't date her, even if he were emotionally capable of that sort of thing right now. Which he wasn't.

What he could do—what he should do—was apologize for the way he'd left things. The way he'd kissed her and touched her and then gone missing, as though none of it had ever happened.

He thought about texting her, but that seemed so cold. So unfeeling. A phone call was better, but not by much.

Instead, he decided to go to her house on his lunch break, when he knew Brittany was at work. He couldn't be sure Lily would be there, but it was likely she would be, given that she worked from home.

When he arrived at her place on Lodge Hill, he was relieved to see that Lily's car was parked out front and Brittany's wasn't. He was less relieved to realize that meant he actually had to go through with his apology.

He got out of his car and had to wait for a flock of wild turkeys to pass before he could make his way up the driveway and to the front door.

He rang the bell, and as he waited, he reflected that he really did still feel like shit. He was up and around, sure. He was getting up in the morning, showering, eating, doing his job. He was functioning. But all the while, he couldn't help thinking about how Molly was doing none of these things.

She should be flourishing in a career, maybe thinking about getting married and having kids. She should be there for him to call, to talk to. She should be present at every family dinner, every holiday, every birthday party. She should have been a part of it when they were creating Bridge Street Wellness, but she wasn't.

Because of him.

She was the other half of him, and since she'd been gone, he'd felt like an essential element of him had died with her.

He couldn't see how that would ever change, but he had to keep going anyway. He had to keep trying anyway. He had to be a decent human being anyway, which meant being here and making this apology.

By the time Lily opened the door, he was psyched up for it. He was as ready as he would ever be.

"Shane?" She blinked at him, obviously surprised to see him. She was wearing shorts and an oversized T-shirt, her hair piled up on her head in a messy bun. She looked adorable, but that wasn't something he could or should say to her.

"I wondered if we could talk for a minute."

"Um ... now?"

Okay, so he'd caught her unprepared. Nothing to do but press forward.

"If you've got a moment."

"Okay." She stepped aside and held the door open wider to let him in. Lily ran her hands down the front of her T-shirt, then patted her hair. "Do you mind if I just …?" She pointed vaguely toward the back of the house.

"Of course."

She left and came back a few minutes later wearing a pair of jeans and a sweater, her hair down from its bun. She looked beautiful, but he'd liked the way she looked before, too—messy and natural, just being herself away from anyone else's eye.

Even a brief glimpse of the real Lily was worth the effort he'd made to come out here.

"Um … I have coffee. Or tea. Or water, I guess, if you'd prefer. Can I …?" She looked toward the kitchen in question.

"No, thank you. I have to get back to the office. This will only take a moment."

"Okay."

"Can we sit?" he asked.

She nodded, and they sat side by side on the same sofa where he'd touched her and tasted her.

"I came here to apologize," he began. "After that day, I just vanished, and that wasn't right. I was having a rough time—it's nothing to do with you—and I just … I wasn't up to talking to anyone. So, while it might have seemed that I forgot about what happened, or that I didn't care, I wanted you to know that I didn't forget. And I do care."

She stared at him with those big eyes of hers, and her full lips parted. And God, he wanted to kiss her again. He wanted to re-enact their earlier experience on this same sofa, but without Brittany and Finn storming in the door.

"That's …" She cleared her throat. "Thank you. I appreciate it."

He found it adorable how she stammered when she talked to him, how she clearly was put off-balance by him. He'd heard her talk to Brittany, to his brothers, and he knew she wasn't always that way. She usually spoke easily and eloquently. But something about him sent her into a spin of self-consciousness. Was it her attraction to him? Was it that powerful? He wanted to believe it was.

But he had no right to wish for that. No right at all.

"Shane?" she said. "Whatever it is … I mean, the thing that upset you … If you want, I could … You could talk to me. That's all. You could tell me about it."

And he found that he wanted to. He really wanted to. But what purpose would it serve to burden her with his problems? With his grief and guilt?

"Ah, thanks. But I'd rather not. It's not you, I just … I don't talk about it. With anyone."

"Maybe you should." She shifted a little on the sofa. Nervous. "Maybe even if it's not someone you know. A therapist? You could—"

"Did Finn talk to you?" He said it more sharply than he'd intended. "Did he say anything to you?"

"No. No! I did ask. But he … It's none of my business, he said. But, you know, he's Finn. So he said it in a nicer way than that. Still."

It made him feel a rush of love and gratitude toward his brother. All the more reason he couldn't make a move on his brother's ex. At least, no more of a move than he'd already made.

Shane nodded, looking at his shoes instead of at Lily. "Okay. Well. That's all I have to say, I guess. Just that I'm sorry I treated you that way. You didn't deserve it. And … I really liked kissing you, even if it can never happen again."

———

I REALLY LIKED KISSING YOU.

Somehow, that was the part Lily kept focusing on, the part that was replaying in her head. Not the apology. And not the fact that he'd said it could never happen again. She knew that part. She'd been going over it in her own head, and she didn't need him to tell her.

He'd liked it—that was what echoed in her mind long after he'd said it.

"I liked it, too." Her voice was barely a whisper.

They looked at each other, some sort of electrical charge

drawing them toward each other. They'd both liked kissing each other, and it was about to happen again, despite what Shane had said, despite what Lily knew was the right thing to do. Her heart beat faster, her palms started to sweat, her breathing sped up, and then …

"Well. I'd better go."

Shane broke the spell, got up, and walked out the door.

———

HOLY SHIT.

Shane had come here to fix things—to make things right. Instead, he'd nearly kissed Lily again. And if he'd done that, there's no telling where things might have gone.

Neither Brittany nor Finn would have barged in on them this time, and Shane wasn't certain he'd have been able to stop himself from ravaging Lily if she was willing, and if no outside forces came to interrupt him.

And she really did seem willing.

He got into his car, sat behind the wheel, and rubbed at his face with both hands. What was he doing?

It's a distraction. You feel like shit, and you're using Lily to get your mind off it.

Using was such a harsh word, though. So negative. What he'd been about to do with Lily didn't feel negative, it felt right. The thought of being with her felt … *healing*.

But just because it might make him feel better, that didn't mean it was okay. It would do damage to so many people. Finn. Brittany. Lily herself, when things inevitably imploded over Shane's inability to work through his problems.

Well, he'd come here to apologize, and he'd done that. Now, there was no reason to ever see Lily Hart again.

Chapter Fifteen

When Brittany started talking to Lily again, it came as a gradual thawing. A word here and there. Brittany was making tea—did Lily want some? Lily was going to the market, and when she asked Brittany if she needed anything, Brittany actually answered.

Lily hadn't apologized about what happened with Shane yet—Brittany had stopped her when she'd tried—but it seemed as though the time was right to attempt it again.

Lily knocked on Brittany's bedroom door one evening after they'd shared a nearly silent dinner at the kitchen table.

"Brit? Can I come in?"

Lily was half expecting her sister to deny her entry. Things were thawing, yes, but they were still chilly and strained.

"I guess so," Brittany said after a moment of silence.

Lily eased the door open. Brittany was lying on her bed, on top of the covers, with a book. Lily sat on the edge of the bed, jangling with nerves.

"Before, when I tried to apologize, you said *not yet.* Are you ready to hear it now?"

Brittany's lips pursed the way they did when she was angry, but not so angry that she was willing to shut you down. "I guess."

Lily took in a deep breath, then let it out. "Brittany, I am so sorry. I didn't mean to hurt you, but I know I did. And I deeply regret it. I love you so much, and I would never … I would never …" She couldn't continue because she was starting to cry.

Brittany's expression softened. "Aw, jeez. If you're bringing on the waterworks just to guilt me into forgiving you—"

"I'm not! I'm not. But … is it working?"

Brittany laughed, and just like that, the tension between them evaporated like it had never existed. Lily reached out and pulled her sister into her arms, and Brittany hugged her back just like she always had.

"You can't do that," Brittany said, still holding Lily. "You can't just … just kiss my ex. There's a sister code, and you broke it."

"I know I did. I don't know what happened."

"What happened is you made out with Shane on our sofa." But she said it without heat, without anger. That had dissipated, leaving behind only Lily's regret.

"I didn't mean to. It just happened." Lily knew it sounded like a lame excuse. Things like that didn't just happen. People decided to do them, then did.

"I mean, I guess I get it." Brittany let go of Lily and sat up straight against the headboard. "Sort of. There was that time I kissed Dan Walker under the bleachers in high school."

Lily's eyes widened. "You kissed Dan Walker? When? Before or after he and I went to prom?"

Brittany winced. "After."

Lily gasped. "You did not."

"I did."

"Whose idea was that? Yours or his?"

"Who knows?" Brittany threw her hands into the air helplessly. "Who remembers? I just know he asked if he could talk to me about something in private, and the next thing I knew, there were lips and tongues, and … and hands."

Lily gaped at her sister. "How did I not know this?"

"You didn't know because I couldn't tell you. I was mortified. I broke the sister code."

"You sure as hell did."

"I know. I was extra nice to you for weeks to make up for it. I even let you borrow my favorite sweater."

Lily remembered the sweater. She even remembered her surprise when Brittany offered it to her. The whole thing took on an entirely new tone in retrospect.

"So I guess you have to forgive me," Lily said.

"Yeah, but Lily? This was worse. We were kids then, and we're adults now. We should know better."

"I do. I do know better. And it'll never happen again."

She didn't tell Brittany that it had almost happened again—and Lily wasn't sure she'd have had the strength to stop it if it had.

———

WITH THINGS more or less back to normal at home, Lily focused on work.

She wrote an article for her newsletter about the annual auction a local organization was holding to raise money for environmental preservation; she proofread a novel for the publishing house that regularly hired her; and she dug into the novel she was writing.

The novel was set in a small town on the Central Coast—one much like Cambria—and despite her best efforts, Lily's own life kept interfering with the plot. She'd outlined the whole thing, planning each story beat, with a chart showing what crisis should happen at what word count and how each of the characters would react to it.

But somehow, one of the main characters kept thinking longingly about her sister's boyfriend, a development that would render Lily's entire outline moot.

No matter how hard she tried to wrestle the events of the story back into the organization she'd planned, the harder her characters rebelled. Her main male character seemed to have lost all interest in the woman Lily had intended to pair him with, while the sister's boyfriend was showing up more and more often, usually with all kinds of unsavory ideas.

"For God's sake," Lily muttered, rereading what she'd written that day. "Who the hell is in charge here, anyway?"

It should have been her, but increasingly, it wasn't.

Frustrated, she set aside the book and turned her attention to her newsletter. She'd been writing and publishing seven to ten articles per week, most of them fairly simple in nature but focusing on issues important to the people of Cambria.

In the absence of other news sources, her subscriber list was growing. It was now up to 1,250. At five dollars per month, that represented a pretty good income—good enough that she was considering hiring a reporter so she could increase the amount of content she was offering.

She'd been thinking about that for a while, and now she decided it was time to take action. She wrote an ad offering part time freelance work and put it up on Craigslist.

She worked a little longer on the proofreading job, then turned back to her novel. The characters still weren't cooperating, so she decided to take a break and go for a jog at Fiscalini Ranch.

———

THE DAY WAS bright and clear, the sun glinting off the water to Lily's left as she set off on the Bluff Trail for her run. Cambria had enjoyed some recent rain—always a cause for celebration in a town plagued by drought—and the bluffs where Lily ran were covered in greenery and wildflowers. To one side of her, the ocean pounded against the rocks below, and to the other, the hillside rose toward the sky, the ground covered in long, deep green grass.

Lily put in her ear buds and selected a playlist, turned up the volume, and set off at a brisk jog, the weather perfect and her spirits lifting as her muscles worked and her breathing found its rhythm.

She used to run regularly when she lived in San Diego, but since she'd moved to Cambria, she'd let it slide. As a result, the beginning of the run was a little harder than it would have been if she'd kept up with it, but she knew it would get easier as she warmed up.

The perfect weather made her wonder why she didn't do this more often. She resolved to get out here at least three times a week —it was good for her fitness and her state of mind. Maybe she could even train for a 5K if she—

Lily didn't see the dog until she was already tripping over it. An unleashed terrier of some kind, it had gone straight for her legs, attempting to run between them. Lily tried to jump at the last second to avoid it, but she was too late. The dog squealed as her foot hit it, and Lily tumbled over the small and frightened animal, extending her left arm to break her fall.

The arm was what broke instead.

Lily lay on the trail, her arm screaming in pain, the dog licking her face tentatively. Apparently, he didn't hold a grudge.

"Oh, God," Lily moaned. Her knees were skinned and bleeding, but she wasn't worried about that. She was more concerned that she couldn't move her arm or even her hand without a sharp, searing pain.

"There you are, Brownie. Oh, no. What did you do?"

Lily heard the dog's owner before she saw him. Then he was standing over her, reaching out to try to help her up.

The man was in his sixties, probably, with gray hair under a ball cap, a leash held uselessly in one hand. Whether Brownie had gotten loose from it or if it had never been attached to him in the first place, Lily didn't know.

"I'm sorry about that. Brownie likes to run around a bit, you know. Hates the leash. I didn't see any harm in it." He was holding her good arm, pulling her up to stand as she cradled her injured arm to her body. "Oh, gosh. You're really hurt."

Lily was wincing in pain, gritting her teeth and trying not to cry out as she moved. "I think I might be, yes." Then she took a step, her arm shifted, and she let out a wail.

Lily pondered what to do as the man caught Brownie and put him on his leash. She needed to go to the hospital, but the nearest one was more than twenty miles away. She couldn't drive herself, but her injury didn't seem urgent enough to merit an ambulance.

Then she remembered what she'd learned about Bridge Street Wellness during the interview: they had their own X-ray equipment so they could deal with routine injuries without sending patients all the way down to San Luis Obispo.

Routine injuries like simple broken bones. She just had to hope hers was simple—if it wasn't, she'd be going to the hospital anyway.

"What can I do?" Brownie's owner was hovering anxiously, obviously guilt-ridden over the trouble he'd caused.

Lily looked him over and decided he was neither a serial killer nor a sex offender.

"Do you have a car? Can you drive me to Bridge Street Wellness?"

———

LILY CALLED Brittany at the salon on her way to the medical practice. No matter how simple the break was, she'd need help. Help getting home, help getting her car back from Fiscalini Ranch, and moral support.

Brittany, sounding alarmed, promised to leave work and get to the medical office as soon as she finished the client she was working on. She couldn't very well leave the woman with half-cut hair.

"It's okay, there's no rush. I'm in someone's car, and we're on the way over there."

"Whose car?"

Lily looked at the man behind the wheel. "I didn't catch your name."

"Charlie. Charlie Frank."

"It's Charlie's car," Lily told Brittany.

"Who's Charlie?" Brittany sounded more worried than ever.

"He's the guy whose dog tripped me."

"But, Lily—"

"I'm really so sorry," Charlie said.

"He's sorry," Lily reported to Brittany. "He's not going to rob me and leave me by the side of the road. Are you, Charlie?"

"Well, no, I hadn't planned to."

"There you go," Lily said. "Anyway, we're almost there."

Brownie, who was standing on the floor of the car at Lily's feet, was whimpering gently and patting at Lily's leg with his tiny paws.

She got the distinct impression Brownie was sorry, too. She hung up the phone and rubbed his head—then cried out when the car went over a bump, jostling her arm.

"Don't worry," Charlie said. "We're just about there."

———

LILY DIDN'T HAVE AN APPOINTMENT, which meant she might not get in to see Shane, which meant she might end up waiting for Brittany to come and drive her to the hospital.

Bridge Street Wellness didn't accept walk-ins—not officially—but Lily hoped her association with the Brodys would help her bend the rules.

Of course, given what had happened with Finn, it might actually work against her.

Charlie stayed with Lily in the waiting room, Brownie in his arms, as Lily spoke to the receptionist about whether Shane could squeeze her in.

"I'm afraid Shane is booked solid," the receptionist told her. "But Rowan might be able to see you."

"Rowan? He's a pediatrician."

"That's right. And that means he deals with more broken bones than Shane does, by far. Kids are always managing to break something."

That made sense. Lily nodded gratefully. "Okay, Rowan, then. Thank you so much."

Given that the practice was cash only, Lily didn't have to fill out any insurance paperwork. She did, however, have to fill out a form giving her personal information and her annual income. Based on that, she would either pay today's fee on a sliding scale, or she could sign up to pay for a monthly membership which would allow her to seek care at Bridge Street Wellness as needed.

"The membership's a better deal," the receptionist told her. "Especially since you'll be needing follow-ups."

Lily had health insurance—she'd signed up for COBRA benefits when she'd left her job—but she'd neglected to switch plans when she'd moved to the Central Coast. Which meant the nearest doctor who'd accept her coverage was two hundred miles away.

She stood there at the reception desk, wincing in pain and wondering what to do. The receptionist, who Lily knew a little from when she was dating Finn, reached out and put a hand on Lily's good arm. "You know what? We can deal with this later. You look like you're in a lot of pain."

Lily nodded gratefully, trying not to cry. She found a seat and settled into it, moving slowly to avoid jostling her arm.

Charlie sat next to her.

"Oh, you don't have to stay," she told him.

"Just until your sister gets here," he said. "I'd feel better."

Brownie wiggled in Charlie's arms, trying to get to Lily. She reached out with her good hand and rubbed his head. "Don't feel bad," she told the dog. "You didn't mean to do it."

He licked her fingers in response.

———

SHANE WAS WALKING from his office to an examining room, passing behind the reception desk as he went, when he saw Lily out of the corner of his eye and did a double-take.

"What's she doing here?" he asked Iris.

"Broken arm," she said. "At least, it looks like it. I know you're busy, so I put her with Rowan."

"Rowan?" Shane was appalled. "Like hell. Give her to me."

"Where?" Iris indicated the appointment schedule on her screen. "You don't have any open spots."

"I'll work through lunch," he said.

"Are you sure?"

"Yes, I'm sure."

"Well, I can put her in after Mr. Ferguson."

"No, I'll take her now. Push back Mrs. Waters."

"But—"

"She's in pain, Iris. Mrs. Waters is here for a check-up. She can wait. I'll take Lily now."

———

WHEN THE NURSE called Lily back, she fully expected to be brought into a room decorated with superheroes and Disney princesses. Instead, she was brought into an examining room designed with an understated taste that kept the house's Victorian roots in mind.

And instead of Rowan Brody walking in to examine her, the doctor now looking her over was Shane.

"How did you do this?" he asked as he gently handled her arm.

"I was jogging. A dog tripped me."

"Ah. Would it happen to be the dog out in the lobby right now?"

"Yeah. Brownie. He's a good little guy. He didn't mean any harm."

"I'm sure." Shane said.

He asked Lily to wiggle her fingers and rotate her palm, both of which caused enough pain to make her nearly pass out.

"Yep, I'd say this is broken," he said. "Good thing it's your left arm."

"Well ..."

"Well what?"

"I'm left-handed."

———

LILY EMERGED into the lobby one X-ray, one cast, and one prescription for pain medication later. By then, Charlie and Brownie were gone and Brittany was waiting for her. Brittany helped Lily fill out the paperwork to begin her monthly membership payments to the practice, and then the two of them headed home in Brittany's car.

"I need to get my car. It's at Fiscalini," Lily said.

"Well, we'll have to figure something out later," Brittany said. "You can't drive like this."

"What am I going to do?" Lily wailed. "I can't do anything like this. How am I supposed to work? How am I supposed to put out my newsletter or get my proofreading work done, or … or …" She felt tears coming on, and she fought them back. It was just a broken arm, and not even a bad one at that. She hadn't needed surgery or a painful realignment of the bone. She'd just needed a cast. It could have been so much worse. And yet here she was, about to blubber about it like a child.

"You'll be all right," Brittany said. "We'll work it out."

"We?" Lily sniffled through tears. "After what I did? Brittany, I don't deserve—"

"Oh, shut up." Brittany waved her off. "You're my sister. Of course it's *we*. I'm here, and we've got this. You're only going to be in that cast for six weeks, and then you'll be fine. So don't panic."

Now Lily was crying. Not because of the pain, but out of love for her sister. "Brittany, you're the best. I mean it."

"I know," she said. "Now, let's get you home."

Chapter Sixteen

The rest of the day, Shane couldn't stop thinking about Lily.

When he'd seen her in the lobby, injured and in pain, he'd only wanted to fix what had hurt her. Now that he'd done that, he couldn't seem to stop worrying about her.

A break in her dominant arm. She was going to need help. She would have trouble doing basic things for herself until she adjusted. He could go over there after work. He could—

No.

If he did go over there, he'd have to explain to Brittany why he was giving Lily special treatment beyond what he'd provide for any other patient. And no matter what he said, Brittany would think it was because of what had happened on the sofa that day when she and Finn had caught him with Lily.

And she'd be right.

An extra-articular, nondisplaced distal radius fracture didn't require him—or anyone, really—to show up at Lily's bedside and nurse her back to health. The arm was in a cast, and she would be fine. She wasn't in any danger, and the challenges she would face would mostly be inconveniences. She'd have Brittany's help. And she would adjust and learn to do things with her non-dominant arm.

And yet every instinct in him said he should be there for her, at her house, helping her do whatever needed to be done. Some sort of male savior complex, probably. He felt a strong need to save the damsel in distress.

He needed to stop thinking about that—about Lily—so he could get back to work. Squeezing her in had put him a half-hour behind schedule. He didn't regret it, of course, but now he had little time to ponder Lily or Brittany or anything else.

He'd worked through lunch, as he'd told Iris he would do. He had a couple of house calls to elderly patients who could no longer drive, and that gave him a welcome chance to get out of the office.

Then he had a follow-up appointment with Caitlin Jacobs, the woman who looked so much like Molly that it made him break out in goosebumps whenever he saw her or even thought about her.

He reviewed her chart before he went into the examining room: she'd come in a week ago for joint pain, which he'd thought was likely the flu. He'd sent her for blood work, and the results were in. The CBC showed she was anemic.

Maybe not the flu, then.

"Ms. Jacobs?" Shane shook her hand as he came into the room. "How have you been feeling?"

In the week since she'd seen him last, the joint pain had not gone away. She'd been unusually tired, and now, on top of every-thing, she had developed sores in her mouth. Shane took a look with a tongue depressor and a mini flashlight and saw red ulcerations on the inside of her lower lip and on her tongue.

Beginning to suspect this was more than just anemia, he took another look at her lab results. Her urine test was positive for protein. Also, interestingly, the sunburn on her cheeks that he'd noticed last time was still there.

"You been getting some more sun?" he asked, indicating the areas of redness.

"Not since Mexico. You'd think the sunburn would be gone by now."

Shane peered at it and began to think it looked more like a rash than a sunburn.

What had started out looking like the flu was now starting to look a lot like lupus.

"I'm afraid I have to send you back for more blood work," he told her.

"Why? Was there a problem with the last blood test?"

"This is a different one. It's called an ANA test. It's to look for any kind of autoimmune disorder. With your combination of symptoms—along with the fact that your CBC showed anemia—I think that's where we need to start looking."

Her eyes filled with tears and she said, "You think this is lupus, don't you?"

Shane's eyebrows rose in surprise. "What makes you say that?"

"I know how to Google." She wiped her eyes and took in a shaky breath. "Oh, God. I don't need this right now."

He put a reassuring hand on her shoulder. "We don't know that. Not yet. Let's get the ANA test, and we can take it from there."

When she was gone, Shane worried about what would come next for her. She didn't have health insurance—that's why she'd come here. If she did, indeed, have lupus, she'd need to see specialists—a rheumatologist, at the very least, and maybe also a cardiologist, nephrologist, gastroenterologist. The list went on from there.

Aidan was a cardiologist, so they could deal with that here if needed. But the others? What would she do? He wasn't about to just cut her loose when his part was done, hoping for the best. That wasn't what they were about here.

And it wouldn't be acceptable to Shane, even if his patient didn't look eerily like his sister.

———

LILY WAS STILL in some pain, though not much. What bothered her more was the fact that everything she did—from taking a shower to getting dressed to making herself something to eat—took at least twice as much effort as it had before.

It also took a certain amount of planning.

For instance, Lily used to take her shower after Brittany left for work. Now, though, she had to get it done while her sister was still there to help her tape a plastic bag over her cast and then get it off again.

"Duct tape. It's got a thousand uses," Brittany remarked as she wound tape around Lily's arm, over her elbow, to seal a plastic grocery bag over her cast.

"Too bad Shane couldn't just slap some onto the bone so I could be done with this."

Brittany looked over her handiwork, tugged on the bag a little to make sure it was secure, then put her hands on her hips. "I guess I have to stop being mad at him now that he's taken care of you. Squeezing you in without an appointment and all. That was decent."

"It was. There are going to be follow-up visits, that sort of thing. Are you okay with that?"

"Am I okay with you getting proper medical treatment? Yes. I think I can deal with that."

"I just meant—"

"I know what you meant. Listen, Lily. Is this thing with you and Shane over? Not the medical part, but the romantic part?"

"There is no thing with me and Shane. Just that moment—what you saw. That was it. And, yes, it's over."

"Okay. That really hurt me."

"Oh, Brittany, I—"

Brittany put her hand up to stop Lily. "I don't want to bemoan the whole thing again. I'm just saying, it hurt. But if you're not going to do it again …"

"I'm not. I swear."

"Then, I guess I'm just glad you had a good doctor available when you needed one."

In the shower, with hot water running over her and steam clearing her head, Lily thought about what she'd just promised. She wouldn't kiss Shane again, on the sofa or elsewhere. She wouldn't let him kiss her. And she absolutely wouldn't think about anything else involving him other than her own health and healing.

She could keep the no-kissing promise. She knew she could. But the part where she wouldn't think about him? That would be a lot harder.

She was thinking of him now, in fact. She'd been thinking of him pretty much every day since the sofa incident, remembering how he'd tasted, how he'd felt pressed against her body.

No one had made her feel that way since … well, since Trevor. And that had ended in disaster and heartbreak, so maybe physical arousal shouldn't be her top priority in looking for a man.

Still. She wanted Shane. She wanted him so much it was clouding her brain, so she would just have to stay away from him if she wanted to keep her promise to Brittany.

Not that she was especially sexy right now, with her arm encased in plaster.

She thought about Shane on the sofa, and then she thought about him gently examining her arm, his eyes full of concern.

"You almost done in there? I have to get to the salon, and I need to cut you out of your bag before I go," Brittany called through the door.

"Just about," Lily called back.

Brittany's voice interrupting her reverie about Shane made her feel awash with guilt. She would not betray her sister again, no matter how attractive Shane Brody was.

———

SHANE WAS TRYING to keep his Lily impulses in check. He did not go to her house after work the day of her injury, the way he wanted to. But he couldn't seem to keep himself from stopping by during his lunch break the next day.

When she opened the door, she looked like an adorable mess—sweatpants, a T-shirt, hair askew, her face free of makeup. She looked surprised to see him, her eyes wide.

"Shane. What are you doing here?"

He held up the paper bag in his hand. "I thought you might need lunch. It's got to be hard doing things like making meals with your arm in a cast."

"You … you brought me lunch?"

"Just a sandwich from Sandy's. Turkey and provolone. I hope that's okay."

"I … ah …"

"Have you already eaten?"

"Well, no, but—"

"Great. Can I come in?"

Lily glanced back at the sofa, the site of a very fond memory for Shane. Then she relented. "I guess so. Aren't you"—she hesitated, twisting the hem of her T-shirt in the fingers of her good hand—"I mean, you've got to be busy, right? With work."

"Lunch break. I brought a sandwich for myself, too. Have you got anything to drink? A Coke, maybe?"

———

THE LAST THING Lily had expected this day to bring was lunch with Shane Brody. If she'd known this was coming, she'd have been dressed in something other than sweatpants. And she'd have done something with her hair. Not that she could do anything with her hair with only one arm to work with. And not that she had the option to wear anything else. She'd tried to put on a pair of jeans but had not been able to get them up and buttoned with just the one hand.

Now, sitting at the kitchen table with him, she felt rattled. She didn't like feeling rattled, but that seemed to be her dominant feeling whenever Shane was around.

"I'm a mess," she blurted out as Shane took their sandwiches out of the bag and put them on the table. "My clothes and my hair. I can't even do a ponytail with only one hand."

He gave her a wry half grin. "Not to make light of how hard that must be, but I think you look great."

"I don't." She put a hand to her hair self-consciously.

"Besides, I didn't come here because I expected you to get all dressed up for me."

"Then why did you come here?"

He slid her sandwich across the table to her. "I was worried about you, and I wanted to help."

He was worried? Worry implied that he was thinking about her, and nothing good could come of that.

"Well, I mean, that's really nice of you. But Brittany—"

"I promise there will be no repeat of the sofa incident. This is just lunch. That's all."

Lily didn't know whether to be relieved or disappointed.

"Good," she said. "Because I don't want … I mean … I want …" What was she trying to say? And why was she so inarticulate around him?

"What?" His voice was soft now. Gentle. "What is it you want, Lily?"

"Um." She swallowed hard, looking into his gorgeous, dark eyes. Thinking about what had happened on the sofa and where that had nearly gone. What might have happened if they hadn't been interrupted. Remembering his hands on her. She closed her eyes and tried to get herself together. She couldn't be having these thoughts. She'd promised Brittany.

She'd *promised*.

"I want …"

"Mmm?"

"Just lunch, I guess."

It clearly wasn't what he'd expected her to say, but he recovered quickly. "Well, you're in luck, then. You think you can hold this sandwich together with one hand? It's packed pretty full."

Chapter Seventeen

After Lily ate her sandwich, Shane cleaned up the mess, said goodbye, and got out of there before Brittany could show up and catch him with her sister again.

Not that he'd done anything wrong, but he'd been thinking it.

The whole thing had him keyed up and unsettled. Lily looking fresh-faced and natural, all tousled as though she'd just gotten out of bed; the way she'd looked at him, wide-eyed and intimate, when she'd almost said what she'd wanted; the way the tension had risen between them as they'd both remembered the sofa incident—it all tormented him as he drove back to the office.

What the hell game was he playing, anyway? He wanted her so much his entire body ached with it, but he knew better than to think he could have her. Of course he couldn't. Not when it would hurt so many people—Finn, Brittany, and Lily herself once things went badly, which they always did.

He came to a stop at a red light and closed his eyes just for a moment, thinking of Molly.

If you can't have this, if you can't have love, then I don't deserve it, either.

He'd thought he could make things work with Brittany, but that was before the anniversary and the way he'd fallen into the dark place where he went every year. He'd known it would happen, but he'd thought …

Hell, he didn't know what he'd thought. That this time would be different? That this time, he wouldn't feel so awful? Wouldn't hate himself so much?

He knew better. But what would it hurt if he checked on Lily now and then? Just until she healed?

He needed to talk to someone about all of it. Generally, when he had a problem that he chose to talk about—which he usually didn't —he went to Finn. He was the psychiatrist of the family, after all, so he knew how to listen. But this time, it couldn't be him.

Shane mentally went through an inventory of his friends and family members, trying to decide who might best offer insights into Shane's problem.

In the end, he chose Rowan.

Why? Because Rowan had made more mistakes with women than all of the rest of them combined, and he'd be the last person to judge Shane. And even if he did decide to turn judgmental, no one would take him seriously.

AT THE END of the work day, Shane suggested to Rowan that the two of them go have a drink at Ted's, if Rowan didn't have plans.

"What makes you think I don't have plans?" Rowan asked, still dressed in his white coat, his stethoscope still slung around his neck. "Whatever would make you imagine that I don't have one or more women lined up for tonight?"

"Because it's after five and you're still here," Shane said. "Usually when you have one or more women lined up, you hit the sidewalk at 4:59."

Rowan frowned. "Am I that predictable?"

"Yes. Now, are you going to drink with me or not?"

BECAUSE IT WAS EARLY on a weeknight, Ted's was mostly empty, which was how Shane preferred it. If the place had been jumping, Rowan would have been too focused on the various women in the building when Shane needed him to be focused on him.

The place was dimly lit and reasonably quiet, as Ted hadn't turned on the stereo system yet. Two guys played darts at one end of the room, and an older woman sat alone in a booth toward the back. Behind the bar, Ted was lining up glasses and checking the taps in preparation for the rush he'd get later that night.

Ted nodded at them as Shane and Rowan took seats at the bar. "Docs. What'll you have?"

Ted had 805 beer on tap, so they got two mugs of that, and Ted plunked a bowl of pretzels down between them. Shane plucked a pretzel out of the bowl, wondering how many people had touched it before him.

"You chose the right man," Rowan said, taking a sip of his beer.

"What? What are you talking about?" Shane asked.

"To get advice. For your lady problems." Rowan waggled his eyebrows. "No one in our family—hell, no one in the world, probably—has as much experience and wisdom regarding women as I do. So, go ahead. Shoot."

"I never said I had lady problems. Which makes it sound like I have menstrual issues, now that I think about it. Could we come up with some other term for it?"

"Sure. Woman issues. Romantic dilemmas. Entanglements with the opposite sex. You choose."

"Yeah, fine. But I still never said—"

Rowan held up a hand. "You didn't have to. Lily called the office to say you left your jacket there. When you saw her. At her place. This afternoon." He did the eyebrow thing again, which somehow made Shane want to punch him. Not an uncommon reaction to Rowan.

Shane couldn't punch his brother, so he threw a pretzel at him instead. The pretzel bounced off Rowan's forehead. "Hey, asshole. Whatever you think happened, it didn't. I was checking on her to see how she's doing with the arm. House calls are part of what we do now, in case you weren't aware."

"Oh, I'm aware. I'm also aware that you were hoping your tender loving care might lead to you feeling her up on her sofa again. Or, even better, in her bed. The fact that it didn't happen just means you're inept, not that you aren't lusting in your heart."

Shane got up from his stool and took out his wallet, putting some bills on the bar. "Screw this. I should have known better than to come to you."

Rowan grabbed Shane's arm and tugged him back toward his stool. "Ah, sit down and don't get your panties in a bunch. I'm just joking around. I'm here to listen. Really."

Shane stood there, undecided. Rowan really could be a dick. On the other hand, he could also be sensitive, insightful, and loyal—even if he took pains to hide that part of himself from the world.

"Yeah, okay." Shane eased himself back onto his barstool. "But could we try not to talk about Lily like she's … you know. Some conquest?"

"That's fair, since neither you nor Finn managed to conquer anything where she's concerned."

"Rowan …"

"Fine. Fine. I will speak of her with decorum and respect."

"Thank you."

"Now, the way I speak of you, on the other hand …"

"Shut up and let me talk, will you?"

"Sure." Rowan took a slug of beer. "I'm all ears. What's up?"

———

BY THE TIME Shane was done telling it, they'd both finished their beers and Shane had ordered another round. He'd laid it all out: how he felt about Lily, how he knew it couldn't go anywhere because of Finn and Brittany, how he knew he'd ruin it even if it did go somewhere, the way he'd ruined things with Brittany and other women before her, and how he wanted to stop thinking about Lily but couldn't.

The advice he wanted, he told Rowan, was how to shut down the thoughts. The wanting. How to make himself stop feeling things for Lily.

Rowan's eyebrows shot up. "You think I know how to shut down sexual impulses for a woman? If I could do that, I could have saved myself a hell of a lot of trouble. Including that time Joe Leonard beat me to a pulp."

Shane winced. "He really cleaned your clock. In fairness, he did catch you with his wife. In his own bed."

Rowan shrugged. "That's why I didn't press charges. The point is, I'm not known for shutting down my desires. I'm more known for … you know. Indulging them."

Shane's shoulders fell, and he turned to face the bar instead of facing his brother. He looked into his beer, feeling dejected. "Yeah, you're right. And even if you weren't, I can't expect you to fix my problems."

"I didn't say I don't have advice. I just said I'm not an expert in self-denial."

Shane looked at his brother. "Okay, so what's your advice?"

"Well, you're not like me," Rowan said.

"That's not advice. That's an observation."

"Shut up, dumbass, and let me finish. What I'm saying is, you have a tendency to get involved with women not because it's fun or because you're horny, but because you have real feelings for them. Which makes you not like me."

"Okay …"

"So if you can't stop thinking about Lily, there's probably something real behind it, and not just you wanting to scratch an itch."

"Therefore?" Shane said, prompting him.

"Therefore, maybe you shouldn't fight it. Maybe you should just spend some time with her and see how it goes."

"Are you kidding?" Shane gaped at him.

"No. I'm not."

"I can't do that. She dated Finn."

"So what?"

Shane stared at him incredulously.

"Look," Rowan said. "I'm as down with the brother loyalty thing as anybody. I'd do anything for any one of you guys."

"And yet you think I should date Finn's ex-girlfriend?"

"I think you shouldn't base your decision about it on Finn, for one reason."

"Which is?"

"Simple. He didn't love her, and she didn't love him, and everybody involved knows it. Same with you and Brittany. It was never gonna work, not long term, so it shouldn't come into play now."

"But——"

"This isn't about brother loyalty, is all I'm saying," Rowan went on. "If you end up with Lily, it's going to hurt Finn's feelings, but it's not going to hurt him in any way that matters. It's not you or Lily or anybody else breaking his heart. It's just etiquette."

Shane considered that—really considered it—and could see the sense in it. But that didn't solve his other, bigger problem.

"But what about … you know."

"The fact that you go to the dark place and shut out any woman you happen to be with until she dumps your ass?"

"Well, I wouldn't have put it that way, but yes."

Rowan tilted his chin down and looked at Shane in a way that meant business. "Look. Shane. I can't fix that for you. But it seems to me that one day, you're going to meet a woman who can go into the dark place with you and drag you back out into the light. If that woman is Lily? Well, I hope to hell you'll give her that chance."

———

LILY DIDN'T TELL Brittany about Shane coming to see her that afternoon. She felt bad about not telling her, as though she was keeping some sort of shameful secret. But telling her would only get Brittany angry with her again, just when the two of them had worked out their differences.

So she hid Shane's jacket in her closet until she could give it to him, and she glossed over the subject of lunch entirely when she told Brittany about her day.

"It was okay," she said. "I managed."

"I worried about you while I was at work," Brittany told her. "I was going to come home and check on you, but a regular client needed me to squeeze her in, so I was slammed."

Lily was horrified that, had it not been for that client, Brittany might have come home and caught her eating sandwiches with Shane. Which made *eating sandwiches* sound like some sort of code for sex. Which it absolutely wasn't.

"You didn't have to," Lily said. "I was fine. I'm getting by."

Brittany looked her over. "But you had trouble doing your hair. And, from the looks of it, getting on any pants that don't have an elastic waistband."

"Do I look awful?" Lily thought about Shane seeing her like this, and her cheeks reddened.

"No, no. You just look like you need a little more help than I gave you. I'll make sure to stay until you're dressed and your hair's done tomorrow. Oh, and food. Did you manage to make yourself some lunch today? It wasn't too hard?"

"I ate lunch," she said. Which wasn't a lie.

"Good. You'll get the hang of this. In the meantime, I'm here for you."

Lily felt herself tearing up. "Brittany?"

"Hmm?"

"You're the best sister ever. I love you."

She hugged Brittany and wondered how she could ever have contemplated betraying her with Shane.

<h1 style="text-align:center">Chapter Eighteen</h1>

<hr>

The plan for Brittany to give Lily more help lasted for a couple of days.

Until their mother called.

"Honey," Janice said when Lily answered the phone. "I have some good news. And also, a favor to ask."

The good news, it turned out, was that Janice had sold her house. She'd put it up for sale barely a week before, and none of them had expected it to sell so quickly. The favor was that she needed help packing 1,400 square feet of accumulated belongings.

"It already sold?" Lily asked.

"For above asking price. Can you imagine? For this old place?"

If the house she'd sold had been the one Lily and Brittany had grown up in, there might have been feelings for Lily about her lost childhood, her memories, the sorrow of time's inevitable passing. As it was, Lily was thrilled about the sale because it meant Janice could start looking for a place on the Central Coast.

"That's so great, Mom. I'm going to send you the names of some Realtors in Cambria. I can't wait for you to move here."

"I can't, either. But first, I've got to get this place sorted out. Do you think you can come and help me pack?"

That was when Lily had to admit to her mother that she'd broken her arm. Neither she nor Brittany had told her.

It wasn't that Janice was incapable of handling bad news. It was just that it was so much easier for everyone if she didn't have to. Brittany and Lily both found their lives to be much more peaceful if their mother didn't know about their injuries or health issues.

At first, Lily hedged the truth.

"Oh. Wow. I'd love to come and help, but I'm just swamped with work. I'm not sure I can get away."

"Well, but I thought, since you do most of your work remotely."

"Right. I do. But—"

"Lily Elizabeth Hart. You're hiding something, and I want to know what it is."

Lilly sighed. Now that her mother had brought out the big guns—her middle name—she had no choice but to fess up.

"Okay. You're right. There is something. Don't freak out when I tell you."

"Lily, I swear …"

"I had a fall a few days ago, and I hurt my arm." She carefully avoided saying the word *break*. "I'm fine—it's going to be fine—but I'm under doctor's orders to rest it. I wouldn't be much good to you when it comes to packing and lifting and all that."

"Why didn't you tell me?" Janice asked. "Oh, Lily. How bad is it?"

"Not bad at all, Mom. I just have to—"

"Is it just a sprain? Oh, it's not broken, is it?"

Having been asked the direct question, Lily didn't have it in her to lie.

"Well, it's a little bit broken, yes."

Janice gasped. "A little bit broken? How can something be a little bit broken?"

"A little bit broken means it wasn't too bad. I didn't need surgery, or—"

"Surgery!"

"I *didn't* need that. The doctor didn't even have to reset the bone or anything. I just got a cast, and it doesn't even hurt anymore. It's just inconvenient."

"But how did you fall?"

For the next ten minutes, Lily had to recount the accident and the injury, reassure her mother that her limb would return to one hundred percent function, explain that she would, in fact, survive, and fend off Janice's repeated offers to come to Cambria immediately to nurse her back to health.

"I swear to you, Mom, I don't need help. I'm fine," Lily said. "But I'm sorry I can't help you pack up."

"Well. I'll see if Brittany can get some time off. Oh, but if I do that, you won't have her there to help you if you need it, so …"

"I'm fine," Lily said for what seemed like the fifteenth time. "If Brittany can get off work, I can absolutely manage without her."

That conversation had been a few days ago. Brittany hadn't left town yet, but she had rescheduled a week's worth of appointments—passing some on to other stylists and trying to cram the others into the next few days so she'd be clear to leave—which meant she was going to work early, coming home late, and skipping lunch breaks to make it work.

And that was how Lily ended up alone at home barely a week after the injury, wondering how the hell she was going to manage with one arm, an editing deadline, a newsletter to write, and no sister to help her.

———

SHANE HAD the perfect excuse to see Lily—the jacket he'd left behind—but he'd been reluctant to use it. What if Brittany was there? How could he explain leaving the jacket at her house? It was possible Lily had told her about their lunch, but what if she hadn't?

He could handle himself with Brittany, but he didn't want to inadvertently start a fight between the sisters.

He liked the jacket, and he liked Lily, and with each passing day, his resolve began to crumble.

Finally, he came up with a plan. He'd go to her house, and if

Brittany was there, he'd simply claim he was doing a routine follow-up on Lily's arm. If Lily didn't mention the jacket, Shane would assume she hadn't told Brittany about the lunch. In that event, he simply wouldn't mention it, either.

When he got there at around noon, bearing lunch as he'd done before, he decided that no subterfuge would be needed. Brittany's car wasn't here, and Lily's was the only one parked in front of the house.

He went up the walk and reminded himself he was here for his jacket and to check on Lily. He wasn't here for any couch shenanigans. Though, if shenanigans happened …

———

LILY WASN'T EXPECTING COMPANY, so when the doorbell rang, she looked like hell. Without Brittany's help this morning, she'd decided not to try to do her hair or put on makeup or wear real pants. Why bother? It wasn't like she was going anywhere. And it wasn't like a ridiculously handsome doctor was going to show up at her door.

Except, one did.

When she opened the door to find Shane Brody standing there, holding takeout and looking more delicious than anything he might have in that bag, she had some kind of out-of-body experience that allowed her to view herself from a distance. Or, at least it seemed that way. Maybe it was just the extreme anxiety caused by her dream man seeing her at her worst.

When she looked at herself, what she saw wasn't pretty: bare face with a breakout of pimples on her chin; sweatpants that should have been washed two days ago; T-shirt with no bra underneath; hair that had barely had a brush dragged through it and which had gone frizzy in the damp, foggy weather.

She was so horrified that she didn't say *hello* or *what are you doing here*, or even *go away*. She just stood there, gaping at him.

"Hi, Lily," he tried.

She didn't speak.

"I came here to get my jacket. And to bring you lunch. In case you'd prefer not to manage making your own with your bad arm."

She blinked twice but still didn't say anything.

"Can I come in?" he asked.

"Oh, God," she moaned.

His brow furrowed with concern. "So, you're not all right? What is it? What can I do?"

Then she burst into tears.

———

SHANE WAS A FAIRLY SENSITIVE GUY, so he didn't go stupid at the sight of a crying woman. He knew what he was supposed to do: listen, be supportive, provide comfort. But at the moment, he didn't know what, exactly, he was providing comfort for.

Still, he tried gamely to provide it anyway. He eased his way into the house, closed the door behind them, led Lily into the living room, set the food on the coffee table for later, and sat her down on the sofa, trying not to think about the wonders that had occurred there.

"Lily? Tell me what's wrong. Are you in pain? Is it your arm?"

For once, she didn't stammer or fumble with her words when she talked to him. She just blurted it all out.

"No, I'm not in pain! Not the kind you're thinking of, anyway. I just … Brittany's working long hours, then she's going to be out of town for a week, and I can't even get dressed in real clothes without her help, and my hair, and I have pimples, and I look awful, and here you are, looking … *like you*, and I always imagine that when you show up at my door I'll look perfect and sexy and beautiful, but instead, for the second time, you've shown up and I look like this. I'm not even wearing a bra!" She grabbed a tissue from a box on the side table and honked into it.

And from that moment on, if he hadn't been before, Shane was enchanted. He wanted to scoop her into his arms and tell her she was perfect and sexy and beautiful just as she was.

She wouldn't believe him, though, not if he said it.

So he decided to show her instead.

She sniffled a little and wiped her eyes with her hands. She looked at him, her breath shuddering, her full lips parted.

Then, he simply grabbed her and devoured her.

———

LILY HADN'T EXPECTED to be kissed, given what a mess she was. And she certainly hadn't expected to be kissed so thoroughly, so well, so expertly, that the kiss was in some other category than any kiss she'd had before.

With Shane's mouth on hers, his arms around her body, she forgot to cry. She forgot to be upset or self-conscious. She forgot how she looked and what she'd said and whether it was a good idea to be kissing her sister's ex. Her body knew what it wanted, and it wanted him.

He plunged his hands into her hair and she let out a little moan of pleasure as his lips tasted hers, his tongue brushed against hers. His breath mingled with hers. Her entire body went warm and liquid, her heart pounding, her belly aching with longing.

How was it that she always seemed to end up on this sofa with Shane, kissing him and wanting to do so much more?

"Lily."

He murmured her name into her ear as he took her earlobe between his teeth, and a thrum of hot desire pulsed through her. If he kept going, she wasn't going to be able to stop him this time. She wouldn't want to.

———

SHANE DIDN'T KNOW if this was smart. He didn't know if he would regret this later. Probably it was some kind of ethical violation, given that she was his patient. Hell, her arm hadn't even healed yet.

But he didn't care about any of that. All he cared about, all he knew, was that right now, in this moment, he wasn't sad anymore.

He couldn't remember the last time he wasn't sad at some level, even if he kept it deeply hidden. But now all he felt was good and alive and happy.

When he'd come in the door, seeing her in a T-shirt with no bra, her curvy body on display, had turned him on so much he'd gotten a hard-on right there. Now, he couldn't help himself. He slid his hand under her shirt and upward to cup one full breast. He ran his thumb over her rock-hard nipple, and she moaned and arched toward him in response.

It was just the way he'd imagined she would respond to him. Just like this, with this kind of pleasure and need.

He pulled the T-shirt off over her head, and it got hooked on her cast. He tugged it free and discarded it on the floor.

She tried to undo the buttons on his shirt with her one hand, but she was having trouble, so he helped her, unbuttoning the shirt and tossing it aside with hers.

At that first press of his skin against hers, he was lost.

———

SHANE'S HANDS were on Lily, and his mouth was on her, and for the most part, she couldn't think of anything but that. The electric surge of pleasure running through her veins made her brain short-circuit.

Except she must have had some capacity for rational thought, because it occurred to her that Brittany might come home any moment. She probably wouldn't—she had planned to work through lunch to clear her schedule for her trip—but she *could*, and that was enough for Lily to make the one sensible decision she would make that day.

She told Shane they needed to move to the bedroom.

"Not here," she said. "Brittany."

It was all she managed to say while Shane was kissing her, but it was enough.

"Okay. Where?"

"Bedroom. Down the hall."

He got off of her in a second, and she was about to follow him, but before she could, he scooped her up into her arms like some prehistoric man hauling his mate off to the cave.

It was incredibly hot.

"Wait," she said when they were halfway down the hallway.

He stopped, carrying her against his body. "Oh. If you're not sure—"

"The clothes!" She pointed back toward where they'd been, indicating the two shirts lying in a pile on the floor—a telltale bit of evidence should Brittany come home unexpectedly.

He set her down onto her feet—a development she didn't particularly enjoy—ran back into the living room, grabbed the two shirts, and brought them back with him. Then he pulled her into his arms again, kissing her in the hallway.

"Which room?" he murmured.

"That one." She pointed to her room, and he headed that way without letting go of her, opening the door, pushing her inside, closing the door with his foot, and pressing her against the wall without pause.

With the wall to her back and Shane to her front, Lily felt deliciously trapped, and the last thing she wanted was to be released. Shane put his mouth on her neck, using his tongue to taste her, and slipped his hand down the waistband of her sweatpants. His fingers slid between her legs, and her knees went weak.

"Oh, God."

A finger went inside her, and now her legs started to fail her. She might have slumped to the floor if he hadn't been holding her in place with his body.

"You're so wet," he whispered into her ear. "I love how much you want me."

He wanted her, too—she could feel his hardness pressing against her. She wanted to put her hands everywhere, but she only had one to work with, so she had to prioritize. She couldn't manage to undo his pants with just the one, non-dominant hand, so she pressed her palm against his erection outside of the fabric, and he drew in a ragged breath.

He added a second finger to the first, sliding it into her, and everything in the world now existed in that one spot at the center of her.

Lily hadn't felt like this since—well, since a time she preferred not to remember. She'd been playing it safe. Dating men she liked, but not too much. Seeing—and sleeping with—men she liked but who didn't have the power to hurt her.

And it was fine, it really was. But this was so much more.

Shane hooked his fingers into the waistband of her pants and slid them downward until they, along with her panties, were puddled at her feet. He picked her up in his arms and Lily wrapped her legs around his waist as he pressed her back into the wall.

He reached down with one hand—apparently, he was better with one hand than she was—and she heard a belt buckle, a snap, a zipper.

"Yes?" he whispered into her ear. "Lily, say yes."

"Yes." It came out as a gasp, and she gasped again when he pressed into her.

She closed her eyes, feeling the sensations of his body and her own, his mouth on her, his hard length moving inside her, the pressure of pleasure building in her belly and her chest.

"Lily, look at me."

She let out a whimper.

"Lily? Open your eyes and look at me."

She did. And somehow, looking into those dark, fathomless eyes made everything seem so much more intense—and so much more frightening.

Oh, God. Oh, God. I'm having sex against the wall with my sister's ex-boyfriend.

She closed her eyes again, because what else could she do? How else could she face what she was doing?

If she'd had her faculties, she might have asked him to stop, but she was too far gone for rational thought.

He buried his face in her neck and increased his pace, moving inside her harder and faster while she held on tight with her one available arm, the cast on the other thrown over his shoulder.

She was so close, so close. The pressure built inside her, the heat, the need. Then he reached down with one hand to the place where their bodies met. He pressed the pad of his thumb against the hard nub of her clitoris and moved it in slow circles as he thrust into her.

"Ah … ah … Shane … oh my God …"

And then the wave broke. She spasmed and shuddered, clasping her legs around his waist, the orgasm so intense that she saw stars behind her tightly closed lids.

He thrust into her hard and fast a few more times, then stilled as his body trembled.

When it was over, neither of them moved. She couldn't, because she was trapped between him and the wall. And he was still recovering, holding her tight and shuddering.

Eventually, he released her, and as she lowered her feet to the floor, the enormity of what they'd done hit her.

She'd screwed her sister's boyfriend.

Well, ex-boyfriend. But Brittany was unlikely to take any comfort from that distinction.

Oh, God. Oh, God.

Not only had she done it, but it had been the most earth-shattering sex of her life.

"Lily?" Shane touched his hand gently to her face. "Are you okay?"

"I don't know. It's just …"

"Did I … If you didn't want …"

"I wanted it, Shane. It's not that." Suddenly aware of her nudity, she went to the bed, pulled a throw blanket off the foot of the mattress, and wrapped it around herself.

"It's Brittany, then." His face was grim as he went into the adjoining bathroom. Lily heard water running, then he came out with his pants done up, belt firmly in place.

"Sort of." But it wasn't just Brittany, was it? It was also the fact that the last time she'd had sex even a fraction as good as this, she'd been put through a hell of emotional abuse she'd been unable to escape.

As though good sex was all it came down to. Shane made her

feel things. Things she hadn't felt in a long time, maybe ever. And those feelings took away her strength, took away her ability to make smart decisions. As today's events demonstrated.

She'd sworn to herself that she would never give a man that much power over her again—not after Trevor. And yet here she was, feeling utterly helpless against her feelings for Shane.

She stood there with tears welling in her eyes, pulling the blanket around her. Shane was so beautiful, and so … so *moving*. Something in him had called to something in her from the moment they'd met.

She'd been able to stuff that down for Brittany's sake when the two of them had been a couple, but now, she was no longer able to tame the beast.

"I think you should go," she said.

"Lily, I didn't mean to—"

"I know. You didn't. Just, please go."

Chapter Nineteen

S hane would have liked to have said he had no idea why Lily was upset and had sent him away. If he'd been entirely clueless about why she'd reacted the way she did, then he could have claimed he hadn't known what they'd done wrong.

But he did know. Shane had just had sex with his brother's ex. And Lily had just done the same with her sister's.

It wasn't the kind of thing you did when you loved and supported your sibling and didn't want to hurt them.

Shane hadn't been thinking about Finn or Brittany. He'd only been thinking about himself.

And the thing was, it felt good.

He'd betrayed his brother, his ex-girlfriend, and hell, his sister, too. He should feel terrible. He should feel like the worst kind of lowlife scum, the kind of person who put his own pleasure above everyone else's needs.

Instead, all he could feel was wonder and a kind of optimism he hadn't felt in a very long time.

He thought about all of that as he got into his car and drove back to the practice to attend to his afternoon patients. The sights of Lodge Hill and then Bridge Street passed by, but he didn't really see them. All he could see was Lily.

The entire time he was with her, the weight on his chest had been lifted. He hadn't felt guilt or pain or grief. He'd just felt … like himself. But the best version of himself—one who had never made mistakes or hurt anyone. One with no regrets.

He hadn't known he could feel that way, or that he would feel that way ever again. And now that he'd felt it, he just wanted to feel it again.

He came back into the office feeling fundamentally different than the person who'd left an hour ago.

And people noticed.

"Well, you must have had a good lunch," Iris commented as he came in the door and headed toward his office.

"What makes you say that?"

"I don't know. You just seem sort of perky."

Perky wasn't a word he would usually use for himself, but at the moment, it felt apt.

The next person to comment on his perkiness was Finn.

"What the hell happened to you?" he asked as they passed in the hallway.

"What do you mean? Nothing happened to me."

"Don't get me wrong. Whatever it was, you should do more of it. You were in a pissy mood this morning—nothing new there— and now you're practically skipping."

"I am not skipping."

"Not literally. But inside, you're skipping."

Finn was right. Inside, he was skipping.

Not that the guilt wasn't starting to creep in, though. The fact that Finn had just told him to do more of whatever he was doing— when what he was doing was having spectacular sex with Finn's ex- girlfriend—made him feel like a shitty brother.

Which meant that while he had been feeling entirely good, now he was only feeling partly good. Still, any level of good was more than he was used to.

He went into his office, took off his jacket, and replaced it with his white coat. Then he poked his head out into the hallway. "Iris? Who's next?"

———

WHEN SHANE WAS GONE, Lily went through the arduous process of bagging up her cast and sealing it with duct tape—one-handed—so she could shower off what she'd done with Shane.

She needed to scrub all traces of him away, not because she hadn't liked what they'd done, but because she really, really had.

How could she have done this to Brittany? And how could she have done it to herself? To put herself at this kind of risk again? It wasn't just stupid, it was reckless. Self-sabotaging. Masochistic.

Oh, what she'd felt so far was pleasure instead of pain, but that would change. It had changed with Trevor, and it would change with Shane. She was sure of it.

Even if Brittany never found out, which she would, Lily was still in the position of having feelings—strong ones—for someone who could potentially crush her heart.

And when that happened, when her heart was inevitably destroyed, who would she have? Not her sister, who would be so enraged by how Lily had betrayed her that she'd likely never speak to her again.

"Oh, this is bad. This is really bad," she muttered to herself over the sound of the water. "God, Lily, what did you do?"

And that led to thoughts about exactly what she'd done, and with whom, and how it had felt. And she wanted to do it again! What kind of person did that make her? What kind of person didn't feel remorse about treating her sister this way? Well, she did feel remorse, but not enough. Not enough to stop her from fantasizing about the next time Shane might handle her body the way he had, so masterfully, so …

A series of knocks on the bathroom door made Lily squeal and jump, pressing a trembling hand to her chest.

"Lily?" Brittany called to her. "Are you okay?"

"I'm fine. You just startled me."

"I ran home in between clients to check on you."

Which made Lily feel even worse about what she'd done.

"Well, I'm good."

"Didn't you already take a shower today?"

Lily closed her eyes and willed herself to sound normal. Not like someone who'd just screwed her sister's boyfriend. "Yes, but I just … I spilled coffee on myself, so I needed another one."

Lies, deceit, deception. Where would it end?

"Okay, well, I'll be here for about ten minutes if you need anything."

"Okay. And, Brittany?"

"Hmm?"

"I love you."

Lily's eyes welled up with tears.

"I love you too, Lily. Now stop being weird and come out so I can make you some lunch."

Oh, shit. Lunch. Shane had brought food. What had happened to it? Was it still sitting on the coffee table? And if so, how would she explain it?

He'd probably taken it with him, she reassured herself. Of course he had. He'd have been smart enough to eliminate the evidence, wouldn't he?

———

WHEN LILY CAME out of the shower, a fluffy bathrobe wrapped around her and her arm still duct taped into a plastic bag, Brittany was holding the bag of sandwiches Shane had brought, and Lily froze.

"Huh. You've already got lunch," Brittany said. She peeked into the bag. "It's from Soto's."

"Yeah, I …"

"Why didn't I remember before that they deliver? That's what we should have been doing from the beginning. But why did you get two sandwiches instead of one?"

Lily scrambled for a lie that would work. "I wondered if you might come home, so I got one for you."

She was going to hell, certainly. No question about it.

"Oh, that was nice of you. I'm starving. What kind did you get?"

She had no idea. She took the bag from Brittany and went into the kitchen. She took the sandwiches out of the bag and began unwrapping them.

"Lily? I asked what kind you got."

"Hmm?" Lily said, as though her arm injury had also affected her hearing.

"Chicken? Turkey? Vegetarian? What?" Brittany said.

By then, she had them unwrapped. "One veggie wrap and one turkey and provolone on a roll. Which one do you want?"

———

WHEN BRITTANY WAS GONE, Lily flopped onto the sofa, the turkey sandwich sitting heavily in her stomach. This is what it had come to. Lying to her sister about sandwiches.

Should she come clean? Should she tell Brittany what she'd done, even if it meant risking a break in their relationship that might never heal?

That would only be necessary if she and Shane were going to keep doing what they'd done. Which they absolutely were not.

It was a one-time thing. Well, two-time, if you considered the time they'd made out on the sofa. Was it worth hurting Brittany for a one-time (or two-time) thing?

Of course it wasn't. The only person it would help would be Lily, because she'd be relieved of the weight of her secret. It wouldn't do Brittany any good at all. So, she wouldn't tell. Ever. And she would hope that Shane wouldn't, either.

———

ONCE THE INITIAL high wore off, Shane started to worry about

Lily.

The way she'd rushed him out of her house after their encounter bothered him. He knew he hadn't pressured her to do anything she didn't want to do, but if she was feeling regret now, that wasn't something he felt good about.

And now that he thought about it, he didn't feel good about bringing her into something that would ultimately cause her pain once Shane started showing her how damaged he really was.

He saw his afternoon patients, including a house call in Pine Knolls, went back to his house on Happy Hill, made himself a sandwich, ate it with a bottle of beer, and thought about Lily.

When he was done eating, he took out his phone and texted her.

Are you okay?

She answered a few minutes later.

Yes. I'm fine.

You seemed upset. After.

I was thinking of Brittany.

Of course she was, and he should be, too. And he should be thinking of Finn. He should feel terrible about what this might mean to both of them. And he did feel terrible. But comparing this terrible feeling to the one he'd been feeling before his encounter with Lily? No contest. This was a nagging guilt, while that had been a deep, dark hole that threatened to swallow him alive.

If he had to choose his terrible, was it so wrong to want this one?

He sat at the kitchen table and stared at his phone for a while, trying to figure out what to say. Trying to convince himself not to say what he wanted to say.

In the end, he said it anyway.

I want to see you again.

He waited, feeling the flutter in his belly that people the world over felt when they were waiting to hear from the person they were infatuated with.

I'm not sure that's a good idea.

It's not, he fired back. *In fact, it's a horrible idea. But let's do it anyway.*

She didn't answer, and he took that as a hopeful sign.

Chapter Twenty

Brittany left for their mother's house in Ohio a few days later, once she'd cleared her schedule at work. Which meant Lily would have to get by on her own the best she could. And which also meant she could see Shane if she wanted to without Brittany finding out.

Lily just wasn't sure she wanted to.

On the matter of getting by, Lily was fairly confident. She'd had practice with her non-dominant arm, and she could dress herself in real clothes, wrap up her arm for her shower, make food for herself, and even drive. Most of those things took longer than they otherwise would have, but she could do them.

She was even managing to do her job, more or less. She was getting good at one-handed hunt-and-peck typing, and she'd switched to voice recordings rather than handwritten notes when she did interviews for her newsletter.

So, practical matters were pretty much under control.

It was the very unpractical matter of Shane Brody that worried her.

He'd been texting her the last couple of days, and she couldn't put him off much longer. She had to either declare that she didn't want to see him anymore, or that she did.

Neither one seemed viable. Seeing him again would be a betrayal of her sister and a cruelty toward Finn. But not seeing him again would mean that this longing, this painful yearning, would go on and on.

Better to end it now, though, because the yearning and the longing will be so much worse if you fall in love with him and then he leaves you.

When Trevor had left her, she'd been gutted, even though it was, in the end, a mercy. She'd needed to get out so badly, and yet it had wrecked her when it had finally happened.

Why would she want to put herself through that again?

Lily had just about convinced herself nothing was worth that.

Then Shane showed up at her door again.

BEFORE, Shane had gone to Lily's house during his lunch break, and at least one of those times had turned out well for him. Why not try it again?

On both previous occasions he'd brought sandwiches, so this time he went for salads. It made sense to switch things up.

He felt optimistic about how it would go until Lily opened the door and he saw the expression on her face.

"Oh, Shane," she said.

The expression was an amorphous, changing thing. First alarm, then what might have been pleasure or desire, then dismay.

The negative emotions on her face were outnumbering the positive ones.

"I came to see how you're getting along. And I brought salads." He held up the bag. "Instead of sandwiches, in case you were getting tired of those."

"You shouldn't have come," she said. She leaned against the door jamb, blocking his way.

"I'm just here to inquire about your well-being. I heard Brittany left, and you're alone, so I wanted to make sure you were getting along okay."

"Well, I am."

And that made him worry that he really had pushed her into something she didn't want to do.

"Lily, are you okay? About what happened last time, I mean? I know I came on strong, and I hope I didn't pressure you. If I did . . ."

Her shoulders fell, along with her defensive posture. "Oh, Shane. No. You didn't pressure me into anything. I wanted it as much as you did, in case you didn't notice."

"Well, I did notice, but I didn't want to be ungentlemanly about it."

That made her laugh, and her laughter was a beautiful sound.

"Look, you'd better come inside before the neighbors see you and somebody says something to Brittany. But we're just going to talk and eat salad. Nothing else."

LILY NOTICED that the sex between herself and Shane had accomplished one thing: she was able to talk to him without stammering now. Apparently, the awkwardness had been a buildup of sexual tension. Now that it had been released, she was finally able to make coherent sentences.

Not that she intended to do much talking to him once she explained that this could not continue.

Shane took the bag of food to the kitchen table and began rooting around in drawers in search of forks, as though he lived here. She supposed some of that familiarity came from the fact Brittany had invited him here more than a few times.

Oh, God. Brittany.

Now his head was inside the refrigerator. "Do you want a Sprite? Or sparkling water?"

"Shane—"

"I'll probably have the sparkling water, if it's okay."

"Yes, it's fine. But—"

"I should have brought drinks, but it seemed like you usually have some, plus they're pretty expensive at the restaurant."

"Shane—"

"Here. Sprite." He brought a can to the table and set it down next to Lily's salad.

She'd meant to launch into her reasons why they couldn't be together, right up front and before the salad, so there wouldn't be any misunderstandings. Somehow, she hadn't managed to get the words out.

Well, fine. They'd eat salad—she really was hungry—and then she'd say it. Surely he knew it was coming.

"So, how's your arm?" he asked as he sat down at the table across from her and opened the container that held his salad.

"It's fine."

"No pain?"

"No. Not anymore. It does itch, though."

"Yeah, that'll happen. Don't stick anything inside the cast to scratch. That's a good way to get an infection."

Lily opened her container and peered at her salad, which looked good. Nestled onto the greens were two plastic containers of dressing—ranch and Italian. It made her smile to think Shane had been careful to cover all of the bases.

"Is that common? An infection because someone stuck something inside their cast?"

"It happens. People use coat hangers, mostly. If you break the skin, the bacteria builds up in there, and you've got a problem."

Lily had been looking longingly at a coat hanger just that morning, for that exact reason. Now, she was glad she'd suppressed the urge.

"And how are you getting along?" he asked.

"Oh, fine." Lily shrugged. "I'm learning to type with my right hand. Do buttons. That sort of thing."

Shane's mouth quirked up into a whisper of a smile, and Lily imagined he was thinking about when she'd tried to *undo* some buttons on his shirt. She felt her cheeks redden at the memory.

"I guess Brittany's helping a lot," he said.

"Well, she was. But now she's in Ohio helping our mom pack up her house. She's planning to move to the Central Coast to be closer to us."

"Oh. Is that a good thing?"

"Yes. It's a very good thing."

They each ate another bite of salad before Shane addressed the point they were both thinking about.

"So, Brittany's out of town. For a while." He shot a significant look at her.

"Yes. She is."

"So, if someone were to be … I don't know, say, kissing on the sofa, there's absolutely no chance she'd come home unexpectedly and catch them." His voice was casual, as though it were a completely hypothetical question.

"There's no chance of that, no. But that's not going to happen."

"Understood." He nodded and took another bite of salad.

They ate in silence for a while, then he tried again. "If it's not going to happen because of Brittany—"

"Partly because of her, but for other reasons, too."

"For instance?"

"For instance, because we're not in a relationship. I usually only do … *that* when I'm in a relationship with someone. Last time, I got carried away and, well, things happened. But you and I are not boyfriend and girlfriend, we're not partners. We're just exes in law. And a person shouldn't sleep with their ex in law."

"I don't think *ex in law* is even a thing."

"Of course it is. It's us. It's exactly what we are."

Shane smiled. "Well, at least we're something there's a name for. Even if you just made it up."

He was being charming, and she didn't need him to be charming. His charm would make it so much harder to push him out the door when lunch was over.

———

YES, Shane had come here with the hope of sleeping with Lily again. And yes, she was shutting him down, showing that of the two of them, she was the one with good sense.

The rejection should have made him sad, or discouraged, or something other than happy, which was what he felt.

As it turned out, just sitting here eating a salad with her was enough to lift him out of the funk he'd been in and make him feel optimistic and good for a change.

His hypothesis had been that the sex had done that, but maybe it was just her.

Interesting.

Lily was taking longer than he had to eat—it seemed that stabbing salad with a fork was harder when you did it with your wrong hand—so he sat and waited, satisfied just to be here in the same place as her.

When she was finished, she closed her empty container, got up from her seat, and threw away her trash. Then she turned to face Shane.

"Okay, we ate. We talked. Now you have to go."

"Right. I will. But before I go …"

"Shane."

"Before I go," he tried again, "are you sure there isn't anything you need done that you can't do with one arm? Take out the trash, maybe?"

Lily paused, looked at Shane, then looked at the full kitchen trash container.

"You're sure you don't mind?"

———

SHANE TOOK OUT THE TRASH, put a new liner in the kitchen garbage can, and rolled the outdoor garbage cans to the curb. Then he swept the kitchen floor—something remarkably hard to do without both arms—and put a load of Lily's laundry into the washing machine.

When he was done, a sense of satisfaction hummed through him. It felt good to be useful to a woman who needed his help.

"Anything else?" he asked.

"Well …"

"Come on, out with it. I'm here and I'm able-bodied. What do you need?"

What she needed was someone to go grocery shopping with her. The house she shared with Brittany was up a steep slope from the street—which was the only available parking—and up a flight of stairs after that. Carrying grocery bags with just one arm meant twice the number of trips up from the street.

Shane couldn't do it right now—he had to get back to the office for his afternoon patients—but he offered to come back after work to do the shopping with her.

"You don't have to do that," she said. "Really. I'm sure after work you just want to relax and—"

"I want to." And it was true—he really did.

"Well, okay. Thank you."

"See you about six?" he said.

"Yes. Okay."

She walked him to the door, and he paused before leaving.

"Thank you for lunch," she said. "And for taking out the trash. And putting in the laundry."

"No problem." His voice had gone low and soft, and he seemed to be looking at her full lips instead of at her face.

"I really …" She cleared her throat. "I wish we could do more. I really do. But …"

"That's fine." It sounded like a purr.

"So I'll … see you at six?"

"At six." He moved toward her. Her lips parted and her eyes closed, and she leaned in. Using all of the self-control he had, he bypassed her mouth and brushed a gentle kiss to her cheek.

Then he left before he could attempt to do what she'd asked him not to.

Chapter Twenty-One

Lily spent the rest of the day waiting for six and trying not to think about the kiss on the cheek.

Yes, it had just been the cheek, but it had been nearly as erotic as everything else they'd experienced together. The kiss had sent a jolt of pleasure and anticipation through her body, all the way down to her toes.

No wonder so many people made stupid sexual mistakes. Desire like this took you out of your right mind. It made you stupid and reckless.

She should call Shane and tell him it was off—she could do her grocery shopping without him. If she had to carry multiple bags of groceries all the way up the slope and then up the stairs one at a time, she would. Her arm might be out of commission, but her legs were fine.

Then again, it was just grocery shopping. She hadn't made a sex date. She and Shane wouldn't be going out to an intimate dinner after which they would spend the rest of the night naked in her bed.

And, oh, imagining that last phrase was a mistake, because it had Lily all fluttery and agitated when she was supposed to be working on a proofreading job with a rapidly approaching deadline.

Lily sat at her desk with the pages of the manuscript in front of her, reading the text with a pencil between her teeth, ready to painstakingly mark up with her wrong hand any errors she might find.

She read a sentence, then realized she'd been so focused on Shane that she hadn't absorbed a word of it. She got up, went into the kitchen, made herself a cup of tea, and brought her mug back to her desk. She sat down and tried again.

She got through a few paragraphs before her mind began to drift back to Shane. Specifically, to a moment they'd shared the day they'd slept together, when he'd put his finger on her—

Damn it.

How was she supposed to finish her work this way? How was she supposed to make a living and pay her bills if she couldn't get her mind off of things like sex and Shane and how lovely it had been when the two of those things had blended together?

She grabbed the pencil and threw it onto her desk. It bounced off the manuscript and clattered to the floor.

Lily needed to focus. She was an adult woman with responsibilities. She could hardly ignore her work to daydream—and wallow in guilt—about Shane Brody all day.

It's just grocery shopping. It's not sex. It's an errand. I need help and I'm accepting help. That's all it is.

Surely no one could blame her for that.

———

SHANE WAS FAIRLY good at compartmentalizing his feelings when it came to his work. Even when he was in the worst of his moods, he could still focus on his patients when he needed to. He could still do his job.

That ability came in handy that afternoon as Shane saw patients, did paperwork, and did what his work demanded of him.

He made another house call to see Orin Delaney—a follow-up to discuss how the cholesterol medication Shane had prescribed was working and whether he'd made the necessary changes to his diet.

He treated one patient with asthma, another with digestive issues, and another with a suspicious mole that required a referral to a dermatologist.

He checked phone messages and returned patient calls, then endured an interminable call with an insurance company. (While Bridge Street Wellness didn't accept insurance, the specialists to which they referred patients did, and Shane had to persuade an insurance provider that a referral he'd made was medically necessary.)

The whole time, he kept an eye on the clock. He didn't want to be late for Lily.

"Hey, Shane, you want to go to Ted's after work?" Aidan asked as they met at the coffee pot in the break room between patients.

"Can't."

"Why? What have you got going on?"

He hesitated to answer, given the fact that his motives weren't entirely pure. But if he lied, Aidan would know. He had a knack for that kind of thing.

"I said I would help Lily Hart with a few errands. Because her arm's in a cast. I agreed to go along." He kept his tone as casual as possible, his eyes on his coffee mug and not on his brother.

"Lily Hart? Really." Aidan's tone held both suspicion and surprise.

"Yes, really."

"I don't think running errands is part of the service we provide, even to our concierge patients. Which, now that I think of it, do not include Lily Hart."

Shane shrugged. "I'm doing a favor for a friend."

Aidan scoffed. "Since when is she your friend?"

"She's Brittany's sister, and I still care about Brittany even if we're not together anymore. So I'm helping out. Do you have an issue with that?"

"Well, not when you put it that way."

"Good."

Shane returned to his office feeling like a manipulative asshole.

Claiming he was helping Lily for Brittany's sake? When he actually had betrayed Brittany once and might do so again?

Shit. What am I doing?

The question didn't stop him from driving to Lily's house the minute he finished at Bridge Street Wellness.

————

LILY ABSOLUTELY WAS NOT GOING to kiss Shane, or get naked with him, or do any of the things she'd previously found so diverting.

Which was why she was taking absolutely no care with her appearance in anticipation of his visit.

She'd been wearing yoga pants all day, so that's what she was wearing now. Tank top with a slouchy sweater over it? Check. She barely ran a brush through her hair, and she certainly wasn't about to put on makeup.

She was making a statement regarding her intentions, and with that statement in mind, she looked at him with defiance in her eyes when she opened the door to him at ten after six.

"Are you ready to go?" he asked doubtfully.

"Yep. Absolutely." She jammed her feet into a pair of flip-flops, grabbed her purse, and came onto the porch, locking the door behind her.

————

SUDDENLY, Shane was feeling overdressed in the dress shirt, slacks, and tie he'd worn to work.

He was feeling other things, too.

For some reason he couldn't explain, Lily drove him to distraction whenever she was messy and unkempt like she was today. He'd seen her in business casual clothes during his time with Brittany, and he'd seen her dressed up when she'd been going out with Finn. She always looked good, but like this? With her hair askew and her face bare, looking like she'd just rolled out of bed?

It was all he could do not to pick her up, carry her to her bed, and tear those stretchy pants off of her.

He couldn't have said exactly why that was. Maybe it was the contrast from the usual expectation for how women were to present themselves. Maybe it was the honesty of it—the lack of pretense. Or maybe it just reminded him of how Lily had looked after he kissed her on the sofa—and after he'd done so much more to her in her bedroom.

Whatever it was, his thoughts were going places they shouldn't as he drove her to the Cookie Crock then pushed her basket up and down the aisles as she chose produce and canned goods, bread and pasta, and placed everything into the cart.

"You're not saying much," she observed, a box of cereal in her hand.

"Oh. I just have a lot on my mind, I guess." He shrugged.

"Anything you want to talk about?"

"Not really."

How could he talk about it, when what he had on his mind was the way her ass looked in a pair of Lycra pants? Or the way her hair, all loose and wild, looked just the way it had after he'd given her an orgasm? Or the way her bra strap was peeking out from the neck hole of her tank top, making him think about taking it off of her?

She bent over to grab a bag of rice off a bottom shelf, and he had to stand behind the cart to hide the sudden bulge in his pants.

What the hell was he doing? Nothing about this was going to end well. If Finn found out …

"Well, I think that's about it," she said. "Let's get checked out, then you can take me home."

God help him.

———

IT WASN'T that she'd bought so much. After all, she was just one person. But some of the things she'd bought were heavy or bulky—a gallon of bottled water, an extra-large bottle of liquid laundry detergent, a size chosen to save money—and she really could use his help bringing everything in from the car.

So Lily was appreciative as Shane brought in the last items, setting things down on the kitchen counter.

"Thank you," she said. "Really. Thank you."

"No problem." He leaned his butt on the edge of the counter, his arms crossed over his chest. "Now, I figure you need some help making dinner."

"Oh, no. I'll be fine."

"I'm here. I came to help. You might as well let me."

When he put it that way, the logic was hard to argue against.

"Well …"

He began rolling up his sleeves, then washed his hands at the kitchen sink. "Pasta okay?" he asked.

"Pasta's fine. It's just … you don't have to. I got some frozen meals. I can just put something in the microwave and—"

"As your doctor, I can't support you eating that much sodium and that many artificial ingredients. Not when I can just make you something."

She arched an eyebrow at him. "So you're just doing this for my medical benefit?"

"Strictly."

Conflicted, she didn't answer for a moment. Then, she sighed. "All right. Thank you. If you really don't mind."

———

AS SHANE SAT down across from Lily at her dining room table, plates of steaming pasta in front of them, he felt pleased with how things were going. He'd turned an initial rejection into what could, conceivably, be considered a date.

After all, dates often involved sharing a meal. And here they were, doing just that.

It wasn't that he wanted to pressure her into doing anything she didn't want to do. He wasn't one of those guys, and he had no intention of becoming one. It was just that he felt better when he was with Lily, even if he wasn't touching her, even if they were just shopping for cereal or eating a meal.

Even if nothing more than that happened, he would still have a couple of hours in which he didn't feel like shit. That seemed like something worth pursuing.

Okay, having a relationship with Lily would betray both Brittany and Finn. But what if he and Lily were just friends? What if he could just talk to her and eat with her and spend time with her and feel better, without doing any of the physical things that would be so upsetting to the people in both of their lives?

"This is delicious." Lily chewed a bite of pasta, her eyes closed in bliss. "Where did you learn to cook?"

He resolved not to think about how the pleasure on her face resembled the pleasure he'd made her feel on other occasions.

"My mother taught me. I don't have a wide range of dishes I can cook, but she always said a man should have a good pasta, a good chicken dish, and a good soup recipe at his disposal, and she made us all learn them."

"She's a wise woman."

"She is. So, how are your mom and Brittany doing getting the house packed up?"

Lily talked about that for a while. Janice had hired movers to deal with the big things—the furniture and whatnot—and to haul the boxes to a storage unit Janice would be using until she found a new, permanent place. But she and Brittany had to sort through ten years worth of belongings, deciding what to keep and what to sell or donate while dealing with the emotional ramifications of all of it.

"And your dad?" Shane asked.

"He died three years ago. He and my mom moved to Ohio for his work—he was an agricultural engineer—and then, lung cancer. He was a heavy smoker."

Which, Lily told him, meant Brittany and their mother were coming across the emotional landmines of George Hart's photos and mementos that had been lying dormant all this time.

"How's she doing with it? Brittany?" he asked.

"Oh, okay. I think. She's trying to keep her mind on the task at hand."

Talking about Brittany somehow gave this evening a kind of innocence, a Good Housekeeping Seal of Approval, that it otherwise might not have had. Would he be asking about Brittany if he planned to ravage Lily after dinner? Of course not. And Lily wouldn't be talking about Brittany if she planned to be ravaged.

Lily had bought a bottle of red wine at the Cookie Crock, and they were drinking it now with their spaghetti marinara. Shane had made the sauce from scratch.

Lily took a bite of pasta, and now she had a tiny spot of marinara at the corner of her mouth. Shane wanted to lick it off. Instead, he reached out with a napkin and dabbed it away.

Which turned out to be a mistake, because the gesture was more intimate than he'd intended. They locked eyes for a little too long, then Shane cleared his throat and tried to focus on his meal.

———

HOW WAS it that Lily seemed to keep eating meals with Shane?

This couldn't continue. And yet here she was, eating pasta and drinking wine and talking to Shane as though they were on a date.

They were not on a date.

"This isn't a date," she blurted out, then plunked her wineglass back onto the table.

Shane looked at her with surprise. "Of course it's not."

"Good. I'm just making sure. Because with the wine and the food and everything, it seems like it might be a date. But it isn't."

"No."

"It can't be. Because what kind of person would I be if I waited for my sister to leave town and then started dating her ex? A horrible person, that's what kind. So … no. This is just you helping a patient to function during healing. Which is going above and beyond, obviously, but that's just because you're a good and caring doctor. That's all it is."

He looked at her for a moment, then dabbed at his mouth with his napkin and put the napkin back down in his lap.

"That's not all it is," he said. "And we both know that."

She stared at him. "Shane—"

"I agree that it's not a date," he went on. "A date is planned in advance with the express intention of romantic possibilities. And that doesn't quite match the description of what we're doing here."

"Okay …"

"But it's not just me helping a patient. You know how many patients I've made dinner for before this? None. You know how many patients I've wanted to make dinner for?"

"None?"

"That's right. None."

Lily's mouth was dry, and she'd stopped breathing.

"I like being with you," he said. "You make me feel better. More like my old self, before …" He stopped without finishing his sentence.

"Before you lost your sister," she finished for him, her voice barely a whisper.

"You know about that."

"I do research on my subjects before I interview them. It's standard practice." That much was true. She didn't mention that she'd done more research on Shane than was standard because she'd wanted to know. She'd wanted to learn everything she could about him.

"Oh. Well, yes. Before that."

He looked so vulnerable that she wanted to help. She wanted to heal him the way he was healing her. She reached out and put her hand over his on the table, and he turned his palm upward so he could wrap his hand around hers.

"This isn't just me being a doctor," he said.

All of Lily's good intentions, all of her resolutions to let him help her and then send him away, were blowing away like so much dust in a windstorm. All she wanted was to take him in her arms. To hold him and stroke his hair. To be whatever he needed her to be to help him feel okay again.

"This is dangerous," she said, her voice weak. "This is going to hurt people."

"Yes," he said.

"We really should stop this now," she said.

"Yes."

And then he leaned forward, across the table, and kissed her, and she forgot everything but him.

Chapter Twenty-Two

Before Shane knew what he was doing, he'd pulled Lily out of her chair and had settled her across his lap. He had his hands in her hair, and he was kissing her as though his very life depended on it.

It felt to him like it did.

Feeling the delicious weight of her on top of him, he caressed her mouth with his, sweeping his tongue over hers. Some cold, painful thing inside him broke, and all he felt was acceptance and pleasure.

"Shane—"

"Please." He whispered it against her skin. "Please don't send me away. Even if we don't do anything, I just want to be here with you. Please."

He pressed his face to her neck and breathed her in, and she let out a shaky breath.

"I need you, Lily. I'm not okay, and you make me feel like I am. Please …"

He felt the moment when her resistance broke. The tension left her body, and she wrapped her good arm around him, relaxing into him.

He was so grateful he almost wept.

———

IN A MOMENT, Lily went from being someone to whom things were happening to being someone who acted. Who took a chance. Who made a choice that might burn her world to ash.

If it did, so be it.

There was no way she could turn him away now. Her heart wouldn't allow it. And so she held him and kissed him and whimpered when he ran his hands down her body.

Before she knew what was happening, he picked her up and set her down on the table, their dinner dishes shoved aside. She wrapped her legs around him—she wanted to wrap all of herself around him—and he slid his hands around her waist, under her shirt.

Later, Lily could not have said at what point she switched over from thinking she absolutely, positively was not going to sleep with Shane again to thinking that he was worth every risk, every possible heartbreak, even those that were not her own. But somehow the switch had happened, because right now she wasn't thinking about Brittany or Finn or even Trevor, she wasn't thinking about what was right or wrong. She was only thinking about Shane's hands on her body and how magnificent this felt, how right.

Yes, it was true that in the past, this kind of desire had only led to pain for Lily. But that didn't mean it would always be true. Wasn't it possible that this could be different?

It wouldn't be. Lily felt that in her heart. Shane was going to cause her nothing but pain and heartbreak. But right now, she didn't care. The threat of pain wasn't enough to outweigh the promise of pleasure.

She went to work on his tie with her right hand, loosening it and taking it off over his head. Then she started in on the buttons of his shirt.

"You're getting better at that," he observed, his voice husky, as she undid one button after another.

"Practice."

"Right."

When she'd undone all of the buttons, he shrugged out of the shirt and let it fall to the floor. She ran her hand over his skin and felt him shudder beneath her touch.

Then, with what she could only think was skill that came from practice, he lifted her up from the table just long enough to slide her pants down over her hips.

Something about both of them being half dressed—him naked above the waist, her below it—felt more erotic than if they'd both been nude. More illicit. As though they were stealing this delicious moment before life intervened.

He touched the wet, hot core of her with his fingers, and she whimpered with need, her face pressed to his neck.

Then he was unbuckling his belt, unfastening his pants, and she wrapped her hand around his hardness and guided him toward her.

The sensation of him moving inside her made her feel weight-less, boneless. Everything in her was liquid heat concentrated low in her body, at their point of contact.

Maybe it was the circumstances—the way he was taking her on the dining room table—or maybe it was the fact that she hadn't stopped thinking about him and wanting him since last time they were together. Whatever it was, it didn't take her long to rise to climax. She clung to him and shuddered as her body spasmed.

"Not so fast," he whispered into her ear. "I'm not ready for this to be over."

So he took his time, laying her back on the table and thrusting into her, his hands on her breasts beneath her shirt, his mouth on the hollow of her throat.

And oh, it felt divine, being worshipped like this, being devoured by him.

And now she was rising again, the delicious pressure building, her body writhing in response.

"Oh, God. Shane—"

When she came, it felt like the world blowing apart.

She felt limp, spent, floating on a cloud of bliss as he stiffened and stilled above her, groaning with his own release.

———

SHANE HAD LOST all sense of his surroundings, so when he came back to his senses, he was mildly surprised to find that he and Lily were sprawled across the dining room table with some of the used dishes from their dinner shoved aside, another one smashed on the floor.

He couldn't remember the last time he'd wanted someone so much that he'd had to have her right there, wherever *there* was. Had he ever, before this? Generally speaking, Shane was the kind of man who went into relationships sensibly, thoughtfully, with care and intent. But this thing with Lily was different. This thing with Lily was like a runaway train that had jumped the tracks and was heading toward a populated town.

And everybody knew there was no way to stop a runaway train, other than the inevitable crash.

He kissed Lily tenderly on the cheek and lowered himself off of her and off the table, just now noticing the shards of a broken plate on the floor.

"Wait," he said when she began to get up. "Let me get this first."

He went into the kitchen, found a broom and dustpan, and swept up the broken plate so she wouldn't cut her feet.

When he was done, she got down off the table, picked up her pants, and went down the hall and into the bathroom. She came back a few minutes later, reassembled. By then, he was dressed again. An uninformed bystander would have looked at the table and thought there'd been an earthquake, maybe—certainly not what had actually happened.

Although it had felt like an earthquake to Shane. A big one that left entire communities in ruins.

As he helped her clean up the dinner mess, he was on the verge of saying something shocking: *I think something bad is happening. I think*

I'm falling in love with you. But he couldn't say that, not now. Not when this thing between them was so new and fragile.

And not when it was so likely that his feelings had more to do with him, with the darkness in his life that was just now beginning to lighten, than with her.

She made him feel better, that was all. Was that love? Was the mere easing of pain enough to bring about that kind of declaration?

He didn't want to be rash with labeling his feelings. He'd been rash enough already, just being here with her.

So instead of telling her what he'd thought of telling her, he worked side by side with her in the kitchen until the surfaces were gleaming and every dish and pan had been put away.

When they were done, he stood in the kitchen with his hands tucked into his armpits, silent.

"Are you okay?" Lily asked, looking up at him with concern.

"Yeah. Yes. Are you?"

"I am. But—"

"But you're going to say we can't see each other anymore," he began, interrupting her. "You're going to say it will hurt Brittany and Finn. Well, I know it will. I know that. But, Lily—"

"That's not what I was going to say."

"Then what?"

She took in a deep breath and let it out in a ragged huff. "I was going to say, I need to tell Brittany about us. And you need to tell Finn."

LILY HADN'T MEANT to say what she'd said. It had just come out. But now that it had, she knew it was the right thing. If she was going to keep seeing Shane—and at this point, she felt helpless not to—it couldn't be a secret. They had to come out into the open.

"Oh." Shane gave her a tight little nod, his lips in a hard line. "I know. You're right."

"Unless you think there's a chance you might want to get back together with Brittany. Or you feel like this thing between us isn't … isn't …"

He reached out and laid his palm on her cheek. "There is no chance that I will get back together with Brittany. And this thing between us? It definitely is."

She blushed, and it made her even more beautiful than she'd been before.

"Then we have to stop keeping secrets," she said.

He nodded, then kissed her. "All right."

"Really?"

"Yes. You tell Brittany, and I'll tell Finn." He sighed. "This isn't going to be easy."

No, it wouldn't be easy. Telling Brittany wouldn't be easy, and neither would the eventual crash and burn of her relationship with Shane—an inevitability, in her experience, when the passion ran so hot.

At this point, though, she felt as though she had no choice in any of it. She had to come clean with her sister, and she had to keep seeing Shane. She had to give in to her relentless need for him, and she had to risk going wherever this thing would go.

That was, after all, one reason she needed to be up front with Brittany. When Shane crushed her, she would need her sister to put all of her pieces back together.

Chapter Twenty-Three

S hane had wanted to stay, to sleep by Lily's side, but she'd sent him home. It seemed wrong to her that the relationship should become that real—that concrete—before she'd told her sister about it.

When he was gone, Lily disinfected the dining room table, then did it again, her cheeks hot with embarrassment over what she and Shane had done there. Or maybe it wasn't embarrassment. Maybe it was remembered passion. Both caused her face to go pink and butterflies to bat their wings in her belly.

After tonight, it was ridiculous to keep pretending that they weren't together. It was disingenuous, and that wasn't doing any favors for anyone involved. This was real. It was happening.

Now she just had to come clean to Brittany.

Lily didn't want to do it over the phone—it seemed like the kind of conversation they should have face to face—but she didn't want to wait, either. The deception was eating at her, and she had to make it right sooner rather than later.

She checked the clock: it was still early enough in Ohio for her to talk to her sister.

She took a shower first, not wanting Shane's scent on her when she confessed to her sister, then sent Brittany a text message.

We need to talk. Is now a good time?

Three dots bounced as Brittany composed her answer.

Sounds ominous. Sure. Are you okay?

Let's do a video chat. I'm calling you now.

Lily took a deep, shaky breath and steeled herself. She settled in on the sofa with her laptop and initiated a video call to Brittany.

Brittany's face appeared on the screen, grainy and poorly lit in the living room of their mother's house.

"Hey. What's up?" Brittany looked concerned. "Are you doing okay? How's your arm?"

"It's fine." Lily adjusted her laptop to position her face closer to the center of the screen. "It's not that. But there's something we need to talk about."

"You're scaring me." Brittany's eyebrows drew together, creating a vertical line of concern between them.

"It's just … I've been seeing Shane. Personally. We've been dating." *Dating* was, of course, a euphemism for screwing on the dining room table, but Brittany did not need to know that detail. "I didn't want to tell you until I was sure it was something. And it is. Something. I know this will probably hurt you, and I never wanted that. I hope you'll be okay with it, but if you're not …" She didn't know what to say after that. If she wasn't okay with it, then what? She couldn't offer to stop seeing Shane. She was too far gone for that.

Brittany got the same facial expression she used to use when they were kids and Lily had broken one of Brittany's toys. Pure outrage. "You did not just say that."

"Brit, I'm sorry. I really am. I never meant—"

"Does it even matter to you that he's my ex? What he and I went through? Do you even care?"

"Of course I do. But—"

"Do you even care how this makes me feel?"

"Oh, Brittany. Yes. I do care. I do!" Tears ran down Lily's cheeks. She brushed them away with her fingertips.

"Just not enough to stop this," Brittany said.

"This isn't just a whim. I have real feelings for him."

"What about *my* feelings? Aren't those real?"

"Look. Brittany. If you could just—"

"Don't *look, Brittany* me. This isn't what sisters do to each other, and you know it."

She did know it—that was the worst part.

"But you didn't really love him," she reminded her sister. "You said that."

"And you do? Is that what you're telling me?"

"I'm telling you that I have feelings. And so does Shane. And we're exploring those."

"Just like you were exploring each other on the sofa that day." Brittany spat out the words as though they tasted bad.

None of this was going the way Lily had hoped, but it was going the way she'd feared. How had she thought it would be any different? Of course Brittany was reacting this way. Who wouldn't?

"I'm so sorry this is hurting you," she said. She grabbed a tissue from a box on a side table, blew her nose, and wiped her eyes.

"Yeah, well. He hurt me, Lily. And he'll hurt you, too. And when he does, don't come to me for help. Because I won't be there for you."

The screen went blank as Brittany disconnected the call.

———

BY THE TIME their mother called to find out what was going on, Lily was miserable, half-drunk on a cheap bottle of wine she'd dug out from the back of the pantry.

"Lily Elizabeth Hart. What did you say to your sister to get her so upset? She's locked herself in the guest room and she won't talk to me. But I know it has something to do with you."

"Oh, it does. But I don't want to talk about it right now."

"You will talk about it. If you don't, how am I ever going to coax your sister out of the bedroom? Now, come out with it."

Janice's authoritative tone had always been hard for Lily to resist. She braced herself and told her mother the truth.

"It's Shane. He and I are … we're seeing each other. I told Brittany, and it didn't go well."

"Oh."

"You said I shouldn't rule him out. You said Brittany didn't love him anyway." Lily felt it necessary to remind her mother of this before the scolding began.

Janice sighed. "Yes, I guess I did say that."

"Well, you were right. I tried not to get involved with him for Brittany's sake, but things happened. And now we're involved. And I couldn't keep it from her. I had to tell her. And now she's so upset, Mom. I don't know if she'll ever talk to me again."

"Oh, honey. She will."

"Are you sure?"

"Of course. Her pride is hurt. And right now, she's questioning your loyalty."

"My loyalty? But—"

"I know," Janice said, cutting her off. "And Brittany knows, too. She will get over this, but you have to give her some space. And I'll talk to her."

"You will?"

"I'll try. But Lily?" Janice paused. "He did make things awfully difficult for Brittany there at the end. Are you sure you're prepared to handle it if he does the same to you?

She didn't know the answer, but she knew that ending things now was not an option.

———

SHANE MEANT to talk to Finn that night after he left Lily's house. But first, he told himself, he would go home, take a shower, and get himself together.

By the time he did all that, it was too late to call Finn, so he vowed to have the discussion the next day. He didn't want to do it at work, though, just in case there was yelling, so he invited Finn to lunch.

"Can't," Finn said. "I've got plans."

"What kind of plans? Do you have a patient?"

"No."

"A date, then?"

"No. I've got errands."

"Errands? What kind of errands?"

They were standing in the break room, waiting with their mugs while Aidan made a pot of coffee.

Finn gestured vaguely with his empty mug. "You know … errands. Picking up dry cleaning. Stopping by the hardware store. Errands."

"I'll come with you," Shane said.

"You want to come with me to buy light bulbs?"

"Sure, why not?"

"The better question is, why?"

"Because I want to talk to you about something," Shane said.

Finn checked his watch. "I've got a few minutes. Talk."

"Not now. It's personal."

"Uh-oh," Aidan said from where he stood at the water cooler, filling the coffee carafe with water.

"Don't you weigh in," Shane told Aidan. "This has nothing to do with you."

"What does it have to do with?" Finn asked.

Shane threw up his free hand. "You keep saying that I need to talk to someone about my emotional health. Now that I want to talk, I get nothing but questions."

"Oh." Finn's eyebrows rose as he regarded Shane. "In that case, meet me out front at noon."

"I'M REALLY glad you decided to talk," Finn said as they got into his car and headed toward Main Street. "It's about time. Although, it's probably better if I refer you to someone. As your brother, I can't be your therapist, so—"

"I don't really want to talk about my emotional health," Shane broke in. "Or, I do, but not in the way I led you to believe. I just said that because I needed to speak to you alone."

"Oh. Is this something I need to pull the car over for?"

"Maybe."

Finn turned left onto Main Street, found a parking space in front of an antique store, and turned off the car. "Okay. I'm listening."

Shane took a deep breath and prepared himself to get yelled at, thrown out of the car, or worse.

"It's about Lily."

"What about her? Are you consulting with me in a professional capacity, or …"

"Not professional. This is personal."

"I see."

What Shane was about to say could hardly be a surprise to Finn after what he'd seen that day at Lily's house. And yet it was hard for Shane to come out with it.

"Well?" Finn prompted him.

"Look," Shane said, diving into it. "I'm seeing Lily. Socially. We're … It's a thing. It's getting to be a thing. And I know that makes you uncomfortable, and that's never been my intention. I didn't intend this. But she … I feel … Finn, I've got to tell you, the time I spend with her is the only time I don't feel like a steaming pile of shit. And I need that. I need to not feel that way. So I'm going to keep seeing her, and I hope that won't be a problem for you. I don't think you and she were right as a couple to begin with, so."

Finn looked at Shane silently, a muscle working in his jaw.

"Finn?"

"Get out of my car," Finn said.

"Wait. That's—"

"Get. Out. Of my. Car."

"Finn—"

"If you don't get out of my car, I'm going to throw you out of it. While it's in motion."

Shane got out of the car and stood on the curb with the passenger door open, leaning in to reason with his brother. "Can't we just talk about this? You like to talk about issues. It's what you do."

"Close the door."

"You're being an ass. You're not—"

"I said close the door, Shane."

So he did. Finn drove off the moment the door clicked shut.

Well, hell. That hadn't gone the way Shane had hoped. Not at all.

———

IN THE WAKE of his talk with Finn, Shane felt crappy but somehow lighter at the same time. He'd hurt and betrayed his brother, and that felt … well, it felt like he'd broken some key commandment, some essential tenet that cast into question his worth as a human being. But having things out in the open? That felt better. Like a weight had been lifted from him.

That was before everyone else in the family started weighing in.

Rowan heard by mid-afternoon. He poked his head into Shane's office and peered at him from the doorway.

"Something on your mind?" Shane asked.

Rowan came into the office and closed the door. "You really screwed the pooch this time. Or, actually, that's not who you screwed."

Shane glared at Rowan, his eyes narrowed, his jaw set. "Watch how you talk about Lily. I mean it."

"I wasn't talking about her—I was talking about you. But it's interesting how you're defending her honor."

"Rowan, you asshole, you're the one who encouraged me to see her. You're the one who—"

"Look, I'm not judging." Rowan perched his butt on the edge of

Shane's desk. "I'm all for it. It's just interesting to see someone other than me pissing everyone off for a change."

"This thing with Lily … it's real. It's worth the trouble."

But a voice in Shane's head taunted him. *You're setting her up for pain. For your pain. And you know it.*

"Time will tell, I guess," Rowan said.

Over the next twenty-four hours, he heard from everyone: Aidan thought he should have waited longer before moving in on Lily; Nolan made a declaration of neutrality, saying he didn't care who dated whom; his father cited some metaphor about trees and sunlight that was supposed to offer wisdom about his situation but didn't; and his mother claimed to be sympathetic to both sides.

By the end of that period, Finn still wasn't speaking to him, which Shane found ironic. Finn usually wanted to talk about every emotion-related situation until the parties involved were ready to throw themselves out a window.

"I'm not sure what to do about Finn," Shane told Rowan when they were both at Shane's house, sitting in front of the TV with beers in their hands.

"What's to do about him? He'll get over it."

"Are you sure?"

"Yes. He's Finn. He doesn't believe in grudges. It's part of his ethos."

The fact that Finn even had an explicitly stated ethos made him the frequent object of ridicule by his brothers.

"Well, he might not believe in grudges, but that doesn't mean he isn't holding one."

"He is now. But he'll let it go as soon as his manly ego has time to heal." Rowan took a drink from his beer bottle. "It isn't as though he loved her. He wasn't going to marry her."

But I might.

The thought popped into Shane's head before he knew he was thinking it. The thought sat there in his brain, alarming and dismaying him. Where had it even come from? How had it gotten into his mind?

Now that it was there, Shane didn't feel the elation one might when one's future has been decided in a favorable way. Instead, he felt as though a train, or maybe a very large truck, was bearing down on him. Did he want to get out of the way, or did he want to just stand there and let it hit him?

He struggled for a way to express all of this to Rowan without sounding like a dick.

"This thing with Lily. I feel like I should put a stop to it," he began. "Not just because of Finn. It might be a disaster waiting to happen. For her. Because of me and my … you know. The Molly thing. But I don't think I can. Put a stop to it, that is. I don't think I want to."

Rowan shrugged. "If your Lily thing and your Molly thing are incompatible, it seems like you've got to let go of one of them. Since only one of those things makes you so depressed you can't get out of bed, I know which one I'd choose." He took a swig of beer. "Food for thought."

Chapter Twenty-Four

Over the next week or so, Shane and Lily saw a lot of each other. Sometimes, Shane just popped by her house to help her with a chore she couldn't do with one arm, and sometimes he came over so they could immerse themselves in carnal bliss.

He took her out to dinner at Robin's one night, and on another, they went to a movie in San Luis Obispo. Afterward, they made love in Lily's bed—never in Shane's. Lily didn't want to sleep with him in the same place where he'd been with Brittany.

At first, Lily tried not to talk about Brittany or think about her when she was with Shane. But that wasn't going well, so she decided to confront Shane's relationship with her sister head-on.

"What happened between you and Brittany?" Lily asked late one night when the two of them were in bed, a sheen of sweat still on their bodies along with the languor of recent sex.

"She didn't tell you?" Shane was lying on his side facing Lily. He reached out to move a lock of hair off of her face with his fingers. "I figured you two talked about me."

"We did. And she told me her part of it—that you were angry

and sad and wouldn't tell her why. I just thought I'd like to hear your side."

"Does it matter now?"

"I think so. If we don't know what went wrong with her, how can we prevent it from happening with me?"

"You're a different person," he pointed out.

"Yes, but you're not."

"No. But I feel different. With you. I feel like a different person."

"Do you?"

"I really do."

The admission made Lily feel warm all over. She snuggled closer to him, her good arm around him.

"Still," she said, "I think it would be good to talk about it. I know it had something to do with your sister, but …"

Shane went still, and his expression hardened. Lily worried that she'd made a mistake by bringing up his sister, but she had to. If not now, then eventually.

"How much do you know about my sister?"

Lily could hear that he was trying to keep his tone neutral, trying to keep the defensiveness out of it. But he wasn't exactly succeeding. Now was not the time to come clean about her investigative efforts, so she said only what she needed to.

"Just that she died. And you and Brittany broke up right around the time of that anniversary."

She didn't tell him what else she knew—that Shane had been driving the car when the accident happened. That whatever had caused the crash, Shane must have thought it was his fault. They would need to talk about all of those things eventually, but for now, she thought it was best to introduce the subject a little at a time, gently, so he wouldn't pull away.

But she hadn't done it gently enough, apparently, because now he was getting up and pulling on the pants he'd discarded on the floor.

"Shane, I didn't mean to—"

"No. You didn't. It's fine. I'm fine."

"Then why are you all the way over there?"

"I just … I need a minute." He went into the bathroom and closed the door.

———

IN THE BATHROOM, Shane splashed cold water on his face, then dried it with a towel. He stared at himself in the mirror and raked his hands through his hair.

He couldn't react like this. Reacting like this was what had pushed Brittany away. Ending things with Brittany had seemed inevitable. But with Lily, he wanted to do things differently.

Yet here he was, pulling away from her, the same as he did with any woman who got close to the Molly situation.

Why wasn't he more prepared for this? Of course she was going to ask eventually. The fact of his sister's death was not a secret. Neither was the fact that he became insufferable on key dates related to it. (Not just the anniversary of her death, but on the birthday he and Molly shared, too—Brittany and he hadn't been together long enough to encounter that one.)

Of course he was going to have to talk about all of it with Lily. And yet, when she'd mentioned Molly, everything in him had said *fight or flight.* Since fighting wasn't an option, here he was, hiding out in the bathroom.

"Shane?" Lily knocked gently on the door. "Are you okay?"

He rubbed his eyes with his fingertips. "Yeah. Fine. I'll be out in a minute, okay?" He struggled to keep his voice from shaking.

Damn it, maybe Finn was right. Maybe he did need to sort out his feelings if he was ever going to be happy with a woman. The thing was, the very idea of him being happy was problematic. He didn't deserve happiness. He hadn't yet suffered enough to atone for what he'd done.

And yet, if he kept hurting the people in his life—kept pushing them away—then he would have even more to atone for.

When he was ready, when his heart rate slowed and he thought he might be able to act rationally in front of Lily, he went back into the bedroom and sat on the edge of the mattress across from where she sat. She was wrapped in a bathrobe now, and he mourned the loss of her nudity.

"I shouldn't have said what I did," she said. "I'm sorry."

"You don't have anything to be sorry for."

"But—"

"I have a hard time talking about her. What happened. All of it. I will eventually, but I'm not there yet."

"Okay."

"Is it really? Okay, I mean?"

"Yes. It is. But there's one thing that's not okay with me at all."

He tensed. "What's that?"

"That you're all the way over there, and I'm over here. And we're both so covered up."

He grinned. "I can fix that."

———

SHANE SLEPT OVER THAT NIGHT—THE first time the two of them had spent the entire night together. It wasn't likely to happen again for some time, Lily thought. Brittany was coming home in a few days, which meant she and Shane would have to go somewhere else. She'd have to get over her issue with sleeping—and doing other things—in Shane's bed if they were to have any hope of spending enjoyable time together.

Lily woke up before he did. She lay in the dim light of early morning thinking about the night before. She'd defused a tense situation with levity and the promise of sex, but eventually, they'd have to confront the issue.

Otherwise, Molly would be like a landmine waiting for one of them to take a wrong step.

At least they'd made a start. She'd brought up Molly, and he'd promised to talk about her eventually. That was something. Lily didn't think Brittany had ever gotten that far with him.

She lay there and watched him sleep for a while. He looked so peaceful, so serene. Only now, seeing him like this, did she realize how tense he looked the rest of the time.

God, he was carrying a heavy weight. She hoped that one day she might help him to finally set it down.

Chapter Twenty-Five

B rittany came home on a Tuesday afternoon, and Lily picked her up at the airport in San Luis Obispo.

Whatever was wrong between them, the two of them were still functional enough that Lily could perform this simple favor for her sister, and Brittany could still accept.

They met at baggage claim, and Lily used her good arm to help Brittany with her luggage. They wheeled her suitcases out to the parking lot and got them loaded into the trunk before either one of them said anything other than the usual polite greetings.

When one of them finally broached the subject of Shane, it was Brittany who did it. She faced forward behind the driver's seat, looking out the windshield, the car still silent and idle.

"So, I guess you spent time with Shane while I was gone."

"Well … yes. I did."

"He probably slept over."

"Brittany …"

Brittany turned in her seat to face Lily. "Look, it's not that I still want Shane. I don't. Breaking up with him was the right decision, and I don't regret it. It's the lack of loyalty, Lily. When I broke up with him, we both should have been done with him. That's the way sisterhood works."

"I know."

"For you to get involved with him? Which means you'll be bringing him around, where I have to see him?" Brittany shook her head. "It's not how it's done, Lily. That's not how a good sister acts."

"I know," Lily said.

"Well, if you know, then why did you do it?"

"Because … because I love him."

Lily hadn't expected to say it, hadn't even realized she felt it. Not definitively. But now that it was out, she knew the truth of it. The whole thing was simple, really. She was in love, and she was helpless against it.

Brittany stared at her in the wake of the admission. "You're joking."

"No. It would be easier if I were."

"Well, God."

They sat in silence for a moment while both of them thought about what Lily had said.

"He's going to hurt you," Brittany said at last. "He's going to go all dark and silent, and he's going to shut you out, and it'll hurt you. Just like it hurt me."

"Maybe." Privately, Lily hoped her sister was wrong, that Lily was different. That she and Shane had enough of a connection that he would change for her, open up to her.

She knew how stupid that was even as she thought it. Rule one of dating was never to assume you could change a man. Lily knew that. And yet here she was, thinking she could change him. That she could heal him.

As though her love was somehow superior to Brittany's. To the love of every woman who had come before her.

"No, not maybe," Brittany said. "He will. And then who's going to put you back together when he breaks you?"

Lily felt tears fill her eyes. "I know you won't be there for me when that happens. I get that, Brittany. I—"

"You idiot. Of course I'll be there. I'm your sister."

Lily blinked, and two fat tears fell. "You will?"

"Yes, you jerk. I love you."

"Oh, Brittany." Lily leaned over and threw her arms around Brittany—even the one in the cast, which made the hug awkward but no less satisfying.

They both cried, and they both wiped their eyes and blew their noses with napkins from the car's console, tidying up in the wake of their shared emotion.

"You're the best," Lily told her sister.

"Yeah, well, I'm still mad at you. And I still think you're making a mistake."

"I might be," Lily admitted. "But I can't seem to help it. He's just ... He's so ..."

"I know," Brittany said. "Let's see if you still feel that way a year from now."

The idea that they would still be together a year from now made Lily glow inside. It didn't feel like the warning Brittany probably intended it to be. It felt like a promise.

————

THEY SPENT the rest of the drive talking about everything but Shane. They talked about Brittany's stay in Ohio, her flight, and Lily's arm and how she was managing.

But mostly, they talked about their mother's plans to come to the Central Coast now that her house was empty and going through escrow.

Janice had to get her car to the Central Coast, so she was driving from Ohio. Brittany had offered to go with her for safety and to share the driving, but Janice wanted to visit a roster of friends and relatives on the way, a prospect that filled Brittany with dread.

Besides, Brittany had to get back to her job, so they'd decided to come west separately.

"I swear, she's stubborn. I even offered to help her sell her car so she could fly out here and then buy a new one. She needs a new car anyway. The one she's got has more than a hundred thousand miles on it. And here she is driving it across the country. She's going to have money from the sale of her house. A lot of it." Brittany shook her head. "But she wouldn't listen."

"With the cost of living on the Central Coast, she's going to need all of the proceeds from the sale," Lily pointed out.

"I guess."

They talked about the logistics of it—where Janice would stay as she looked for a house, what neighborhoods might work best for her, what she would likely love and hate about Cambria.

They each did the other the favor of not bringing up Shane again.

———

WHEN THEY GOT HOME, they brought Brittany's bags into the house, plunked them down on the floor just inside the door, and stood there awkwardly, as though neither of them knew how to proceed with this new relationship in which they had a man in common.

"I wasn't sure you would even let me keep living here," Lily said. "After everything."

"How petty do you think I am?" Brittany jammed her fists onto her hips, scowling at her sister. "Do you really think I'd kick you out onto the street over a guy I'm not even with anymore?"

"But you were so mad."

"Yes, I was mad. Of course I was. I still am. But that doesn't mean we're not sisters anymore, Lily. For God's sake."

And with that, Brittany turned her attention to other things, like unpacking and planning what to have for dinner.

Relationships could be fragile, Lily thought. But maybe not quite as fragile as she'd believed.

———

SHANE STILL HADN'T TALKED to Finn since he'd been kicked out of Finn's car on Main Street.

He wasn't sure he wanted to.

"Tell Shane that Mrs. Bartholomew agreed to come to therapy," Finn told Nolan in the break room, when Shane was standing right there. Mrs. Bartholomew was a patient Shane had who'd answered the standard question, "Is anyone hurting you at home?" in the affirmative. Shane had offered support in a number of ways, within the bounds of his patient's right to privacy, and one of those ways was referring her to Finn.

"Tell Finn I'm glad to hear that," Shane told Nolan.

"Idiots. You're both idiots," Nolan said before taking his coffee and his muffin and storming out of the room.

When he was gone, Finn didn't speak to Shane or look at him, but he made much more noise than necessary in making his coffee and banging around in the refrigerator looking for some unnamed snack.

Shane felt it was his responsibility to try to make things right, so he was the first one to speak.

"I really am glad about Mrs. Bartholomew," he said.

Finn grunted.

"She didn't want to report the abuse to the police, and I can't make her. But I hope she'll come around to that with your help."

"Really? You don't say?" Finn slammed the refrigerator door shut and spun to glare at Shane. "And here I didn't realize my goal was to actually help her."

"Don't be a dick," Shane said, but there was no heat in it. He figured Finn had the right to be a dick if he wanted to.

"You know, not for nothing, it's supposed to be bros before—"

"You'd better not say what I think you're going to say if you're talking about Lily."

"Fine. Bros before romantic relationships. Bros before … anyone who's not bros. And you broke that pact, Shane. You just fucking broke it."

"I know I did."

"And for what? So you can blow the whole thing to shit in a few months like you always do?"

"Maybe not," Shane said.

"What's that supposed to mean?"

"It means maybe this time is different."

"Really."

"I think maybe. Really."

Finn gave Shane the same look he gave anyone when he was trying to figure out whether they were full of shit.

Finally, he said, "I'm not just mad about this because of my male ego."

"You're not?"

"No. I'm also mad about it because I care about her. About Lily. I'm not in love with her, but I also don't want to see you stomp on her feelings as soon as she gets too close to your issues. She's a good person, and she doesn't deserve that."

"I have no intention of stomping on anyone's feelings."

"Okay, sure. I believe that. But do you ever intend it?"

Finn walked out before Shane could answer.

Chapter Twenty-Six

____

Considering that Lily didn't want to use Shane's bed, and also considering how awkward it would be to go to Lily's place now that Brittany was home, Shane did the only reasonable thing a man could do.

He bought a new bed.

He'd considered just replacing the mattress, but what if Lily objected to the overall bed itself? He didn't want to take any chances, so he took Nolan with him to a furniture store in San Luis Obispo on Saturday morning, hoping the way would be cleared for himself and Lily by that night.

"I can't believe you're making me spend my Saturday this way," Nolan said, adjusting his glasses as they walked among the rows of beds frames in all styles: sleigh, platform, four poster, some with storage underneath, some without.

"What else do you have to do?"

"I have things," Nolan said vaguely.

"I asked Aidan," Shane said, "but he's at a cardiology conference this weekend. Finn's obviously out of the question. And Rowan—"

"Rowan would make disgusting comments about headboards and people's heads banging into them," Nolan finished for him.

"Exactly. So you're it."

Nolan fidgeted, his hands in his jeans pockets. "Fine. But you're buying lunch."

"Done. What do you think of this one?" He pointed to a king-sized bed frame in dark oak with a heavy, Mission-style headboard and footboard.

"It's nice, but it's too manly."

"I'm a man."

"Obviously. But Lily isn't, and you're buying this mostly to appeal to her."

Shane considered that and had to concede that his brother had a point. "Huh. Okay, then what would Lily like?"

"Maybe this one." Nolan pointed to a bed with a tufted upholstered headboard in beige linen. "It looks nice, and it's practical because you've got the padding on the headboard in case you want to sit up in bed."

Shane grimaced. "Too girly. I mean, I get that I don't want to go overboard on the masculinity, but this goes too far the other way."

"Something in between, then."

They continued to walk up and down the aisles, browsing. A sales guy offered his help and was shooed away.

"The thing is," Shane said as he inspected the price tag on a maple sleigh bed, "I think I might love her."

"Really?" Nolan's eyebrows rose behind his thick glasses. "But you thought you might love Brittany, too."

"I thought I might eventually love Brittany under the right circumstances. This is different. I think I might love Lily right now, under exactly the wrong circumstances."

"That is different," Nolan agreed.

"But there's Finn," Shane said.

"There is. But he'll get over it. He's already starting to."

"Why?" Shane looked up from the price tag. "Did he say something to you?"

"Not directly."

"What does that mean?"

"It means, he mentioned your name without throwing something or using obscenities, and that's a step forward."

"I guess it is."

Shane came to a stop in front of a bed that was similar to the Mission-style one he'd liked earlier, but with a lighter color of wood and a more delicate frame. "What about this one?"

"Hmm." Nolan inspected it, his hands linked together behind his back. "I like it. It's got the style you like without being too much of a guy bed."

"Exactly."

"It's a combination of masculine and feminine, heavy and light, classic and modern."

"Now you're just making shit up." Shane smacked Nolan on the back companionably. "Come on, let's get that sales guy over here."

———

THE SALES GUY had offered the option of delivery, but Shane was hoping to lure Lily into his new bed that very night, so they decided to load the bed into Nolan's truck and haul and assemble it themselves. It was now tied into the truck bed along with a new mattress and box spring. Shane had already bought new sheets, pillows, and a comforter, so he figured he'd covered all of his bases.

Shane had promised Nolan lunch, so they stopped at Giuseppe's in San Luis Obispo on the way home.

Over plates of spaghetti pomodoro (Nolan) and tagliatelle Bolognese (Shane), they talked about the practice, a baby Nolan had delivered, their parents, and Rowan's latest girlfriend before Nolan brought up a heavier subject.

"Have you told her? About Molly?"

Shane poked at his food, having suddenly lost his appetite. "No, but she knows."

"Brittany told her? Or Finn?"

"Neither. She did some digging."

"Oh. Right. I forgot she's a reporter."

"She is. She brought it up the last time we were together, and it didn't go well."

"Meaning you shut down like the engine on an old Pinto."

"Something like that."

Nolan twirled pasta onto his fork. "Well, if you want this time to be different, that part is going to have to be different, too."

"I know."

"I mean it, Shane."

"I know. I do. I just don't know how to be different."

Nolan nodded. "Then you'd better start learning."

———

THAT NIGHT, Lily got dressed up for her date with Shane. At least, as much as one could get dressed up with a hunk of plaster covering one arm.

She'd considered wearing something that would cover the cast—something with long, loose sleeves—but rejected that idea because the only dress she had that matched that description looked frumpy on her. And frumpy was not the look she was going for.

She opted instead for a sleeveless little black dress, since she wasn't going to be fooling anyone anyway.

It was hard to do her hair with her non-dominant arm, and it was even harder doing her makeup. She cursed to herself as she stood in front of the bathroom mirror, redoing her eyeliner for the third time. At least she hadn't poked herself in the eye yet, which was still a distinct possibility.

She was just about to give up on eyeliner entirely when Brittany poked her head in the doorway.

"What are you grumbling about in here?"

When she saw what Lily was wearing, Brittany scowled. "You're seeing him tonight, aren't you?"

"I'm just going out, that's all." Lily hadn't expected that to be enough, and it wasn't.

"Yeah. Going out with *him*." Brittany crossed her arms over her chest, her eyebrows drawn together.

"Brittany, if this is going to be a big issue with us—"

"It's not. But that?" She pointed at the mess Lily had made with her eyeliner. "That is an issue. Give me that." She held out her hand for the eyeliner tube.

Brittany took a makeup removing wipe out of its container and worked to clean away what Lily had done. Then she repaired the foundation that had also been wiped away and went to work on Lily's eyes.

"Look up."

Lily did.

"This dress looks nice on you," Brittany said as she worked with the eyeliner. "Good call not trying to cover up the cast."

"That's what I thought."

"I mean, he put it on there, so it's not like he doesn't know about it."

"Just two more weeks," Lily said. "Then I get my arm back."

"That'll be handy. No more accidentally thumping Shane in the face during sex, am I right?"

They both endured a beat of awkward silence.

"I'm sorry." Brittany lowered her hands from Lily's face. "That was uncalled for."

"Yeah. It really was."

"I'm trying, but it's hard."

"I know," Lily said.

"It's not that I even miss him, specifically. I miss the possibility, you know? The hope that it might work out. I miss the thought of what the two of us might have been. But we weren't, so I don't even know what I'm sad about."

"You're sad because he hurt you, and I did, too. That's reasonable, Brittany. We deserve for you to be unhappy with us. I just want to know that you won't be unhappy forever."

"Maybe just until you fix me up with one of his brothers." Brittany grinned, and Lily felt the relief of it—the pure pleasure of seeing her sister smile at her again.

"That might not be out of the question," Lily said. "Just not Rowan."

"Oh, God. Rowan." Brittany rolled her eyes extravagantly in a gesture that either referred to his insane hotness or his ridiculous immaturity with women.

"Here," Brittany said. "Give me that mascara."

———

THEY'D PLANNED to meet at Neptune for dinner so Shane wouldn't have to pick Lily up at home, possibly upsetting Brittany. But when Brittany learned of that plan, she called it stupid, insisting it was dumb for Lily to do any more driving than absolutely necessary with just the one arm.

"Of course he can pick you up." Brittany stood in the living room across from Lily, her arms crossed over her chest. "I won't burst into flames. I'll just hide in my room like any rational person would do."

But she didn't hide in her room, and she did see Shane when he came for Lily.

When he got there, Brittany was sitting on the sofa watching TV in clear view of the front door. He didn't come in when Lily opened the door for him, but he did wave tentatively from the doorway.

"Hi, Brittany. How are you?" he asked as Lily gathered her coat and purse from the coatrack near the door.

"I'm swell." Brittany waved to him, then let her hand linger in the air, middle finger extended, before lowering it.

"Nice." Lily glowered at her sister.

"Oh, shit. I'm sorry. I meant to be gracious, but my finger didn't get the memo."

"No, I'm the one who's sorry," Shane started. "Brittany, I never meant—"

"Oh, no. We're not doing that again," Brittany said. "If either one of you apologizes to me one more time, I'm going to puke on your shoes. Seriously."

Brittany turned off the TV and went to the doorway to face Shane. "If you want to make it up to me? Don't hurt my sister." She jabbed one finger into his chest four times to emphasize those last four words.

"I won't," Shane said.

"He won't," Lily echoed. Coat on and purse slung over her shoulder, she ushered Shane out the door and down the front walk, sincerely hoping they both were right.

Chapter Twenty-Seven

Shane had been skeptical about going to Lily's house to pick her up. He'd wanted to—he didn't think it was right to make an injured woman drive any more than she had to—but he also didn't want to start the evening with an ugly scene.

He was relieved that he'd gotten off with the comparatively light consequence of having been flipped the bird.

"Brittany seems okay," he offered as they drove to Neptune, a seafood restaurant on Main Street that was generally regarded to be the most swanky place in town.

"She is. I think." Lily told him about the talk she and Brittany had that evening and about the help she'd given Lily. Then she told him what Brittany had said about fixing her up with one of the Brody brothers.

Shane shot her a look from the driver's seat. "Do we really think that's wise? Between you and me and Finn and Brittany, this thing is already pretty complicated, family-wise."

"It really is. Maybe someone else? Someone you're not related to?"

"I'll think about that." Shane gave her a half smile that made her insides melt. "I didn't get a chance to say it before, but you look amazing."

"Even with the cast?"

"Even if you were encased in concrete from the neck down. Though, now that I think about it, I'm glad that's not the case."

"For obvious reasons," Lily added.

"Speaking of which …"

Lily waited, eyebrows raised.

"I bought a new bed," he said.

She blinked at him. "You did?"

"Yeah." He shrugged. "I thought, if you feel so moved to come to my place sometime, you might like it if there was a clean slate, so to speak. A blank page."

"A fresh start," she added.

"Exactly. Not that I'm assuming anything. It's just, if you feel like it's right …"

The smile she gave him in return was very encouraging.

———

THEY ATE oysters and seafood linguine, drank wine, and talked at a table lit by candlelight. They chatted about his family, the practice, her mother's impending move to the Central Coast, Lily's work. She told him about the novel she was writing and about how it had felt to be laid off from her job. She told him about coming to Cambria, and how she'd initially planned to get her own place, but how that had been put on hold once she and Brittany had fallen into a companionable rhythm as roommates.

"Until I almost ruined that," he said.

"You didn't."

When he held her hand atop the table as they were waiting for the check, she thought the evening had been nearly perfect.

And it wasn't over yet.

"So, where to? Do you want me to take you home, or …" he asked as they sat in his car after dinner.

She leaned over and kissed him slowly, languorously, and with relish. "I think I'll take *or.*"

———

SHANE LIVED in a renovated log cabin on Happy Hill, a neighborhood across the highway from Moonstone Beach that had, in the town's mining days, been a hub of prostitution. Now, it was a charming, tree-lined area full of an eclectic combination of houses ranging from modern to historic.

Shane's place was small and cozy with a stone fireplace in the living room, a galley kitchen with open shelving, oak floors, and furniture that looked like it had been purchased secondhand by someone with a discerning eye for quality.

"Did you do this?" Lily walked around the room, running her hand over the backs of chairs, the surfaces of tables. "It's perfect."

"Not me. My mother. If it were up to me, I'd have gone to the nearest furniture superstore and taken the first matched living room set I saw. This is better."

"She's got great taste. Did you take her with you when you picked out the new bed?"

"No."

Lily gave him a wry grin. "So, can I expect the first matched bedroom set you saw?"

Shane came to her and smoothed her hair with his hand. "Come and look."

The way he said it, his voice a low purr, she was certain they would be doing more than assessing his taste in beds. Which was just fine with her.

———

SHANE TOOK Lily's hand and led her into the bedroom. He pointed out each feature of the new bed as though he were a furniture salesman.

"As you can see, the maple frame is sturdy and will hold up

under even the most vigorous activity." He sat his butt on the edge of the mattress and bounced. Then he swept a hand toward the headboard. "The design incorporates Mission style while hinting at a more modern and graceful aesthetic." He stood and pulled back the comforter and top sheet, swiping a hand over the fabric of the bottom sheet. "The high thread count of the sheets ensures maximum comfort and long-term durability." He lay down on his back. "And the mattress? State of the art. Support and softness. The perfect blend of luxury and practicality."

"Wow. And here I thought you were just going to say, 'Look, comfy.'" She grinned at him, her body already anticipating the feel of his hands on her.

"You want to try?" He patted the spot beside him on the bed.

She slowly walked over to what was, apparently, her side of the bed, kicked off her shoes, and lay on the mattress next to him.

"*Mmm*. I can feel that luxury and practicality you mentioned," she murmured.

He turned onto his side to face her. "And the way it stands up to vigorous activity? I haven't tested that yet." His voice was low and a little rough.

"Maybe I can help you with that."

"You think?"

She shrugged. "We could give it a try."

He slid one hand under her skirt and ran it up her leg. And their light banter ended as he got up onto his knees, slid her panties down her thighs and off of her, and glided his talented fingers into her wetness.

"Oh, God ..." Lily closed her eyes and arched her back, wanting more, wanting it now. But Shane took his time, touching her, teasing her, then lowering himself to press his lips to her inner thigh. With her skirt up over her hips, he kissed and licked higher, higher, until finally his tongue pressed its wet heat to her core, his fingers still moving inside her.

She came so hard her body jolted with the force of it.

Shane murmured, "*Hmm*. First part of the test is a success."

"And the second part?" Lily gasped out.

"I can't wait to find out."

———

IN THE WAKE of their lovemaking, when they were both sated and nude and covered in a light sheen of perspiration, Shane reflected that the bed had held up just as promised.

He also thought this thing with Lily had entered a new phase, one that was more serious. More rewarding. And also more fraught with peril.

If he fucked this up, he was going to do some real damage—both to Lily and to himself. He didn't want to fuck it up, but he didn't know how not to. Fucking up relationships was his default mode.

Lying here with Lily in his arms, he was happier than he'd ever been—but at the same time, that happiness was mixed up with a heaping load of guilt and fear. Guilt, because he didn't deserve happiness if Molly couldn't have it. And fear, because he wanted the happiness even if he didn't deserve it, and he didn't want to lose it.

"Lily?" Shane spoke softly, his lips brushing her forehead.

"*Mmm?*"

"I have … things. That I don't know how to talk about. And those things tend to wreck everything whenever I'm with someone."

She snuggled closer, running a hand over his skin, and didn't look at him. "That's what happened with Brittany."

"Yes. And with other women before her."

"Are you warning me?"

"I'm telling you that I want this time to be different."

She was quiet for a while, and he worried about what she was thinking.

"I have things, too," she said at last.

"Okay."

He didn't ask, and she didn't tell him. Not yet. But there would be time for that. He hoped they would have plenty of time.

Chapter Twenty-Eight

When Lily and Brittany's mother arrived on the Central Coast, she moved into a furnished month-to-month rental house in Morro Bay until she could find a permanent place to live.

Brittany and Lily had both been worried that she would want to move in with them—they loved their mother, but they loved her better at a distance—so they were both pleasantly surprised with the arrangements Janice had made.

"I don't want to cramp your style, girls," she'd said when they asked her if she would need to stay with them temporarily. "And besides, I'm used to living on my own by now. And I like Morro Bay. There's more going on there than in Cambria."

Janice and George Hart had raised their girls in Cambria, so Janice knew the town well. When they'd moved to Ohio for Edward's work, she'd missed the Central Coast, but she didn't miss the sleepy nature of Cambria—its lack of nightlife, not to mention its lack of a Costco. Morro Bay would put her halfway between her daughters to the north and a host of conveniences in San Luis Obispo to the south.

A sweet spot, both personally and practically.

Lily still hadn't gotten her cast off, so she wasn't much help carrying in the bags and boxes crammed into the back of her mother's car. So she stood by on the front walk of the Morro Bay house and watched as Janice and Brittany lugged everything into the house. Once her mother's things were inside, Lily made herself useful by opening boxes and beginning to unpack.

"I wish I could have bought a place before coming out here," Janice said. "It would have been so much easier if I didn't have to have an interim rental. But there aren't many houses on the market right now, and the ones that are …" She shrugged to indicate the expense of the real estate market on the coast. "My budget is good, but it's apparently not good enough."

"You'll find something," Brittany reassured her. "We'll help. I've been looking on all of the real estate sites for something that'll work for you."

"And I've been asking around," Lily added. Janice had said she would be open to a long-term rental, so Lily had been making inquiries, so far to no avail.

"For now, this place is really cute." Lily looked around at the two-bedroom cottage across the highway and back several blocks from the ocean. There wasn't much of a view—a view would have cost another thousand a month—but you could see a hint of water and a sliver of Morro Rock if you positioned yourself at the front window just right.

"Give me your grocery list," Brittany told her mother. "I'll go to the market and pick some things up for you while you and Lily unpack."

"Oh, thank you, sweetheart." Janice wrote up a quick list and handed it to Brittany. "Just a few things to get me settled. Coffee, bread, eggs. That kind of thing." Brittany scanned the list, then promised to be back in twenty minutes.

When she was gone, Janice put her arm around Lily and gave her a squeeze. "It seems like you two are getting along okay despite what's going on between you and Shane."

"We are. Mostly."

"So, what exactly *is* going on between you and Shane?" Janice raised her eyebrows and looked at Lily with expectation.

Lily sat down on the sofa, and Janice sat beside her.

"Actually," Lily began, "I'm not sure. But it's great. It's really great." She was smiling like an idiot, like some kind of lovesick fool.

"Oh, honey. That's wonderful. So you think it might go somewhere?"

"I hope so. I really hope so."

The question of where things might be going was plaguing Lily even as she tried not to let it. Shane had a track record of pushing women away, and Lily's own history was full of relationships carefully chosen to put her at minimal emotional risk. Now, she had let her heart be vulnerable to a man who, by his own admission, had difficulty not shutting out the women in his life.

It wasn't exactly cause for optimism.

Janice must have read the look on Lily's face, because she took her daughter's hand and said, "It's always scary, honey. Love. It's always a huge risk. But it's worth it."

"Were you scared when you met Dad?"

"Oh, my, yes. I broke up with him three times."

Lily stared at her mother. "You did not."

"I most certainly did. He was so handsome, and he made me feel so many things that I just … Well, I was terrified. But he was persistent. Said if I wasn't ready for a relationship, we would just be very good friends—friends who spent a lot of time together and were always there for each other. But, Lily, I didn't want to be just his friend. When I was finally ready to jump, he was there to catch me. And when he died … He was too young. I told him over and over to quit smoking. But still, we never thought …" Janice didn't finish her sentence. She just shook her head, her eyes wet with tears.

"Oh, Mom." Lily hugged her mother the best she could with one arm.

When Brittany came back, the two of them were still sitting there, hugging and crying, and also laughing.

"What's going on in here?" Brittany demanded. "You two aren't supposed to have emotional mother-daughter talks without me."

"We were talking about Dad," Lily said.

"Dad would want you to date," Brittany told her mother without hesitation.

"Date?"

"Yes. You know—see a man socially. Maybe more than one, if it strikes your fancy."

"Honey, my fancy hasn't been struck in quite some time."

"Then it's time to change that, isn't it?" Brittany said. "Let me tell you how dating apps work."

———

FOR ONCE, Shane was beginning to think that both his personal and professional lives were coming together nicely.

He and Lily were seeing a lot of each other, and Finn seemed to have come to terms with that. His mixed feelings about the relationship were bothering him, but maybe a little less than usual. He was doing good work at the practice, and he felt like he was helping people.

One of the people he'd helped was Caitlin Jacobs, his patient who looked so much like Molly. Her ANA test had come back positive, which had led to more testing, which had led to a diagnosis of lupus.

That wasn't good news—lupus was a serious and incurable illness—but now that she knew what she was dealing with, she could get treatment that would allow her to avoid the worst consequences of the disease and give her a normal lifespan.

He'd referred her to a rheumatologist, and Iris was going to help her find low-cost health insurance to cover the care and treatment that fell outside of Bridge Street Wellness's areas of expertise.

Shane hadn't given her special treatment because she looked like Molly—he'd have done the same things for anyone in the same situation—but the resemblance to his sister made him want her to be okay, made him want to fix her the way he hadn't been able to fix his sister.

He'd checked in with her a few times since the diagnosis to make sure she was following up and getting the care she needed.

All in all, he felt like he was on top of things.

Finn noticed and mentioned it one Sunday when the Brodys were gathered for their family dinner.

"You're in a good mood," Finn remarked as the two of them happened to arrive at the Igloo cooler in the back yard at the same time, each of them seeking a cold beer.

"Am I?" Shane said.

Finn pulled two beers out of the cooler and handed one to Shane. "Seems like it. You seem perky."

"Puppies are perky," Shane said. "I am not perky."

"Well, you're something resembling perky. I even saw you smile earlier."

"Which you object to, given what a dick I've been."

"Not at all." Finn screwed the top off of his beer and took a long drink. "I'm a bigger person than that. I'm glad you're doing better. So, you and Lily," he went on. "It's going well, I assume."

Shane wondered if this was a trap—if admitting that things were, in fact, going well would set off Finn, causing a ruckus at his parents' barbecue.

"It's not a trick question," Finn said, as though he'd read his brother's mind. "I'm just asking."

Shane took a swig of beer and shot a look at Finn out of the corner of his eye. "Yeah. Yes, it's going well."

"Then why didn't you bring her?"

Shane's eyebrows shot upward. "What, here?"

"Yes, here. You two are in a relationship. It's standard practice to invite your significant other to family get-togethers. In case you weren't aware of the usual protocol."

Shane kept his voice neutral, casual. "And you'd be okay with that?"

"Hell, I'm the one who just suggested it, aren't I?"

"You're also the one who made me get out of your car and walk back to the office after I told you I was seeing her."

Finn made a scoffing noise. "You had to walk all of three blocks."

"Well, still."

"Look." Finn turned to face Shane, setting his beer down on a patio table. "Did I support this thing between the two of you? No. Was I happy about it? No. But it happened. It's a thing. And now that it is, the last thing I want is for you to be half-assed about it, which would mean you and Lily upset people and stirred up turmoil for no good reason. You're doing this thing? Do it right. Make it worth the trouble. That's all I'm saying."

Finn picked up his beer and walked away, leaving Shane to think about what he'd said.

———

SHANE MIGHT NOT HAVE BROUGHT a date to the family dinner, but Rowan did. He showed up a half hour late with a tall blonde on his arm. The problem was, the tall blonde wasn't the woman Rowan was currently seeing.

"Who's that?" Shane asked Aidan, who was manning the barbecue. He gestured with his beer bottle toward Rowan's date.

"Hell if I know." Aidan flipped a row of burger patties, their father's KISS THE COOK apron around his waist.

"Did he and Ashley break up, then?"

"Not to my knowledge."

Now that Shane thought of it, for Rowan and Ashley to have broken up, they'd have had to have been in a relationship to begin with. Rowan didn't have relationships. He had sex partners.

Which left Shane to wonder whether Rowan had switched one partner for another, or if he was currently juggling two women at once. Which would not have been unprecedented.

He and Aidan were still pondering the question when Nolan came over and joined them.

"That's not Ashley," he said.

"No," Shane agreed.

"Which is unfortunate, because I ran into Ashley today at the Cookie Crock and asked her if she was coming tonight."

Aidan was in the middle of taking a swallow of beer when Nolan said it, and now he nearly choked on it. "Oh, shit," he said when he'd recovered enough to talk. "What did she say?"

"Oh, she might have said that Rowan hadn't mentioned it, but that she'd stop by if she got a chance."

Aidan guffawed. "This should be good."

As for Shane, he was finding it to be a refreshing change that his own love life wasn't the center of the shit show for once.

"Should we warn him?" he asked his brothers.

"What, and ruin the entertainment?" Aidan asked. "Hell, no."

———

FOR A WHILE, they all thought Rowan might luck out and Ashley wouldn't come. But Rowan's luck with women was usually bad, and this time was no exception. Just around the time Aidan started taking burger patties off the grill, calling around to see who wanted what, Ashley poked her head over the back fence, calling out to the Brodys.

"Hey, everyone. Am I late?" She unlatched the gate and came into the back yard holding a plastic container of something that looked, from this distance, like potato salad.

Shane's gaze shot to Rowan, who did a double-take that would have been comic if actual people's feelings hadn't been at stake.

"I've got this." Aidan handed the barbecue tools to Shane and headed toward Ashley at a fast clip. When he got to her, he positioned himself in such a way that in order to face him, Ashley had to turn her back to where Rowan and the blonde were standing. He began talking to her animatedly, with hand gestures and feigned enthusiasm.

"That was smooth," Shane commented. "You'd think he did that kind of maneuver every day."

"We shouldn't enable Rowan," Finn grumbled, always the

psychiatrist. "Let him deal with his messes instead of sweeping them under the rug."

"Do you really want Mom and Dad to have to deal with the bloodshed and hair-pulling that would involve?" Nolan asked.

"Fair point," Finn admitted.

While Aidan kept Ashley busy, Rowan took the blonde by the arm, turned her to face away from Aidan and Ashley, said something into her ear, and then steered her toward the house. He didn't even look back.

Once he was inside, Aidan visibly relaxed, but he shot a meaningful look toward his brothers, either wondering what his next step should be or looking for backup.

At that moment, Shane's phone pinged with a text message. He took the phone out of his pocket and looked.

Rowan.

I've suddenly come down with food poisoning. Bad coleslaw. Please tell anyone who's looking for me that I'm going to have to skip the rest of the evening.

You ass, Shane replied.

He felt bad about lying to Ashley, but he felt even worse about the prospect of dealing with female emotions he hadn't even caused. So he told Ashley the coleslaw story when she came over to him looking for Rowan.

"Oh, no. He's sick?" Ashley's perfectly sculpted eyebrows drew toward one another in concern. "Where is he? Is there anything I can do to help?"

"I'm sure he went home," Shane said.

"I'll go there, then. I'm sure he needs someone to commiserate."

Finn fielded that one, despite his stand on enabling bad behavior. "I wouldn't," he said.

"Why not?"

"I'll tell you something, Ashley," Finn said, as though he were imparting valuable wisdom. "The last thing a man wants is for a beautiful woman to see him hurling into the toilet. Let Rowan keep his pride. Can I get you something to eat?"

"Well, I guess so," she said. "But I think I'll skip the coleslaw."

———

THE NEXT DAY, Shane and Lily met for lunch at Linn's Easy as Pie Cafe, and Shane told her about the farce that had resulted from Rowan trying to manage two women at the same time.

"My parents didn't miss a step," he said, laughing as he picked up his meatloaf sandwich. "They made small talk with Ashley like it was perfectly normal for the evening to begin with one of Rowan's girlfriends and end with another." He shook his head in wonder. "It's amazing nobody's gone after him with a pair of hedge clippers yet."

Lily laughed and expressed wonder and disbelief in all the right places. Then she picked at her salad with her fork and said, "I kind of wish I'd been there to see it."

The rebuke was gentle and subtle, but Shane didn't miss her point.

"I wanted to invite you." He wiped his mouth with his napkin, then folded it beside his plate. "I just wasn't sure, with Finn and everything."

"Right. I can understand that." She nodded. "But if we're in a relationship …"

After the word was out, she realized she didn't know whether that's what this was. Not for sure. Yes, they were seeing each other. Yes, they were sleeping together. And yes, it was good. But was it a relationship? Was she assuming too much?

Lily backtracked as quickly as she could. "Not that this is necessarily a relationship yet. I know that. I didn't mean—"

"It is," Shane said. "At least, I think it is. It feels like one."

"And you're okay with that?"

"I'm more than okay with that. And you won't find yourself being distracted by my brothers so I can hide my other girlfriend," he said.

"Is he always like that?" Lily wanted to know.

"Always. He's been mistreating women since puberty."

Lily stabbed some salad onto her fork. "Maybe Finn had a point. Maybe it's best not to enable him."

"Yeah." Shane nodded. "I can see that. But if we'd just let it happen, Ashley would have been hurt."

"And hurting people isn't what you're about," Lily said. "You like to heal them."

"When I can," he said.

Shane had hurt Brittany, and he might yet hurt Lily. She knew that. But if it happened, it wouldn't be out of carelessness or self-interest. It would be because he kept hurting himself, and that pain kept spilling over onto the people around him.

"I'll bet Rowan will take a certain amount of shit for this," she said, grinning.

"Oh, hell, yes. We've already started, and it won't end until he does something even worse. Which should be any minute now."

———

SHANE HAD BEEN TELLING himself that this thing with Lily wasn't a relationship. He'd purposely avoided using that word, even in his own head. But when she'd asked, the words had just popped out. He'd spoken his truth: Yes, this was a relationship. Yes, this was real.

Once they'd finished lunch and he'd said goodbye to Lily, he had to confront what he'd said and figure out what it all meant.

His thoughts were a mass of contradictions: He wanted to be with Lily. He might even want it long term. But he had proven himself incapable of maintaining things with a woman for more than a few months. His history always intervened. His guilt. His pain.

He had no idea how to change that, which meant things with Lily were ultimately doomed. He would hurt her and himself, and he'd prove to everyone he loved that he was still as irreparably screwed up as he'd always been.

Which was some form of justice, surely.

He wasn't built for happiness. He didn't deserve it. But what if he'd finally decided he wanted it?

He went back to work with a dizzying mix of dread, fear, and hope swimming around in his chest. The dread and fear were familiar, but the hope? That was new. He had Lily to thank for it. He just prayed she wouldn't come to regret it.

————

LILY WENT HOME after lunch that day feeling a range of her own emotions.

She was still hurt that Shane hadn't invited her to the family dinner, but she was riding on a wave of bliss having heard Shane say this was a relationship. She'd known it was for some time, but she wasn't sure he did. Now, knowing they were on the same page, she couldn't help thinking about what their future together might be.

She wasn't naïve enough to start thinking about forever. Not yet. But this wasn't just attraction, wasn't just infatuation. It was love, capital L. The kind that made you do stupid things and give up whole parts of yourself for the other person.

Just as she'd done with Trevor.

That had ended in disaster, but this didn't have to. If she could hold on to the key elements that made her who she was, and if Shane could trust her enough to let her in, well … maybe this time would be different.

Maybe this time, they could both find the healing they needed.

Chapter Twenty-Nine

Lily finally got her cast removed in Shane's office. An X-ray showed the bone had healed properly, so Shane sawed off the plaster with an electric tool that Lily found alarming, considering how close the blade came to her skin.

Equally alarming was how white and vulnerable her arm looked once it was freed from its plaster prison.

"It doesn't even look like my arm," she said, holding it up to compare it to the one that had not been injured.

"It's going to feel a little weak for a while," Shane told her. "And you might have some trouble straightening it at first. Try not to favor it. The more you use it, the quicker it's going to get its strength back."

He offered to refer her for physical therapy, but she declined. She'd had enough of everything having to do with the injury. Surely she could regain full function of her arm on her own.

"That's fine," he told her when she turned down the offer. "Just reconsider if you have trouble getting back your full range of motion."

Lily knew that an examining room was not the place to express her feelings toward Shane—not when he was being completely professional. But she was so happy to have her arm back that she threw it, along with its partner, around him in a burst of happy impulsiveness.

"Oh, my God. I'll be able to take a shower without wrapping myself in plastic bags and duct tape. You never appreciate a thing like that until it's gone."

"I suppose you don't." Shane looked down at her with amusement in his eyes, and she went up on her toes and kissed him. Professional or not, he kissed her back with enthusiasm.

"This probably isn't the best place to be doing this," she said, her arms still around him, her forehead touching his.

"Probably not," he agreed.

"I'm just happy to be whole again."

"I'm glad I could help."

She left his office eager to do all of the things she hadn't been able to do over the last six weeks: take a full-immersion bath, type with both hands, put her hair in a ponytail without assistance, jog.

Although maybe not the jogging, she reconsidered, given the fact that jogging was what had gotten her injured in the first place.

———

"LOOK." Lily waved her arm around for Brittany at the salon as Brittany stood at the sink shampooing a customer's hair. "I'm free! I have two arms again!"

"Yay!" Brittany did a little happy dance, her hands covered in shampoo suds. "I'm so happy for you."

She was probably also happy for herself, given that Brittany had been helping Lily with everything from bagging her arm to doing her buttons and styling her hair. "Thank you so much for everything you did to help me through this," Lily said. "Especially since …" She didn't finish, but she didn't have to. Especially since Lily had stolen Brittany's ex. They both knew what Lily meant.

Brittany finished rinsing her client's hair, then wrapped it up in a towel. She came to Lily and gave her a swift hug. "You don't have to thank me. I'm your sister. What else was I going to do?"

"It feels weird." Lily flexed her arm a few times to demonstrate.

"It'll come back," Brittany said. "Our bodies have an amazing ability to heal."

Lily couldn't help thinking the same was true for relationships, if hers and Brittany's was any indicator.

———

SHANE'S INSTINCTS told him to pull back from Lily before his natural inclination to screw up relationships kicked in, doing untold damage to them both.

But his instincts tended not to serve him well when it came to women, so he ignored them and did the opposite.

For one thing, Lily was right when she'd gently rebuked him for failing to invite her to the Brody Sunday dinners. She wasn't just some woman he was sleeping with. He had feelings for her, and he hoped things between them would last. She deserved to be included in things that mattered to him.

So he began inviting her, and she showed up to eat barbecue, drink beer, and shoot the shit with the Brodys. It was awkward at first, especially with Finn, but by the third Sunday in a row that she came to dinner, things thawed considerably.

Shane kept his distance, keeping a watchful eye on things, as Finn approached Lily one Sunday and offered her a cold bottle of beer. Lily accepted, and Shane could see the evolution in their body language as they talked. First stiff and upright, each of them striving for courtesy, then a subtle relaxation in their shoulders, a certain easing of tension in their faces. Then Finn said something to Lily and she laughed, a hearty guffaw that lit up her face. Finn put a hand on her shoulder and squeezed.

Shane thought that under different circumstances, the exchange might have made him jealous. But instead, he felt relief. The storm had passed, not only with Finn but with Brittany. Shane had gone to Lily's house a few times over the past couple of weeks, and it had been okay. Not easy at first, but okay.

Now the only thing standing between Shane and Lily was Shane's issues.

He'd thought he was doing a good job of cramming the issues down into a little box inside himself that he would never open and never again examine. The folly of that became clear one night when Lily said she loved him.

They were at Shane's house, in bed, having just taken a shower together, their hair damp, both of them smelling of lavender soap and recent sexual bliss.

And then she'd said the words.

"I love you, you know." Just like that. As though it were a piece of information she thought he might like to have.

Of course he knew he was supposed to say it back. He wasn't an idiot. And he could have said it in complete honesty. Everything Lily was feeling for him, he felt, too.

And yet his mouth just didn't form the words.

In the wake of what she'd said, he said nothing. The hurt and embarrassment in her eyes made him feel like a complete dick.

Lily arranged her face in a smile that looked forced, then she got out of bed, her eyes wet with tears. She picked up Shane's robe from where it lay draped across the back of a chair and put it on.

"Lily," he said.

"I'm just going to …" She pointed toward the bathroom. "I'll be back." Then she left him lying there alone, feeling like he'd screwed everything up.

God, he was a fool. He loved her. He loved her so much it scared him. He loved her in the way you read about in sonnets and epic poems. He loved her deep in his soul the way he loved his own life, the way he loved joy itself.

And yet, he couldn't seem to say those words to her, even when not saying them hurt her.

He got up, went to the bathroom door, and knocked gently.

"Lily?"

Through the door, he heard running water and the clearing of her throat. "I'll be out in a minute."

Shane leaned his head on the door. "I didn't mean to hurt you. That thing you said? I do. I do, too."

She opened the door a crack and peered out at him. "You do?"

"I do."

But he still wasn't saying the words. Instead, he was alluding to them in a tangential way, as though he were sneaking up on a bear or maybe a venomous snake.

Which didn't escape her notice.

"You don't have to say that if you don't mean it, Shane. You don't have to say it because you think my feelings are hurt. They're not."

But they were—they both knew that. She went home that night instead of sleeping over.

———

WHEN LILY GOT HOME, she needed her sister. Brittany was the last person she should be going to with her Shane problems but the first person she wanted to talk to for comfort.

Lily hesitated at first, but Brittany drew her out.

"Okay, spill. What's wrong? What happened?" Brittany was sitting on the sofa watching a movie when Lily came in, and she reached for the remote and turned off the TV.

"Why do you think something's wrong?"

Brittany rolled her eyes. "Do you think we've just met? I know your facial expressions. Something happened. Now sit down and tell me."

Lily sank down onto the sofa and sighed. She didn't want to cry, but she felt the tears burning in her eyes anyway.

"I said it. I said the words."

"The words?" Brittany looked at her sister in confusion.

"You know, the words. The *three* words."

"Oh." Brittany gasped and clapped a hand over her mouth. "And what happened?"

"He didn't say them back."

"Oh, God."

The horror on Brittany's face told Lily that her sister understood exactly how mortifying this was, and that gave her some comfort.

"So, what did he say?" Brittany asked.

"Nothing at first."

"Nothing?"

"Nothing. He just laid there."

"Which means you said it in bed. Which is even worse."

"Exactly." Lily raked her hands through her hair. "Then I went into the bathroom and cried while trying to pretend I hadn't gone to the bathroom to cry." She shook her head. "It was horrifying."

"And he never said it back? At all?"

"Oh, he made a lame attempt. 'That thing you said—I do too.' Something like that. But by then—"

"It was too late," Brittany finished for her.

"It really was."

"And now you're here instead of there, where you'd be if he'd just said it back."

"Yes. And now, on top of the mortification, I'm feeling guilt for making you comfort me about this. You're the last person who should have to deal with my Shane issues."

"This is true," Brittany agreed.

"Oh, Brit. I'm sorry. I never should have—"

"Stop it. We've done enough of that already. The question is, do you think he feels it and couldn't say it, or that he doesn't feel it at all?"

Lily had been asking herself the same question, and she considered it carefully before answering. "Honestly? I think he feels it. I really do. You can tell when a guy's all in, as opposed to when he's faking it to get laid. You know? There's a difference."

"There really is." Brittany got up off the sofa, went into the kitchen, and retrieved a bottle of wine and two glasses, which she brought back into the living room with her. She opened the bottle and poured for both of them. "Here." She handed one glass to Lily. "You need this."

"God, yes, I do."

"So," Brittany continued, picking up where they'd left off. "He loves you, and you know it, and he knows it, but he didn't say it."

"That about sums it up."

"Which means that his thing—whatever it was that made him go into his dark place when we were together—is probably standing in the way."

Lily knew what the thing was. Her research into Shane's past had revealed all she needed to know about his sister's death, except for the crucial detail of why Shane believed it was his fault. But Brittany didn't know, and Lily didn't feel that it was her place to tell her.

Brittany read Lily too well, though.

"You know what it is. The thing," Brittany said.

"Maybe."

"Well, what is it?"

Lily winced apologetically. "I don't think I can tell you. I'm sorry. I don't want to violate his privacy."

"Okay, fine. But why does the thing—whatever it is—make it hard for him to commit to a relationship?"

"That's the part I don't know."

"And how does he get past it?"

"That's the part I *really* don't know."

They sat with that for a while, drinking their wine and pondering the unfathomable mysteries of men.

"For what it's worth?" Brittany said. "I never thought he felt it. Love. With me. Not for a minute. It was nice and friendly and companionable. It was … pleasant. And I hoped it might become more one day. But love? It just wasn't there."

"Brittany …"

"What I'm saying is, you don't have to feel guilty anymore. I'm letting you off the hook. It wasn't happening, and it wasn't going to happen, whether you entered the picture or not."

Damn it. Here came the tears again, only this time, they were tears of gratitude. "Really?" Lily asked.

"Really. Now grab that bottle and refill me, would you? This wine isn't going to drink itself."

Chapter Thirty

When Lily was gone, Shane refrained from the impulse to bang his head against the wall until he knocked himself unconscious.

Could he have been any more of an idiot? Maybe there were worse things he could have said or done, but right now, he couldn't think of them. She said she loved him. She gave him that gift. And he threw it back at her like it meant nothing.

It didn't mean nothing. It meant everything, but the prospect of happiness had scared him so thoroughly he'd turned and run from it like he was being chased by a pack of rabid dogs.

He'd deserve it if Lily never came back. If she never wanted to talk to him again.

And that was the point, wasn't it? Punishing himself. As though, if he eventually put himself through enough pain, he could atone for what he'd done to his sister. As though it were a debt he could someday pay.

It didn't work that way, though. Because the more pain he caused himself, the more pain he caused to the people around him. Which meant he had even more to atone for, not less.

He went back to bed, lay down beneath the covers, and tried to sleep, but it didn't work. Instead, he stared up at the ceiling, watching the patterns made by moonlight through the trees outside his window.

Shane wanted to be emotionally healthy. He really did. He wanted to be able to put the past behind him and move on. He wanted to be happy and whole and able to say things like *I love you*. He wanted to stop worrying his family. He wanted to stop pushing Lily away. He just didn't know how to do any of that. He didn't even know how to start.

He'd heard about people who thought they could communicate with their lost loved ones. He'd hoped those kinds of things were true, but he'd never heard from Molly. She hadn't come to him in a dream. She hadn't spoken to him through gestures from beyond—a penny found on the sidewalk, the chirp of a particular kind of bird. He'd imagined that if she could somehow let him know she was happy, that she was okay, then he could be released from this hell of self-loathing.

But Molly wasn't speaking to him from wherever she was. Molly was just gone.

If his parents could forgive him, which they had, then it stood to reason that he should be able to forgive himself, and yet it had never happened. He'd never managed that feat.

After trying and failing to sleep, Shane turned on the bedside light, grabbed his phone, and sent a text to Finn.

You were right. I've got to get my shit figured out.

Of course I was right, Finn responded. *I'm glad you've finally come to your senses.*

I don't know how to start.

You start by talking to someone, Finn said. *A professional. Someone who's not me. I can give you names.*

I don't want any names.

And there he was, resisting it again. Asking for help and then refusing it. Closing down any possible avenue of healing, of moving forward. What was wrong with him?

Fine, Finn answered. *Let me know when you're done steeping in your own misery. Until then, there's not much I can do.*

The answer seemed harsh, but Shane knew he deserved it. And he knew Finn was right—nobody could do anything for him until he was ready to let them.

———

LILY DISTANCED herself from Shane for the next couple of days. She worked on her novel and her editing projects; she interviewed a local restaurateur about a charity project he was leading to provide meals for the homeless; she visited her mother in Morro Bay; and she tried not to think about the disastrous *I love you* declaration and its aftermath.

Not that she could put anything past her mother.

Lily was at Janice's house with her laptop, looking over the local real estate listings, when Janice asked her what was wrong.

"Don't say it's nothing, Lily, because I know better. I've been reading your facial expressions since birth, and I know when there's something bothering you."

Lily closed the laptop and sat back on the sofa, her head leaning against the cushions, looking at the ceiling. "Oh, it's just … Shane. We had a thing the other night."

"What kind of thing? A fight?"

"No, not a fight. Just a thing."

She told Janice what had happened, excluding the naked in bed part, since she was, after all, talking to her mother.

"I was hurt and embarrassed, so now I'm kind of ghosting him. But not really. Kind of a polite version of ghosting, in which I do answer his texts but with distant courtesy. Which I guess I'll keep doing until I can figure out a way to unsay *I love you*."

"Oh, that's just nonsense." Janice waved a hand to dismiss it. "Just because he has trouble talking about his feelings doesn't mean you should. You said something true. Good for you. The world would be a better place if we all did that. Don't you dare try to take it back, Lily. Not if you meant it."

"I did mean it." Lily swallowed hard. "But if he doesn't feel it too …"

"Is that what you think? That he doesn't love you?"

She thought about it, then shook her head. "No. I think he does, he just didn't say it for whatever reason."

"Then maybe he just needs more time." Janice reached over and squeezed Lily's hand. "You can't expect his timeline for emotional things to be the same as yours. Give him a chance to catch up."

Janice was right, and hearing what she had to say made Lily feel better. Sometimes a girl just needed her mom to put things in perspective.

———

AFTER THAT, Lily stopped her courteous ghosting of Shane. She apologized for being distant—exactly the behavior that bothered her so much in Shane—and suggested they get together at his place that night after he got off work. After she texted him the invitation, she waited anxiously for his response, wondering if he was as eager to get past this rough patch as she was.

I'll bring home takeout, he texted her. *How's Indigo Moon?*

She smiled, relief washing over her as she formed her response. *I love Indigo Moon. I'd like something with pasta, please.*

And just like that, her mood went from brooding to elation. She dug into her latest newsletter article, eager to get work out of the way so she could think about her evening with Shane.

———

SHANE GOT the text from Lily about their plans that night while he was at the office, between patients. His brothers were going to be happy about it, because he'd been acting like a grouchy asshole to them all morning. Of course, the grouchy assholery had been about Lily and his worries for their relationship.

Now, unless she wanted to see him so she could break it off for good—which he didn't think was the case—things were looking up. He was actually humming a jaunty tune when he passed Finn in the hallway on the way to his next appointment.

"What the hell are you suddenly so happy about?" Finn peered at Shane with interest. "Earlier today, you were inches away from smashing the coffee pot."

"Well, things have improved since then."

"Meaning you heard from Lily."

It still felt weird talking to Finn about Lily, but he'd asked.

"Yeah," Shane admitted. "I did."

"You seeing her tonight?" Finn asked.

"It looks that way."

"Well, whatever you did to fuck things up before, don't do that anymore." Finn clapped Shane on the back and headed toward wherever he'd been going.

Finn had thrown out the advice in a half-serious way, but he'd been right. He had to not do the thing that had screwed everything up.

Which meant he had to tell Lily he loved her.

That should have been an easy enough thing, because it was true. He did love her, unreservedly and with his whole heart. But saying it meant he was claiming it. Claiming the happiness it represented, the rewards. The moving forward. And if he claimed those things, it was like he was leaving Molly behind. Like he was saying he'd already paid in full for what he'd done to her, and that just wasn't true. There was no way to ever pay in full. Pretending he had would diminish her value, reduce it to a thing that could be marked complete and filed away.

Shane felt all of those things at the same time as he knew it was dysfunctional to be feeling those things. Intellectually, he understood that he was holding himself back to no good purpose. That he couldn't bring his sister back no matter how much he suffered. And that if she were here, she'd kick his ass for being stupid.

His feelings about what he should do were directly at odds with his rational knowledge of what he should do.

In the past, he'd always gone with his feelings. But what if he let rational knowledge take the lead for once? He was, after all, a man of science.

He was still pondering all of that when he walked into an exam room and saw that his next patient was Caitlin Jacobs. She was sitting on the exam table looking so much like Molly that it took his breath away.

———

THINGS WITH CAITLIN had degenerated since Shane had last seen her. She presented with exhaustion, fever, increased joint pain, and sores inside her mouth. The rash on her face—the one he'd at first thought was a sunburn—was worse.

Even more alarming was the fact that she burst into tears the moment he asked her how she was feeling.

"I don't know what to do," she said, her shoulders shaking, tears dripping down her cheeks. "I feel like I'm dying. I can't work, I can't … can't …" She took in a shuddering breath and never finished her thought.

Shane grabbed a box of tissues from the countertop and handed them to her. She pulled a wad of them out of the box and blew her nose, then wiped at her eyes.

"I'm sorry," she said. "I'm sorry. I just …"

"There's nothing to be sorry for." He put a soothing hand on her shoulder. "Let's just back up. Tell me when these increased symptoms started."

As it turned out, Shane had thought all this time that Caitlin was seeing the rheumatologist he'd referred her to. He'd assumed she'd gotten on the right medication and would be experiencing some relief of her worst symptoms by now. But talking to her, he learned that she'd had trouble getting insurance, even through the state exchange, because it was outside the open enrollment period. She'd considered paying cash—money she could not afford—to see the specialist, but she'd called and learned that the wait for a new appointment was more than two months.

"Am I supposed to just feel this way for the rest of my life?" She took another tissue and tore it to shreds in her hands. "Is this what my life is going to be?"

"No. No, it isn't." He wheeled a stool over to her and sat down so he could be at her eye level. Then he reached out and took her hand. "Caitlin? Look at me. We're going to figure this out. We're going to get you help. Do you hear me? We're going to make this work."

The thing was, he had no idea how.

Chapter Thirty-One

He was still thinking about Caitlin Jacobs when he arrived home that night with takeout from Indigo Moon. Which meant he was thinking about Molly. Which meant he was reverting to his default mode of being tight-lipped and sullen. And that did not lend itself to any of the plans he had tonight to tell Lily he loved her. To make himself vulnerable. To break out of the cycle that had kept him miserable for so many years.

When Lily arrived, she took off her coat and hung it on the rack by his front door, her cheeks pink with the cold. She was smiling, happy, and it shamed him. He didn't deserve her happiness.

"I've been looking forward to this all day," she said. "I've really missed you. After … you know, what happened, I had some time to think. And what I thought was, I want to be with you." She went to him and put her arms around him, then pressed her lips to his.

Instead of melting into her, he went rigid, kissing her back in only the most perfunctory way.

"Are you okay?" she asked.

He tried to shake off the mood. "Rough day, that's all."

"Well, come on. You can tell me about it over dinner. That pasta smells amazing."

———

LILY KNEW something was very wrong from the moment she touched Shane. He reacted as though her embrace were some kind of punishment he had to endure. But she tried not to overreact. If she could just stay relaxed and positive, avoid reacting with defensiveness, then maybe they could get past whatever was bothering him.

They sat at his dining room table with the food and two glasses of wine, but he was barely eating. He poked at his food, moving it around on his plate.

"Shane? What happened?" she asked gently. "Maybe if you talk about it ..."

"Nothing," he said. "It's nothing." He looked down at his plate, avoiding her gaze.

Lily put down her fork and decided to try the direct approach.

"Is this a bad night to do this? Would you like me to leave?"

"No. I don't want that."

"Okay. Then you're going to have to tell me what's going on."

Shane put down his fork and pushed his plate away. "I don't want to talk about it."

"Of course you don't." Lily had tried not to get frustrated with him, but it was time they had this out. It was time she said what was on her mind. "You close down when you're upset. It's what you do. And look how well that's worked out for you so far."

"Damn it, Lily."

"I don't know what this is about, but I'd venture to say it has something to do with your sister. Something to do with Molly."

Now that it was out there, Lily wondered if she'd made a tactical error, because Shane looked even more upset now that Lily had mentioned his sister's name. And from the look on his face, he was turning to anger as an alternative to whatever other negative emotions were boiling inside him.

"You need to tell me what you're thinking," she persisted. "I know you don't want to. I know you don't feel comfortable doing that. But it's the only thing that's going to get you past this ... this thing you do of shutting out the people around you. The people who love you. Because I do love you, Shane. Even if you can't say it back. Even if you don't love me too. I love you, and I can help you if you'll just talk to me."

He stood up so abruptly it knocked his chair back a foot. "Is that what you think? You think if I just tell you what I'm feeling, it'll make everything all better?"

"No, but—"

"You think it'll fix this fucked-up medical care system we've got, so the patient I saw today can get the help she needs?"

"Shane—"

"You think if I just cry on your shoulder about my feelings, it'll bring my sister back? It won't. So I honestly don't see the point."

Then he walked into his bedroom, closed the door, and locked her out.

———

ONCE SHANE HAD LOCKED Lily out of his room, she knew the role she was supposed to play. She was supposed to leave, reassess their relationship, then tell him it wasn't working out. That way, he could continue to punish himself the way he always had.

If things were ever going to be different for Shane, somebody had to break the pattern. If he wouldn't do it, she guessed it was up to her.

So, she wouldn't leave. She'd stay here, and she would press him until he talked to her.

"Shane." She called to him through the door, willing her voice to remain calm and steady. "I'm not leaving. I'm right here. When you decide you're ready to talk to me, I will still be here."

Then she went to the sofa, sat down, and waited.

When he hadn't come out fifteen minutes later, she went back to the door.

"Still here," she said. Then she waited some more.

Fifteen minutes after that, she went to the door and decided to try something else—to tell him everything she knew. Then he could respond, or he could choose to keep shutting himself away.

"I know you were driving the car the night Molly died," she said, her voice trembling with emotion even as she tried to keep it steady. "And I know—at least, I think—that you feel responsible. And that's why you push everyone away. You think … I don't know. You think you don't deserve happiness, maybe. But you do. You do, Shane. It wasn't your fault. Accidents happen. It wasn't—"

The door flew open, and Shane glared at her with a look so fierce it made her take a step back.

"You've done your research, have you? Like the good reporter you are? Great. But you missed something. You missed the fact that yes, it was my fault. I caused that accident."

"Were you … did you …"

"I wasn't drinking, if that's what you're thinking. I was *texting*." He threw out the word like it was a vile, hated thing. "I was texting with my girlfriend while I was driving. And Molly told me to stop. But the girl I was dating? We had a fight. I thought she was seeing someone else. So I was distracted, and I was upset, and I let the car drift over the center line. I saw the oncoming car in time to swerve out of the way, but I overcorrected and we hit a utility pole. Most of the damage was on the passenger side, where Molly was. I walked away with cuts and bruises. Everyone told me I was lucky not to have been hurt worse. *Lucky.* I was *fortunate* to have just killed my sister instead of both of us."

Lily's eyes filled with tears. "Shane."

"So, yes, it was my fault. One hundred percent. So the whole *accidents happen* thing? This one happened because I made it happen. Because I was irresponsible and selfish. And you know the stupidest part? My family forgives me. Which infuriates me. I don't want to be forgiven because I don't deserve it. There. I told you. Are you happy now?"

Tears spilled down Lily's cheeks. "Happy? None of this makes me happy."

"Well, that makes two of us. Go home, Lily."

"No."

"I'm telling you I don't want you here."

"And I'm telling you I'm not going anywhere."

He stared at her, his lips pressed into a tight line. Then he went into the bedroom and came out with a jacket. He put it on and pushed past her. "Fine. Then I will."

He grabbed his keys off a table by the front door and left, slamming the door behind him.

WHEN SHANE WAS GONE, Lily stood in his living room wondering what to do next. What could she do? She'd said she wasn't leaving, but there was little point in staying if Shane wasn't here. If he was determined to shut her out.

She had a good cry, then went into the bathroom to blow her nose and wipe away her smudged eyeliner. Then she gathered up her things and drove home.

Lily wasn't in the door five minutes before Brittany read the situation with pinpoint accuracy.

"He did it again," she said. "He did to you what he did to me." She shook her head. "I'm so sorry, Lily."

"But why? I thought when it happened before, with you, it was because … the anniversary …" She sat on the sofa next to Brittany and felt the tears starting to come again.

"He had a patient today who looks like his sister. It must have triggered him."

"How do you know that?"

Brittany put her arm around Lily and squeezed. "Finn called. He saw the patient in the waiting area and thought this might happen. He told me so I could keep an eye on you."

"Oh." Lily marveled at brothers and sisters—the way they would take care of you when you didn't want it and didn't deserve it, but really needed it. "He shouldn't worry about me. Shane's the one who needs him. He tried to kick me out of his house, but I wouldn't go. Then he just left. God knows where he is now."

Brittany pulled her phone out of her pocket and wrote a text.

"Who are you texting?"

"Finn. I'm telling him what you just said. If Shane's out there on his own, upset …" She left the thought unfinished.

"Okay. Good. That's good."

With that done, Brittany turned her attention back to Lily. "Are you okay? You seem upset but okay."

"I am, I think. I'm worried about Shane. But he told me what happened, Brit. With his sister. About the accident that killed her."

"He never said a word about it to me," Brittany said.

"Right. So, even though he got all angry and tried to make me leave, and then ran away himself, he did talk. That's got to be a step, right?"

Brittany squeezed Lily's hand. "I hope so. I really hope so."

WHEN SHANE LEFT HIS HOUSE, he went to Ted's to get drunk off his ass.

Getting drunk off his ass by himself, while in a heightened emotional state, wasn't the healthiest thing to do. But, so what? He couldn't feel like this for even a moment longer, and he needed alcohol to numb the pain.

He was sitting at the bar, two shots of whiskey in him already and a gin and tonic in front of him, when Finn came in the door.

Oh, shit. Just what he needed. His sanctimonious brother, judging him and making assessments of his mental health.

Finn pulled up a stool next to Shane. "Hey. What're you having?"

"Solitude. Go home."

Ted came over and raised his eyebrows at Finn.

"I'll have what he's having," he said, motioning toward Shane's drink. Ted went to the other end of the bar, made the drink, and brought it to Finn.

Finn took a sip. "G&T. Not bad, although Ted uses the cheap gin."

"What do you want?" Shane said.

"I'm here to babysit you. Lily told Brittany what happened, and Brittany told me, and I took a guess about where you'd be. I guessed right."

"Well, fuck off."

"Mmm." Finn pulled a face to indicate that he was considering it. "No. I don't think so."

"Then at least shut up. I don't want to talk."

"Fine."

They drank in silence for a while, Shane sulking, Finn watching him do it. The bar was dark and mostly empty, since it was a weeknight. The sound system played eighties rock at a volume low enough that the few patrons could still hear themselves think. Two guys at the other end of the room played a game of pool.

"Eighteen years," Finn said after a while.

"What?" Shane barked at him.

"It's been eighteen years. Since the accident. If they'd sent you to prison, you'd be out by now. Don't you think it's time you considered your debt paid?"

Shane took a gulp of his drink and turned to face Finn. "But I didn't go to prison, did I? I've been free this whole time. Healthy. Having my career, enjoying my family. Having relationships. Doing all of the things Molly can't do. How is that fair?"

Finn let out a harsh bark of a laugh.

"What?" Shane demanded.

"Who the hell told you life was fair?"

"Finn—"

"I mean it. Who was the asshole who said that? Because I've got a serious issue with them. It's not fair that Molly died. It's not fair that you've punished yourself for a simple teenage mistake ever since. And it's not fair that you keep dumping women you care about for reasons that are no fault of theirs. None of it is fair. Life isn't fair. The sooner you get used to that, the sooner we can all move forward."

"Look, dickhead. I came here to get drunk. I didn't come here for a lecture."

"Well, you need the lecture more than you need the alcohol, so …"

Shane swallowed the last of his drink then turned on his stool to face Finn. "Can I ask you something?"

"Sure. Ask away."

"Why did you forgive me? I mean, all of you. Mom, Dad, everyone. After what I did? Why?"

"Because shit happens, Shane. Sometimes it's because of the things we do, and sometimes it's not. And none of us are perfect. Not even you. You did a dumbass thing when you were a kid, and you know what? That's what kids do. They're dumbasses. Most of us manage to get through it without doing much damage, and that's pure luck. It's not because we're better than you. You're flawed, and you made a mistake, and the worst-case scenario happened. It doesn't mean you don't deserve love. Or forgiveness. Or a chance to move forward. It doesn't mean you're ruined forever. Unless you decide it does."

Finn took out his wallet and left some money on the bar, his own drink barely touched. "Now, come on. I'll drive you home. Lily's not there anymore, so you're safe."

Chapter Thirty-Two

———————————

Lily didn't know what to do about Shane.

She knew she didn't want to abandon him no matter how hard he tried to push her away, but she didn't know how best to go about supporting him and loving him.

Should she give him space? Give him the opposite of space by showing up at his house? Or try some medium area between the two?

Of course, all of that assumed she would be the one to make the first move. As it happened, she wasn't. Just when she was coming up with a strategy to deal with complete silence from him, he showed up at her door the day after their failed date.

It was ten p.m., later than she would expect a visitor. She was just about to go to bed—she was wearing her pajamas, her hair in a messy bun—when the doorbell surprised her.

"Who the hell is that?" Brittany said. "At this time of night?"

"Come with me," Lily said.

"What? Why?"

"I don't want to answer the door alone in case it's a … I don't know. A home-invasion robber or something."

So Lily and Brittany went to the door together, and Lily peered out through the peephole.

"It's Shane." She stared at Brittany. "What's he doing here?"

"I don't know. Ask him." She headed back toward her room.

"Where are you going?" Lily asked, feeling anxious. She'd pondered strategies for dealing with Shane, but she hadn't settled on one yet. She didn't know what to say or how to act.

"I'm giving you privacy," Brittany said, then went into her room and closed the door.

The bell rang again, and Lily opened the door. It was raining, and Shane was soaked.

"Lily. Hi." He shoved his hands into his pockets, his gaze somewhere around her knees.

"Come in. Get out of the rain."

"No, that's okay. I won't be long. I just … I wanted to say something to you."

"Okay."

He looked at her, blinking the rainwater out of his eyes. "I had to tell you I'm sorry. The way I treated you last night, I was an ass."

"Yes. You were."

"I know. You didn't deserve it, and I apologize."

Lily's expression softened. "Are you sure you don't want to come in?"

Rain was falling onto his head, running down his neck and into his collar. "Well, maybe just for a second. Just long enough for me to say what I have to say." He stepped inside but didn't go beyond the front entryway.

Lily closed the door to keep the cold out, then turned to face Shane, her hands tucked into her armpits. "Okay. So, say what you want to say."

Shane nodded, his expression one of grim determination. "Yesterday, before I saw you, something happened at work that upset me."

"Your patient. The one who looks like your sister."

"Yes. Finn would say that triggered me. Then you came over, and—"

"And you reverted to your usual defense tactic of pushing away anyone who loves you," she finished for him.

"Yes. That's … that's what I did."

"Well. I knew all of that before you came here." Lily knew she sounded a little petulant, but she wanted to make him work for it, just a little.

"What you don't know is that I want to change. I want to do better. I don't want things between us to end the way things always have. I'm trying. I want to try. But I'm going to need you to be patient with me, because I don't really know how to fix this."

Lily wanted nothing more than to take him in her arms, but the way he was standing there, feet away from her, looking so miserable and so alone, she knew it wasn't the right time. If she tried, he would push her away.

"Why?" she said, her voice soft. "Why now?"

Shane swallowed hard. "Because that thing you said about how you feel? About me? I feel the same way. About you. And I don't want to shut you out. I don't want to force you away."

"You love me," she said. "That's what you're trying to say?"

"Yes."

"But you can't say the words?"

"I …" He shook his head. "Not yet."

"Oh, Shane." She couldn't keep herself from touching him, so she put a hand on his arm. "You deserve better. So much better than what you're putting yourself through."

"Yeah, that's what I'm trying to make myself believe."

Lily thought about what to say. She could urge him to talk to a professional, but she was sure he'd already heard that from Finn. She could tell him he deserved forgiveness, but she was sure he'd already heard that from everyone who'd ever loved him. She could tell him about the mistakes everyone made, some tragic, some less so, and how they all had no choice but to move forward however they could. But he already knew that. Now, he just had to learn how to believe it.

"I love you," she said. "You might have trouble saying the words, and that's okay. You can say them when you're ready. But I don't have any trouble. I love you, and I can say so, and I am saying it, Shane. I'm here. And I'll still be here, however long it takes you to figure things out."

Please, please don't let it take too long.

"Okay." Shane nodded. "Okay."

Lily reached out, put her hands on his face, and kissed him once, quickly. When she let him go, she sniffled a little, wiped her eyes with her fingertips, and then looked up, startled, when Brittany cleared her throat.

They both looked toward the sound and saw Brittany standing in the hallway outside her bedroom, her arms crossed over her chest.

"You were listening?" Lily asked, affronted.

"I was on my way to the bathroom, and I heard things. For what it's worth, Shane? Lily's right. You don't deserve this. You're not a bad person. It's okay to be happy. The world won't come to an end." Then she went into the bathroom and closed the door behind her.

Chapter Thirty-Three

The thing was, Shane was punishing himself for causing pain by continuing to cause pain. Even the most basic grasp of logic said that made no sense, and it didn't help anyone. He couldn't atone for the damage he'd done by doing more damage.

He just didn't know how to stop the cycle.

Well, Lily had been right. His patient had triggered him. So he would start making positive changes there. He'd start with her.

"Family meeting upstairs after closing," Shane told his brothers the next morning, delivering the message to whoever he saw in the halls or in the break room."

"Family meeting?" Rowan grimaced as though Shane had announced that they'd all be doing a colon cleanse. "What the hell for?"

"I'll tell you at the meeting."

"Well, shit. I'm supposed to go to dinner with Ashley after work."

"Call her and tell her you'll be late."

"Family meeting?" Aidan asked when Shane told him. "Is something wrong with Mom or Dad?"

"Not that I know of," Shane said.

"Then what?"

"Just show up, and I'll tell you what."

When he texted his parents to tell them, his mother, predictably, wanted to make food for everyone. He told her it wasn't necessary. "I'll order pizza," he told her when she called to talk about it.

"Well, but pizza. You boys need better nutrition than that."

"One time eating pizza won't kill us. Bring a salad if you want."

When it was all set and everyone had agreed to come, he already felt better. Calling the meeting was the first step of many, but it was a step.

———

THEY MET upstairs in Finn's waiting room. Shane chose it because it was nicely furnished, with leather sofas and well-thought-out lighting, and he thought the nice atmosphere might make his family more amenable to what he was going to propose.

Everyone was hungry after a long day of work, so Shane waited until they all had paper plates of pizza and the green salad his mother had made, bottles of cold, sweating soda in their hands, before he said why he'd called them here.

"So, let's get to it," Rowan said. "I'm meeting Ashley in an hour. I'm walking out that door in fifty minutes whether you're done or not."

Shane put down his plate and stood up, ready to start his pitch.

"I've been treating a patient whom I've diagnosed with lupus," he began.

"The one who looks like Molly," Finn said.

"Yes." He cleared his throat, emotion thickening it at the mention of his sister's name. "That's right. She doesn't have health insurance, so I treated her pro bono. But where does she go from here? She requires specialists, medications, follow-up care that we can't provide. What we're doing here is valuable—it provides quality care to people who can't afford it, but only in our particular specialties. What do our patients do when they need more than what we offer?"

"I agree, it's a problem," Aidan said. "But we can only do so much."

"What if we could do more?" Shane asked.

Shane's father sat forward in his chair. "What do you have in mind?"

"I want us to form a private foundation to pay for health insurance for our patients who can't afford it and who need more care than we can provide here at the practice. We're all financially privileged. We'd have family wealth even if we hadn't gone into a lucrative field. Between our investments and Mom and Dad's land holdings … Rowan, how much did you make on that health tracking app?"

"More than you'd know what to do with," Rowan said.

"Right. So, I'm proposing that we start with a set contribution from each of us. We'll invest it and use the proceeds to fund insurance premiums for ten patients as a pilot program. If it goes well, we can expand it gradually. The money will be tax deductible, which will help Rowan with the IRS, which you need, God knows."

"I do need that," Rowan agreed. "How much were you thinking from each of us?"

Shane told him. Then he waited for questions, feeling better than he had in some time.

"Who would choose the patients?" Nolan asked.

"We would," Shane answered. "We'd select people based on their income and based on the amount of care they need outside of what we can provide."

"Well … shit. I've got at least three patients right now who need specialists they can't afford," Aidan said.

"We all do," Nolan agreed.

"It's a drop in the bucket," Rowan said. "The health care system in this country is still fucked."

"We can't change that," Shane said. "But we can change the situation for a few people who need it."

"It's not enough, but it's something," Rowan said. "I'm in."

Their parents hadn't said anything yet, so Shane turned to them. "Mom? Dad? What do you think?"

Shane's father scratched at the stubble on his chin. "I think, why stop at ten? The need is bigger than that, and your mother and I can contribute more than what you said."

"If I contribute twice as much, can I choose twice as many patients?" Rowan wanted to know. "They're kids, man." He shook his head. "Sending kids away knowing their parents can't afford the specialist or the medication or the surgery or whatever the hell it is? It kills me every time."

Then they all started talking at once about who they wanted to help and how Shane was thinking too small, and at that moment, Shane thought that he had never loved his family more. He didn't feel whole, but he could see wholeness from here, like some distant light on the horizon.

"All of this because your patient looks like Molly?" Finn asked when the din of conversation was beginning to die down.

"All of this because her looking like Molly reminded me that she's somebody's sister or daughter," he said.

Finn nodded. "Good answer," he said, and clapped his brother on the back.

Chapter Thirty-Four

Lily didn't hear from Shane for the next few days, and she tried not to worry about it—or about him.

She told herself it was healthy to be able to do without him while he figured things out. She told herself nothing good came of being so dependent on a man that she couldn't exist for a few days on her own.

After all, the last time she'd felt that way had been Trevor. And that hadn't ended well.

He'd cheated on her. He'd gaslighted her. He'd encouraged her to distance herself from her friends and her family. He could lift her so high with his gifts and attention and declarations of love, then bring her low when it served him, his cutting criticism and disdain convincing her that no one but him could ever love her.

By the time she finally broke up with him, her self-esteem had been so low that she hadn't even known what was true anymore— what was his fault and what was hers. How much of his judgment of her was right and how much was manipulation?

It had taken her a long time to come back from that, a long time to convince herself she wasn't damaged, wasn't unworthy. She'd been so determined never to get into that kind of situation again that she'd only dated men from whom she could easily walk away.

Until Shane.

Back then, with Trevor, she'd told herself relationships were hard. That they were work. And that you didn't just walk away when things got rough. And that was what she was telling herself now as she waited for Shane.

How did she know this was different? How could she be sure?

"Is this Trevor again?" she asked one day, out of the blue, when she and Brittany were driving to their mother's place to go with her to look at houses.

"Is what Trevor? You mean Shane?"

"Yeah." In the passenger seat, Lily slumped down, making herself small. Just the way she had with Trevor. "Yes. I mean, am I doing the same thing I did with him? Letting myself be treated badly in the hope that if I just give a little more, sacrifice a little more, things will get better?"

Brittany shot her sister a look. "I don't know. Do you think it's the same?"

It's what a therapist would say, Lily thought. Not that seeing a therapist would be a bad idea.

"Yes and no," she said. "Yes, it's true that I'm not being treated the way I want to be treated. And yes, it's true that I'm hanging in there, thinking if I just tough it out, things will be okay."

"And the *no* part?"

"The *no* part is that Shane is taking responsibility for his actions. He apologized. He said he's the one at fault. And he said he's trying to change. Trevor never did that. It was always me, always some character flaw I had that was causing all of the problems."

"That asshole," Brittany grumbled. "If he was crossing the street right now, I swear I'd run him down with my car."

"I love you," Lily said.

"I know."

"I love that you would run him over with your car for me. But that's not really the point."

"I know that, too."

They drove through Cayucos and toward Morro Bay, the day sunny and bright, the ocean a carpet of deep blue stretching toward the horizon, green hills rising to the left of the highway.

"Do you feel the same way about Shane as you felt about Trevor?" Brittany asked.

"No."

"No?" Brittany sounded surprised.

"I feel … I feel so much more for Shane. It's so much deeper. So much more real." She took in a shuddering breath. "But I'm doubting myself. What I felt for Trevor was real, too, in its way. Or at least, I believed it was."

Brittany was silent behind the wheel for a while as she considered the question. Finally, she answered.

"I feel like I have a unique perspective on this," she said. "Because Shane and I dated. I feel like I know him well enough to give you a good answer."

"Okay," Lily said.

"And I really don't think he's anything like Trevor. Trevor was a narcissistic dick, and he was only in that relationship for what he could get out of it. He got off on controlling and manipulating women. But Shane? He's a good guy who's going through some things. I don't think he meant to hurt me, and I don't think he means to hurt you, either." Britany changed lanes to get out from behind a slow-moving RV. "But."

"But?"

"But, his intentions don't matter if the relationship isn't good for you. You know? If it causes you more pain than happiness, then he might as well be Trevor."

It was a good point, Lily had to admit. It wasn't what she'd wanted to hear, but it was worth considering.

"So, how do I know when to let go and when to hang on?" Lily asked.

Brittany shrugged. "I don't know. I guess you just have to know your limits. You have to know what you are and are not willing to accept for yourself, and you need to stick to that. I mean, I know Shane is dealing with a lot. And I know you want to support him.

But supporting him is one thing, and letting him bring you down into the abyss with him is another."

She knew Brittany was right. She just didn't know if she could cut Shane loose if he became an anchor threatening to drag her to the bottom of the ocean.

———

SHANE'S FAMILY already had a lawyer—someone they'd used to set up their practice and who Rowan had used when he'd sold the rights to his app. So Shane was one step ahead of the game when he began the process of forming the foundation.

He consulted the lawyer via an online video chat—the guy was based in Los Angeles, and Shane was too busy to go down there—and was happily surprised to learn that the foundation could be up and running in just a few days. Paperwork was exchanged and signed, and money was transferred as Shane hammered out the details with his lawyer and his family.

There were more meetings in Finn's waiting room as the Brodys established a procedure for how they would choose who to help, how many people they would help, how they would invest the principal, and what would happen if there was any kind of dispute over who would get funding and who wouldn't. They also pondered the question of how long funding would last for any individual patient, and they determined that a patient's status should be reviewed once a year based on a set list of criteria.

When all of that was done, Shane called Caitlin Jacobs and asked if he could come to her home for a visit. He was used to making house calls by now, and this was one he was particularly looking forward to.

"You want to visit?" She sounded more apprehensive than he'd expected. "Why? Did something come up in my lab tests? Oh, God. Is it bad news?"

All at once, Shane realized his miscalculation. Nobody expected an urgent visit from their doctor to be a financial windfall. They expected it to be something else—a spot on an X-ray, a terminal diagnosis.

"It is absolutely not bad news," he assured her. "It's good news, in fact. Very good news."

"Well … okay." She gave him her address, even though it was in her file, and said she'd be waiting for him.

———

CAITLIN LIVED in a rented RV on a property two miles up Santa Rosa Creek Road. When she let him in, he understood why she'd been so reluctant to have him visit. The RV was old, nearly falling apart, with rust patches on the exterior and torn upholstery inside. She was doing her best with it—he could see that. She'd put a small, colorful rug on the floor and a vase of flowers on the tiny dining table. The bed at one end of the RV was covered in a decorative spread, and the place had been scrubbed spotless.

"This place—it's all I can afford," she said apologetically when Shane stepped in. "I'm lucky to have it, actually. I thought I was going to have to move somewhere else, Atascadero, maybe, and drive to Cambria for my job."

She worked the front desk at one of the hotels on Moonstone Beach. The pay was above minimum wage and the work was pleasant, but her wages weren't anywhere near enough to match the soaring real estate values and rents in Cambria, she told him. And, of course, her employer didn't offer health insurance.

"That's why I'm here," he told her.

"What is?"

"Your health insurance. I want to pay for it."

She blinked at him a few times, not understanding. "Maybe we should sit down for this."

———

SHANE SPENT the next fifteen minutes explaining the foundation, the concept behind it, what the Brodys hoped to achieve, and how they hoped to achieve it. Then he told her she'd been selected to be the first of their patients to get a health insurance policy fully funded by the Brody Family Foundation.

As the news sank in, Caitlin put a trembling hand to her mouth, her eyes shimmering with tears. "You want to buy my health insurance?"

"Yes. That's exactly what I want to do."

"You can't be serious. This can't be real."

"It's real, and I'm serious. Caitlin, let us do this for you. With your condition, you're going to need ongoing care. Expensive care we can't provide at the practice. We can't fix the broken health care system, but we can do this. Please say you'll accept."

They were sitting in a booth with a plastic table between them. She stood up, leaned forward, and threw her arms around him, almost upending the vase of flowers.

"Oh, my God. Thank you." She was crying now and laughing at the same time. "Thank you so much. You're saving my life, Dr. Brody."

That was the idea. An idea so obvious he was surprised he hadn't thought of it earlier.

He set her up with an appointment with Iris, who would help her find a policy and go through the application process.

Shane hadn't decided to help her just because she looked like Molly. But now that it was happening, it felt healing for him to be able to do something meaningful for her. To be able to solve her most pressing problem so she could deal with her health. If he'd had to walk away from her—if he'd had to leave her at the mercy of the medical establishment, which for the most part had none—he'd have been failing his sister all over again.

As he was walking toward the door to leave, she stopped him.

"You know something?" she said. "It's not right that you and your family had to do this, though I'm really glad you did. It shouldn't be necessary." She looked at him with eyes so much like Molly's that it made his knees weak. "Everyone deserves a chance to get better from whatever's wrong with them. You shouldn't have to just suffer. Everyone deserves a chance to heal and move on, you know?"

He'd never gotten a sign from Molly. He'd never seen her in a dream, never heard her speak into his ear, never gotten some sort of secret message or coded communication. But right now, it felt like his sister was speaking directly to him through this woman who looked so much like her.

You shouldn't have to suffer. Everyone deserves a chance to heal.

The sensation that Molly was talking to him was so uncanny that, for a moment, he froze.

"Dr. Brody? Are you okay?"

He blinked away tears and cleared his throat. "Not completely. But, you know what? I think I will be."

Chapter Thirty-Five

Lily hadn't heard from Shane in a while.

When he'd come to her house to apologize and tell her he was working on himself, that had been encouraging. But now she didn't know what to think. It had been more than a week without a word.

She didn't want to complain about it to Brittany any more than she had to, so she turned to her mother.

"This is it, isn't it?" she asked Janice one Saturday morning while they were perusing the real estate listings and planning which houses Janice would ask her Realtor to show her. "He's gone. When he said he was going to work on himself, he meant long term. He meant he's going to do therapy for, like, a year, and he'll call me when it's over. Maybe. If he still remembers me."

"Oh, honey. It hasn't been that long. Give him a chance."

They were sitting at the kitchen table at Janice's rental house with cups of tea and a laptop. The fog that had blanketed Morro Bay matched Lily's mood—gloomy.

"I am. I am trying to give him a chance. But what if he never calls? What if part of his effort to change means leaving me behind?"

"I don't think that will happen," Janice said in the voice she'd used to soothe her kids since their births. "But if it does, you'll be okay. You'll move on."

Except Lily didn't think she would move on. She'd come to realize that Shane was the love of her life. He was The One. If he decided he didn't want her—if he somehow came to the conclusion that he couldn't heal with her in his life—she wasn't sure she'd recover. Oh, she'd get on with her life. She'd survive. But surviving was different than living. Than thriving. She didn't want to just stay alive, just keep breathing in and out. She wanted the life she imagined with Shane. She wanted everything she knew he could give her.

"Lily, you're sulking," Janice admonished her.

"I deserve to sulk. The man I love is off doing whatever he's doing, and I'm just supposed to wait patiently. I'm just supposed to trust that it's all going to work out. But it might not, and if it doesn't …" She left the thought open, unnamed pain and tragedy implied in the pause.

"If it's meant to be, it'll be," Janice said.

"You don't really believe that. The whole fate thing." Lily scowled at her mother.

"I most certainly do."

"But Mom—"

"I do!" Janice insisted. "I firmly believe that your father and I were meant to be, and if you and Shane are meant to be, then it'll all work out. The universe works in mysterious ways, Lily. Why, I wouldn't be surprised if Brittany dated Shane just so you could meet him. Not that I would say as much to Brittany, though I believe she'll come around to that conclusion herself eventually."

"She won't if this thing between me and Shane crashes and burns in a fireball of doom and despair."

Janice gave Lily a withering look. "You do have a dramatic way of stating things, Lily."

"I know. I know I'm being overdramatic. But I need him, Mom. I need this to work. Not just because I love him, which I do. But because, after Trevor …"

"You lost your confidence, and you need to get it back," Janice finished for her.

"Yes. I really do." Lily's shoulders fell. "I can't take another loss, Mom."

"You're stronger than you think, Lily." Janice squeezed her daughter's hand. "But for what it's worth? I don't think you're going to lose."

———

SHANE KNEW he was on the borderline of having waited too long to talk to Lily. He hadn't wanted to leave her hanging, but he needed to get his head together before he saw her. He needed to know he wouldn't freeze up again, wouldn't panic and turn angry and brooding on her just when he needed to get closer instead of further away.

And he needed her to know that things were going to be different from now on. He needed her to know he meant it. That he was in this all the way.

He'd been thinking a lot about his next step, and that next step scared the hell out of him. But scared or not, he was making progress. A year ago—hell, even three months ago—the step would have been so frightening it would have been unthinkable. The fear would have driven him into a depression that would have affected his family and everyone around him.

Now he actually thought he could do it. He just needed to psyche himself up.

"You seem good," Finn told him at a Brody Sunday dinner as their father turned ribs on the barbecue despite the rain. The barbecue was set up under a large patio umbrella, and Finn and Shane stood under the patio cover and watched while the rest of the family stayed warm inside.

"You sound surprised," Shane said.

"Honestly? I am."

Shane sipped a beer and wondered how much to tell his brother.

"A thing happened," he said. "With my patient. Caitlin Jacobs."

"Uh-oh. A medical thing?"

"No. A personal thing." He steeled himself and continued. "When I told her about the foundation, about how we'd be covering her insurance costs, she said a person shouldn't have to keep suffering. A person deserved to be able to heal."

"She's right," Finn said.

"She is. But something weird happened. And you can tell me I'm crazy if you want to. But … it was Molly. I'm not saying Caitlin looked like Molly. I'm saying that in that moment, I felt … God, I really am crazy. But I felt like Molly was talking to me through her. That she was talking about me. How I shouldn't have to suffer. How I deserved to heal. And since then? I've felt different. Better. Like some of the weight has been lifted."

Finn didn't say anything for a while. He just stood there and looked out over the rain-soaked yard, toward where their father was grilling ribs.

"You think I've lost my mind," Shane prompted him.

"I didn't say that."

"But you're thinking it."

"No." He shook his head. "No, no. I'm not."

"Really?"

"Listen, Shane. In my practice, I can't tell you how many times I've heard grieving patients say they've gotten signs from the people they've lost. I don't know what that is. I don't know if it's real, or wishful thinking, or what. But I've seen it enough times to know not to dismiss it."

"Really?"

"Yes, really. And I'll tell you something else. If it helps you or anyone else deal with their grief, I'm all for it. If it allows people to move on, to move forward, then I don't care if it's real. Even if it's not, it's still a good thing."

"So you're saying I might be crazy, but whatever works."

"No." Finn turned to face him. "I'm saying, maybe you're just ready, and talking to that patient is what made you realize it. If so, I'm grateful as hell, whether she was a voice from beyond or not."

They stood together thinking about that, sipping beer and listening to the rain on the roof.

"So, Lily," Finn said.

"Yeah. Lily."

"I have to wonder, if you're feeling better about things, and you're maybe ready to move forward, where the hell is she?"

"I wanted to talk to you about that," he said. "I have a thought, but I need to make sure you're okay with it."

"Well, tell me."

Shane did.

"No shit?" Finn asked when he was done.

"No shit. The only thing holding me back at this point is you, and how you might feel about it."

"I think I feel fine," Finn said. "You know what? I definitely do."

Shane grinned. "And then there's Brittany. I'll need to talk to her first."

"I guess you will," Finn said. "Good luck with that."

Shane appreciated the sentiment. He was going to need the luck.

———

SHANE'S CONVERSATION with Brittany was awkward, but he supposed it had to be. He didn't want Lily to know about it, so he went to the salon where Brittany worked and talked to her as she applied dye and little sheets of aluminum foil to a client's head.

He told her what he wanted to do, trying to keep the emotion out of his voice and the nervous tremor out of his hands.

"I'd like you to be there, if you want to be. You're the most important person in Lily's life—well, you and your mother—and I think Lily would like you to be there."

"Oh, that's so romantic." The client, a woman in her fifties, beamed with enthusiasm, her hair halfway wrapped in foil.

"It's only romantic until you realize he's my ex and Lily's my sister," Brittany said to her.

"Yikes," the woman said. "I can see how that would change things."

"Yes, but Brittany and I were never right for each other," Shane told the woman. "She and I both knew that. But Lily and I are … we're it. We're perfect together. She's my One."

"Your One." The woman said it on a sigh.

"He dumped me," Brittany said to the woman.

"No, I didn't. You dumped me."

"Okay, I dumped him. For good reasons. And now I'm supposed to watch him do what he said he's going to do in front of his whole family, and that's not supposed to be humiliating for me?"

"Well …" the woman said.

"It won't be humiliating," Shane said. "Or, at least, only if you let it be. You dumping me led me to think about things, and because of that, I'm going to change, Brittany. I'm going to do things right this time. I'm determined to. You dumping me might have been the best thing that could have happened to me, and I'm grateful to you, so there shouldn't be any hard feelings between us."

"There'll be hard feelings if you treat my sister like crap." She pointed the brush she was using to apply the hair dye at Shane.

"I won't." He put his hands up, palms out, in a gesture of submission.

"You'd better not."

"And anyway," Shane went on, "that's another reason for you to be there. What if things go south and Lily needs you?"

That got through, as he knew it would. "You asshole."

"So you'll come?"

Brittany let out a heavy sigh. "Yeah. I'll come."

"Great. Thank you. I won't let you down. I won't let either of you down. Oh, but you can't tell Lily. You just have to kind of … show up."

"Now you've got me lying to my sister."

"Not lying. Surprising her."

"Oh, Brittany. He's a dream. How did you ever let him go?" the woman asked.

"I wish it had been off the side of a cliff," Brittany said, but she was grinning slightly, a hint of a curve to her lips.

"No, you don't," Shane said.

"You want to find out? Hurt my sister and we'll see."

Shane left the salon feeling optimistic for his future, a thing he hadn't felt in a very long time.

———

THAT NIGHT, Lily fretted over the fact that she still hadn't heard from Shane.

She didn't want to be that woman who sat by her phone all night willing a man to call, so she urged herself not to do that. She tried putting her angst into her novel, but after two pages, she found her mind drifting and she pushed her laptop away at the kitchen table.

"This is pathetic," she said, half to Brittany and half to herself.

"What is?" Brittany was in the kitchen making dinner, and she paused with her hand on the knife she was using to chop vegetables.

"Me. I can't write. I can't focus. I can't do anything except wonder why Shane hasn't called. It's like I'm sixteen. Next thing you know I'm going to be doodling his name on my notebook."

"He'll call," Brittany said.

"You don't know that."

"Actually, I do."

Lily turned in her chair to face her sister. "What? How? What do you know and how do you know it?"

Brittany shrugged, looking a little flustered, as though she'd said something she shouldn't have. "I don't *know* it, exactly. I just ... I would bet that he will, that's all."

"You're hiding something." Lily pointed one finger at her sister.

"What would I be hiding?" It wasn't an answer—it was a deliberate non-answer—and they both knew it.

———

LILY HAD to wait just two more days until Wednesday evening. She and Brittany were just settling down to a pizza that had been delivered when Shane came to the door.

"Shane." Lily stared at him, not knowing what to expect. It had been so long since she'd heard from him that at this point, he could be here to break up with her. "Come in."

"No thanks, I'll only be a minute."

He looked nervous. Nervous wasn't good. It meant he was about to say something he was unsure about, which could definitely be a breakup. Lily's stomach fluttered with nerves of her own.

"Well, okay, then," she said. "What's going on?"

"This." He reached out, pulled her into his arms, and kissed her. The kiss was thorough and passionate, but brief. He let her go a moment later, but by then, her knees were already shaking, her palms already sweating, her body already yearning in response to him.

"Well, I … wow," she said. "Now you really do have to come in."

He grinned at her, and it made her warm all the way to her toes. "No, I can't. I just came here to do that and to ask you to come to this week's Brody Sunday dinner."

Lily felt awash with relief. If he was inviting her to dinner with his family, this wasn't a breakup. It was maybe the opposite of a breakup.

"I'd love to."

Now Shane's smile lit up his whole face, and only then did Lily realize she'd never seen him smile unreservedly before. Not even once. Now that she'd seen it, she wanted to see more and more of it.

"Great. That's great. Five o'clock?"

"I'll be there."

"I can't wait." He kissed her again, quickly this time, then turned to go.

When he was gone, Lily went back to the table. "That was Shane," she told Brittany.

"Oh?"

"Yeah. He wants me to come to Sunday dinner this week."

"Mmm," Brittany said.

Now Lily knew her sister was keeping something from her.

"Brittany, what do you know? I swear to God, you'd better tell me."

"I don't know anything. Now, would you just shut up and let me eat?"

Chapter Thirty-Six

Shane had everything ready by four thirty on Sunday. Flowers, champagne, the ring. The plan was, he would propose to Lily in the back yard after she arrived, and when she said yes, he would lead her into the house, which was elaborately decorated for an engagement party. He'd even arranged for Brittany to bring her mother. The two Harts would wait in the house until they received a cue that the proposal was imminent, then they would come outside to surprise Lily.

The living room of his parents' house was ready to go—white balloons, flowers, streamers. There would even be a dinner catered by Neptune, though Shane's father had insisted on grilling some steaks anyway.

As Shane waited for Lily to arrive, his whole family in attendance, he kept fiddling with the ring box, flipping it open to stare at the ring, then slapping it shut again. His heart was hammering so hard it felt like it was going to come out of his chest.

"Here." Rowan came to where Shane was standing and put a drink in his hand. Whiskey, two fingers. "You need this. You're fidgeting like a five-year-old in church."

"Thanks." Shane took the drink and swallowed it in one gulp, feeling the welcome burn in his throat. "I see you brought Ashley this time. Have you broken up with the other one, then? What's her name?"

"Paige. Not yet."

"Rowan, you're such a dick."

"Look, I'm going to do it. I've decided. I really like Ashley, so I'm going to tell Paige it's off. I just haven't figured out how to tell her yet."

"With words," Shane said.

"Yeah, yeah."

Finn came over to clap Shane on the back and ask how he was holding up.

"Okay, I guess. I just hope she says yes."

"She will."

"You don't know that."

"I can guess. I'm a psychiatrist. I can read people."

Nolan and Aidan came over to wish him luck, then his parents, and before he knew it, he was at the center of a crowd of congratulatory Brodys. Ashley, who'd helped him decorate the house, came over to give him a kiss on the cheek.

"After all of this, I'm going to look like an idiot if she shoots me down," Shane said.

She couldn't shoot him down. The thought was impossible, unthinkable. He needed this. He needed a win.

He'd asked Lily to text him when she got here, though he hadn't said why. When the text came in, he signaled to his family to disperse and act natural.

"Get out of here." He waved frantically at his family members, including his mother, who was busy adjusting his collar. "Go on, you guys! Dad, go grill something."

Everybody spread out across the yard, pretending to do whatever it was they usually did during a family barbecue, making a big show of paying no attention at all to Shane, or to Lily when she came through the side gate and into the back yard.

That's the woman who's going to be my wife, Shane thought as he saw her. He went to her and pulled her into his arms.

"Well, that's a nice welcome," Lily said. "You seem … I don't know. A little jittery. What's going on?"

"I'm just happy to see you, that's all. I've missed you."

"I missed you too, Shane. So much." She kissed him, and then everything happened fast after that.

———

"I HAVE something to say to you," Shane said. "Something to ask you. Something I've been thinking about the whole time we've been apart."

He gave the signal to Nolan, who opened the sliding glass door and brought out Brittany and Janice. The Brodys and the Harts gathered around Shane and Lily.

"Mom?" Lily asked, confusion in her voice. "Brittany?"

"I wanted them to be here for this," Shane said. "And I thought you might like it, too."

"What's going on?" Lily asked. "Shane?"

Heart jackhammering in his chest, Shane reached into his pocket and brought out the ring box. Lily saw it and gasped. Then, gathering all he had of courage and optimism for the future, Shane lowered himself onto one knee in front of Lily.

And then, everyone's attention shifted when a voice called out, "Hi, everybody! What's going on? Am I interrupting something?"

They all looked up and saw Paige coming through the gate leading to the back yard. She made her entrance just as Rowan was wrapping his arm around Ashley's waist and nuzzling her ear.

"Paige?" Rowan said, letting go of Ashley as though she were burning him.

"Rowan? Who's that?" Paige pointed at Ashley.

"What are you doing here?" Rowan asked.

"You invited me," Paige said, her voice steely.

"Oh, shit. Did I? I guess I forgot."

"Who is she?" Ashley demanded, stepping away from Rowan and glaring at him.

"Oh, shit," Aidan murmured.

"Shane?" Lily said, reminding him that he'd stopped cold right in the middle of a marriage proposal.

The moment ruined, Shane got up off his knee, put the ring back in his pocket, and walked toward Paige.

"Okay," he said, "let's just all stay calm."

"Fuck calm," Paige said. "Who's the whore?"

"*Whore?*" Ashley's eyebrows shot up and she turned to Paige, feet set apart as though she were preparing for a fistfight.

Chaos erupted. Paige and Ashley started yelling at each other about who was Rowan's girlfriend and who wasn't, Rowan made placating sounds that nobody paid attention to, the various Brodys tried to step in between the two women to prevent possible violence, and Aidan called Rowan a dick. Brittany and Janice rushed to Lily's side to offer whatever support might turn out to be necessary, and Shane's dad kept manning the grill in fear that the steaks might burn amid all of the distraction.

It wasn't long before Paige and Ashley decided that yelling at each other was counterproductive, and they both started yelling at Rowan.

Insults flew, then Ashley called Rowan a bastard. When it came to light that he'd slept with both of them in the same twenty-four-hour period, Paige slapped Rowan so hard that the sound made everyone in the back yard wince.

"That's enough." Finn took control of the situation, grabbing Paige by the arm and leading her back toward the gate from where she'd come. Aidan followed his lead, putting an arm around Ashley and taking her into the house, muttering validating things to her about how Rowan really was a bastard and how she deserved better.

Rowan watched them go, a red handprint forming on his face.

"Did I really invite them both?" he asked nobody in particular. "I must be losing it. Shit. I should know better."

Nolan put a glass of amber liquid in Rowan's hand—whiskey, because beer wouldn't be enough—and Rowan slugged it back.

"You should be ashamed of yourself. Those poor girls." Shane's mother scowled at Rowan as she went inside, presumably to see how Aidan was faring with Ashley.

"Oh, my God," Lily said in awe, a hand over her mouth, staring at Shane.

———

IN ALL OF THE COMMOTION, Lily had become distracted from the fact that Shane was, apparently, planning to propose to her. But now, with the crowd dissipating and the threat of further violence averted, the fact of it hit her. He was going to propose. He'd planned a whole thing, with her mother and Brittany here, with the whole Brody family as witnesses.

"Shane, were you—" Her question was interrupted by the sound of breaking glass coming from inside the house.

"Oh, crap." Shane ran into the house and Lily followed him.

When she got into the living room, the first thing that struck Lily was the sight of Ashley throwing full glasses of champagne at the wall while Aidan alternately ducked and tried to restrain her. Ashley yelled, "Fuck that fucking asshole dickhead bastard" as Fiona called out that she was going to dial 9-1-1 if things didn't calm the hell down.

Once Ashley dissolved into tears and no longer posed a threat, Lily noticed everything else: the flowers, the streamers, the balloons, and the fact that there had been a tray of full champagne glasses in the first place. She turned to Shane. "What is all this?"

Shane sighed. "I was going to propose to you in front of everyone, and when you said yes—which I really hoped you would—I was going to bring you in here for an engagement party. I've been planning it for days."

By now, Brittany and Janice had come inside, and they were standing nearby, listening.

"Get on with it, then," Brittany prompted him.

"Now?" Shane looked over toward Ashley, who was crying as Aidan ineffectually patted her back.

"No time like the present," Janice said.

"Well … okay." Shane took the ring box out of his pocket again, decided not to go down on one knee because of the broken glass and spilled champagne, and opened the box, showing the glittering diamond ring to Lily. "Lily, I love you," he said. "I couldn't tell you that before, but I can now. I love you more than I've ever loved anyone. So much that I want to be better for you. I want to be whole and happy again, and I want to make you happy, too. I know it's not that simple. I know I can't just say I'm going to heal and then do it. It's going to take work. But I'm going to do that work. I've already made an appointment with a therapist to talk about everything, and I'm going to keep going and keep talking. Whatever happens, I want you with me. And I want to be there for you, too, whatever you're going through, whatever you need. Always. Please, Lily. Marry me. Be my wife."

Lily didn't even realize she was crying until she spoke and heard the tears in her voice. "Yes. Of course I'll marry you."

Shane slipped the ring on her finger and took her into his arms, and the Brodys Lily hadn't even realized had gathered around them erupted into hoots and cheers and applause.

"I'd offer everyone some champagne, but …" Aidan said.

The next few minutes were filled with hugs and congratulations, happy tears and welcomes to the family.

Lily hadn't realized how unhappy Shane had been until now, when he wasn't. His face was alight with joy, and he seemed like a new man.

And Lily wanted him—the new one, the old one, any version of himself that he wanted to be. But she really hoped happy Shane was here to stay, and she promised herself she'd do everything she could to make that happen.

Chapter Thirty-Seven

In the commotion following Shane's proposal and Lily's acceptance, Shane all but forgot that Ashley was there and still visibly upset. But now, as things started to settle down, he looked over to where Ashley and Rowan were standing in the corner of his parents' living room, talking intensely, Ashley with her arms firmly folded over her chest, Rowan gesturing in a way that Shane supposed was intended to be soothing.

"Do you think she'll be okay?" Lily asked.

"She'll be better off, probably." Shane shrugged. "Ashley strikes me as the settling-down type, and Rowan … isn't."

"How long has he been dating two women?" Lily wanted to know.

Shane scoffed. "Since high school."

But Shane didn't want to talk about Rowan. He wanted to talk about Lily, and his future with her.

"You know, we don't have to wait until we get married to move in together," he said.

"I suppose we don't."

"If you don't like my place, we can look for somewhere else. A house we can buy together."

"I love your place. It's adorable. I've coveted it since the moment I saw it."

"Have you?" Shane grinned at her. "Well, you won't have to covet it anymore. It's yours now. Ours."

That word—ours—made him feel warm all over.

One by one and in small groups, the Brodys and the Harts came over to inquire about when the wedding might happen, where it might happen, what kind of dress Lily might wear, and whether they might have kids.

"Whoa, whoa," Lily said, laughing, when her mother posed all of those questions in what sounded like one breath. "The engagement just happened. We haven't even talked about any of that yet."

"We should, though." Shane turned to her. "Soon."

"We will."

"Oh, Lily. A grandbaby …" Janice went on, as though Lily had never said what she'd said about not knowing the answers.

"Mom, there's no grandbaby," Lily said. "Although, when Shane's ready …" She left the thought out there, a smile on her lips, a glow of happiness all over her.

Before Shane could say anything, Janice threw her arms around Lily and squeezed her so hard Shane wondered if Lily could even breathe.

Someone from the catering staff was cleaning up the broken glass and spilled champagne, and Aidan turned on some music—a romantic playlist on Spotify that Shane had chosen in advance.

When the music began, something soulful and soaring, Shane held out his hand to LIly. "Would you care to dance?"

"Here?" Lily asked.

"Why not?"

She put her hand in his, and he led her to the center of the room. He put his arms around her, and they began swaying to the music. Was this what happiness felt like? Shane was so unfamiliar with the sensation that he couldn't be sure. But he knew he wanted to feel more of it. And he wanted to give more of it to Lily.

———

LILY LAID her cheek against Shane's chest and moved with him to the music. She couldn't remember ever having been this content.

It wouldn't be easy, and it wouldn't be perfect. Shane still had issues to work through. He still had grief and unresolved guilt, and he still would have a tendency to shut out the people who loved him when those things got too intense. But now she'd be here to help him through it. And he'd have to let her help. He was pledging to spend his life with her, and that meant all of it—the good and the bad.

"We should have a long engagement," she told him. "So you have time. Time to deal with things. In therapy. If you really meant that you'd go."

"I really meant it," he said, and she felt the vibration of his words through his chest.

"And the part about kids?"

"Mmm?"

"I do want them. Do you?"

"If it's with you, then yes. I want the kids. I want the family. I want it all. But Lily?"

She lifted her head to look at him.

"I'm still scared." He swallowed hard. "I'm still … It's still hard. To be happy. To accept that, knowing …" He left the last part open, but she knew what he was trying to say.

"I know. Just don't shut me out, Shane. That's all I'm asking."

"I won't. I promise."

As they danced, Shane's mother and father joined them on the makeshift dance floor. Then Finn asked Brittany to dance, then Aidan moved into a waltz with Lily's mother.

Lily noticed that one couple was conspicuously absent from the festivities. She looked over Shane's shoulder to where Rowan and Ashley were still talking, Ashley's face pinched and angry, Rowan's open and pleading.

"Do you think she's going to take him back?" Lily asked Shane.

"Who knows?"

"Does he even want her to?"

"Again, who knows? Rowan's thought process when it comes to women is a mystery."

When the song ended, Shane took Lily's hand and led her out of the room.

"Where are we going?" she asked.

"Someplace where I can kiss you."

"Lead the way."

———

SHANE TOOK Lily upstairs and into a spare bedroom, locking the door behind them. It might have been awkward if he were taking Lily into his childhood room—music posters on the walls and memories of his teen girlfriends in the air—but he'd never lived here, so the room was bare of history. He and Lily would make their own memories.

He took her into his arms and kissed her, and this kiss felt different from those they'd shared before. Those had been kisses of passion, of lust. This was a kiss of love.

Her lips were warm and soft beneath his as they parted for him. Her tongue brushed against his, her breath playing with his.

He reached behind her and drew down the zipper on her dress, then slid his hand over her bare skin.

"Oh, God," she murmured at the feel of his touch.

He slid the dress off her shoulders, and it fell into a pool of fabric at her feet.

"Here?" Lily said. "Your parents—"

"Are busy with the party," he finished for her.

"But—"

"Do you want me to stop?" he asked.

She paused, her lips red from being kissed, her face flushed with desire. "No. I don't ever want you to stop."

He picked her up and carried her to the bed.

Given the circumstance, neither of them had the time to go as slowly as they wanted, to be as leisurely with each other's bodies as they would have preferred. Eventually, someone was going to come looking for them, so Shane got right down to business. He stripped off his clothes, drew Lily's panties down and off, and lay beside her, his hands roaming over her before his fingers found her warm, wet core.

At his touch, she tipped her head back, eyes closed, a low moan coming from her throat.

"I love you, Lily." He kissed her neck, her cheek, her lips.

"I love you," she said. "So much."

Then he moved on top of her and slid inside her, holding her to him. Lily wrapped her legs around his body and moved with him, and Shane wished he could make this moment last a lifetime. If Molly couldn't have love or happiness, then Shane would have to have enough of both for the two of them.

Shane rolled over onto his back, bringing Lily with him, and she sat astride him, her eyes locked on his, her body finding its rhythm.

He liked seeing her like this, transported by pleasure and knowing he'd given that to her. He sped his pace and she matched him until she gasped and shuddered, and he followed right behind with his own release.

Afterward, she collapsed onto him, warm and sated in his arms.

"We should probably get back," she murmured.

"Probably." He brushed a lock of hair from her face.

"Do you think they'll know what we were doing?"

"Definitely."

"Oh, God."

"But we're engaged," he reminded her. "And my parents want grandkids, so …"

"So it's not like anyone will disapprove," Lily said.

"I certainly don't."

Shane didn't disapprove at all. In fact, he wholeheartedly endorsed it.

———

WHEN LILY GOT DOWNSTAIRS, having put herself back together

the best she could, she waded through the crowd of Brodys to find Brittany.

She found her standing in a corner of the living room, drinking a glass of champagne and chatting with Shane's father. When she and Lily locked eyes from across the room, Brittany raised one eyebrow at Lily.

Lily waited for Declan to excuse himself and move away before she approached her sister.

"Hey," Lily said, filling the space Declan had vacated. "Some day, huh?"

"I'll say. You couldn't even wait for the party to be over?"

"What do you mean?" Lily feigned innocence.

Brittany let out an unattractive snort. "You think I don't know what you were doing for so long upstairs? Plus, your dress is on wrong."

"What?" Lily looked down at her dress, alarmed.

"The collar's all folded and weird. Here. I'll fix it." Brittany put down her glass and straightened Lily's collar. "There."

"Thank you. Do you think Mom knows what we were doing?"

"She had two kids, so, probably."

Lily turned to Brittany and took hold of her hands. "Brit, are you okay? With all of this, I mean? Me and Shane, and the engagement?"

"Of course I am. I'm over it."

"Really?"

"Yes. Did you think I was going to pine away over him forever? We weren't even a match. We tried it, it didn't work. It does work with you. So." She shrugged.

"Oh, Brittany. Thank you. Thank you for being okay. For accepting everything. If I had to choose between him and you—"

"I'd lose," Brittany said. "And I get that. You're going to marry him. I *should* lose."

"Having to make that choice at all would kill me. It would absolutely kill me. I'm so glad I won't have to." She reached out and impulsively hugged her sister. When she let go, both of them had tears shimmering in their eyes.

"Crying?" Shane came over and looked at both of them in alarm. "There's not supposed to be crying. This is supposed to be a happy occasion."

"It is, you jerk." Brittany playfully smacked Shane on the arm. "I've always wanted a brother. I just didn't think it would end up being someone I've slept with."

"Well, it's awkward when you put it that way," Lily said.

"It's not awkward. It's fine. It's all fine. I need another glass of champagne," Brittany said, then she went off to find one.

"Speaking of crying." Lily looked meaningfully to where Ashley and Rowan were having an intense conversation at one end of the room. Ashley was dabbing at her eyes with the corner of a napkin. Lily would have expected Ashley to have gone by now, given everything, but she hadn't. She supposed that was good news for Rowan.

"If they're still talking, maybe that means they're not breaking up," Shane said, as though reading Lily's thoughts. "Though why she wouldn't dump him is beyond me."

"Maybe she loves him," Lily said. "Or maybe—"

Her sentence was interrupted when Rowan, his face a mask of shock, yelled at Ashley, loud enough for everyone to hear, "Are you freaking kidding me? You're *pregnant*? Is it even mine?"

For the second time that day, a woman's hand hit the side of Rowan's face so hard it sounded like a gunshot.

"Uh oh," Shane said.

•••

To see where Shane Brody's story started, read *Then, Now, and Always* from Linda Seed's Otter Bluff series. Learn more at lindaseed.com.

www.ingramcontent.com/pod-product-compliance
Lightning Source LLC
Chambersburg PA
CBHW021647110726

47902CB00007B/1862